The

Fury

Frontier

Fire Fury Saga

Amanda Rose

Fire Fury Frontier

© 2019 Amanda Rose

Cover by Daniel McCutcheon

Amanda Rose

Dedication

To all the science fiction lovers.

Fire Fury Frontier

After a long voyage...

Chapter 1: Adrift

"... 280 years ago, a handful of people tried to save the world we used to live on, but it was too far gone. They bought us time, though. Corruption, power, and greed almost lead to our own extinction; when personal gains outweigh all other considerations, we are lost. The C.D.F.P. corporation ignored and hid vital scientific findings about global warming that was affecting the planet and that decision ultimately sealed our fate.

"About 240 years ago the people living on our world realized the end was coming, that things had become too dire to sustain life. Plants wouldn't grow, animals were dying off, weather patterns shifted, and the extreme heat and cold were killing us off. Seismic tremors were tearing the land apart, and it drove our ancestors to devise of our ship, the *Saisei*. It was a race against time to build it before there was nothing left to save. All resources were pooled from around the globe, scientists were pushed to their limits, and after many failures, the Saisei was built and launched into space 227 years ago.

"All that once existed on our home world no longer exists. Just a few years after the Saisei launched, the long-range sensors of the ship detected a massive energy surge on our homeworld, and the best scientists determined that the planet had violently split apart. Only what we preserved on this ship has survived; our history, literature, genetic materials... we almost wiped out our own existence as a species.

"We remember the past, so that we are not doomed to repeat it. The Empire is now governed by a democratic council, to keep singular desires and motives from affecting the whole. While we search for a new planet to make our own, it's crucial you keep these lessons from our past in mind, and pass them down to the next generation," Hiroshi stopped pacing for a moment, and leaned against his desk, facing his students.

Hiroshi took in their faces, to see if his words were getting through to these teenagers. Most stared back blankly, a few took notes, and a couple were bored. *Ah, do they even care about a world they've never set foot on? Some will. I guess I do.* Hiroshi thought. "Ok," he picked up a data pad off his desk, and opened up a book on it, enlarging the cover on the screen, and then held it up for the students to see, "read chapters 8 through 10 tonight from 'How We Brought Down the C.D.F.P.' Class dismissed."

The students lazily packed up their books and made their way out of the classroom. Hiroshi sat at his desk as they did and began to mark papers on his data pad. After all the students had filed out of the room, Hiroshi set down the pad, pulled off his glasses, and rubbed the bridge of his nose. He stretched leisurely then put his glasses back on. Hiroshi was in his early forties, tall, with black hair, salted with a few stark-white greys. He was incredibly handsome, with sharp cheekbones, and green eyes.

Hiroshi began to grade the papers again, but found his mind wandering. He pulled the tab back up with the book he'd assigned to his students. *If only you had all taken down the C.D.F.P. sooner, maybe we wouldn't have to live like this...* Hiroshi took a deep breath, then stood up from his desk, and walked over to the window. Stars, far off in the distance, slowly passed by, twinkling like diamonds against the black ink of space. Hiroshi put his hand against the cold glass and sighed.

|

Suki lay awake in her bed, staring at the air duct running across the ceiling above her. She had always loved the natural curves, divots, and imperfections in the metal hull of the ship, and so she'd left her room sparse. Suki's mother had wanted to cover it up, saying it felt "...too cold and impersonal," so she'd used fabric draping's to cover the rest of her families living quarters. But Suki took refuge in her barren room. Her bed, desk, chair, and dresser were all she had, and all she wanted in her space. She spent hours looking over every nook and cranny; it helped her think.

Suki was 17, but she'd always been more mature than her age. She only had a few close friends, as she enjoyed her solitude far too much. As she laid there, she grabbed her long braid of chestnut-brown hair and began to undo it; the tight braid had been pulling on her scalp. Once her hair was free she ran her fingers through it, it was soothing, and helped her relax.

The book bag she'd brought home from class was slumped on the floor, against the bedpost near her feet. After gathering the energy, she sat up, and opened the pull rope on the bag, and riffled through the data pads which were loaded up with books. She pulled out *How We Brought Down the C.D.F.P.*, and then laid back in her bed. Suki enjoyed history class and found Hiroshi to be a very interesting teacher. She opened the book to chapter 8 and began reading.

A half-hour later Suki laid down the book on her chest and shook out her arms. The blood had drained down, and made her arms hurt, from holding the book overhead; despite the aggravation, she always read this way. While her arms recuperated, Suki tried to imagine life on the homeworld of her ancestors. It seemed such a foreign concept to her to live on a planet. She was born on the Saisei, and aside from a couple excursions to planets the ship had stopped at to collect resources, she'd lived her entire life aboard the spacecraft.

Even on the few planets they'd visited, there'd been no breathable atmosphere, so she'd had to wear her spacesuit the entire time. She had no concept of what it was like to feel a breeze, the warmth of the sun on her skin, or the earth beneath her bare feet. Her environment was one of stability, perfect climate control, and recycled oxygen. Suki had come to rely on the stability, after all, it was all she'd ever known. Still, she allowed her imagination to wander, and fell asleep dreaming about living on a planet.

I

"Empress Hiroshu," before the councilor could say another word, the empress rose her hand to cut him off.

"Please councilor, Jona, we've discussed this before, the formalities are unnecessary."

Jona stood unmoving and silent in-place for a moment, unsure of what to do. The government assembly was in full attendance for the quarterly status updates, and all eyes were on Jona. "Uh, right... well, Norita, the inventories are in ship-wide. Food production is excellent, the hydroponics bays are producing a surplus this quarter. Fuel reserves are at 67%, oxygen backups are full, however our water reservoir is running low," Jona explained while reviewing the data pad numbers in front of him.

"How low?" Norita asked.

"We're down to 13%," Jona said sheepishly.

Murmurs of shock and dismay sounded from around the room, "How can that be?" "Why didn't we know sooner?" "That's terrible!" came the outcries from around the room.

Norita raised her hand to hush the room, "Please, everyone, let's stay focused. We all know the last 2 planets we visited had no water to replenish our stores with. Jona, at 13% how long will that last?" she asked calmly.

Jona flipped through his paperwork, "Uh, at current consumption rates, about 7 months."

Norita nodded, "Ok, good. Jona I want you to get a long-range scan done of all nearby solar systems, and have it analyzed by the scientific division this week. In the meantime, we need to extend the supply we have, so water rationing will go into effect immediately. Get the word out and have a ship-wide announcement this evening. We will meet back here one week from today to review our options, thank you everyone."

Chatter commenced as the government officials began to get up from their seats and collect their things.

|

"... fighter pilot drills at 0600 tomorrow morning. Dismissed, Omega Squad," General Takeo Yamamoto bellowed.

"Yes sir!" came the responding reply from the Omega Squadron. They began to disperse.

"Lieutenant Saito, a moment," Takeo said, walking up to him.

Raiden Saito turned around to face the General, "Yes, sir?"

Takeo paused for a moment before he spoke, evaluating the lieutenant. Takeo was a thoughtful man, though he came across as somewhat gruff, and often intense. The General was well kempt, less for his rough short beard, which always looked like a 5 o'clock shadow. Raiden waited patiently, his years of intensive training allowed him to stay focused, and in control. Takeo finally spoke, "I want you to take point in tomorrow's drills. We're going to practice the raven maneuver."

Raiden nodded, "Yes sir, thank you sir!"

Takeo smiled, "Go rest up Lieutenant."

Raiden saluted, and then walked away. His mind was abuzz with ideas for the next day. When Raiden turned the corner into the corridor, he found Freya waiting for him.

"So, what was that all about?" she asked.

"Guess who's leading the drills tomorrow?" Raiden grinned.

Freya punched his arm playfully, "Shut up, really?! Ha, congrats man. But don't you be barkin' orders at me."

"Lieutenant, that's 'don't be barkin' orders at me, *sir*,'" Raised teased.

Freya pushed him, "Don't start man, haha!"

Raiden smiled, "I'm going to go look over the flight plan and maneuver sequencing."

"Right, I'll come with," Freya nodded, and they headed off the control room together.

Later, after they'd finished their work, Freya and Raiden walked towards the mess hall. Freya and Raiden had grown up together, their quarters had been right next to each other on the Saisei. Freya had always been a tomboy and hadn't gotten along well with the other girls. Raiden had always been quiet, reserved, and focused, and had a hard time making friends. When they met, they instantly had a rapport, and became inseparable. In their late teens they applied to be a part of the military on the same day. They always had friendly competition against each other as they progressed; both competitive, and both skilled, they achieved advancements at the same pace. Their friendly competition kept them both focused.

Freya walked into the mess hall like she owned it, her confidence never lacking. Freya felt at home in the military, the rules made sense to her, and she fit in. She had a dirty sense of humor, quick wit, multiple tattoos, and short blond hair. Above all, Freya was driven to be the best, and so she never showed weakness in front of her peers. Freya walked over to one of the tables that some of their fellow Omega Squadron buddies were sitting at. Freya took a seat, and put her feet up on the table, then rested her head in her hands. Raiden sat down next to her.

"What took you guys so long?" Koji asked, taking a swig of beer. Koji was a year older then Raiden and Freya but had joined the military 2 years year after them. He was level headed, easy to get along with, reliable, and held the rank of corporal.

"Raiden got cherry-picked to run the drills tomorrow," Freya grinned. Raiden rolled his eyes.

"That's fantastic, congrats!" Koji said emphatically.

"Gotta drink to that," Masato, who sat bleary-eyed next to Koji, raised his glass.

"Shit Masato, you look like you've already had enough," Freya said, swiped the glass from his hand, and chugged down what was left.

"Hey!" Masato objected.

"Dude, she's right, early morning tomorrow, take 'ere easy," Koji agreed.

"Yeah, yeah…" Masato pouted.

"So, what's for dinner?" Raiden asked, his stomach rumbling.

Raiden and Freya grabbed their dinners, and another pitcher of beer for the table, and then came back. The group stayed long after supper, playing cards, and chatting. At 9PM the ship-wide speaker system came online with a *BEEP!* and a moment later a voice came on with an announcement, "Attention all citizens. This is a ship-wide announcement. Effective immediately, we are implementing water rationing. Each citizen is granted 2 liters of drinking water per day, and 1 liter for washing. Shower systems are banned. Departments requiring water usage will be sent individual water allowances. Water rationing will be in effect until further notice. Thank you." *Crackle!* The speaker system turned off.

"Seriously?!" Masato sighed.

"Guess you're going to be feeling that hangover even longer than you thought, private," Koji jived.

Freya and Raiden shared a look of concern with one another. Koji caught their look, "What is it?"

Freya quickly changed the mood, "Just terrified of having to smell you without a shower, Koji."

Koji flipped her off, and they both laughed. After the card game, they went home for the night, and Freya and Raiden walked back towards their cabins together. "Something must be up," Freya said, as they walked.

"Yeah... I don't know why, but I have a bad feeling about this," Raiden agreed.

"Think Yamamoto knows anything?" Freya asked.

Raiden shook his head, "Nah, the General gets orders, just like us."

Freya huffed, "Fuckin' politics..." They arrived at Freya's quarters, in the barracks. Freya looked Raiden in the eye, "Keep your ear to the ground, man."

Raiden nodded, "You too."

Raiden walked off towards his bunk. *Water rationing... I don't think they've ever done that before, not that I can remember... Things must be bad...* His mind continued to juggle possibilities, but in the end, Raiden didn't know enough to make any concrete assumptions, so he gave up thinking about it, and focused on the flight plan for the morning.

|

Norita was burning the midnight oil, sitting at her desk in her office, going over figures, charts, and reports. After a while she picked up a hot cup of tea and took a sip, then sat back in her chair. Her mind was awake, but her body was tired. A gentle tapping knock on the door stole her attention. "Yes?" Norita called out.

"It's Jona," came the voice behind the door.

"Come in," Norita called back, then took another sip of her tea.

Jona came in and closed the door behind himself, then bowed to Norita, "I'm terribly sorry for coming by so late, but you said once we had any information to let you know right away..." Jona began to explain himself.

"Jona, it's alright, I'm awake anyway. What is it?"

Jona slapped down a data pad in front of Norita, on her desk. "The long-range scans came back. No planets, but we've found one asteroid with water at the furthest ranges of our scans. It's going to take over two months with the neutrino engine running non-stop for us to get there. The problem is that it's almost entirely ice, -107°F in the sun and -373°F in the shade, so collecting it isn't going to be easy. On top of that it's not just water, it's an H2O and methanol mix. On my way here, I contacted Dr. Takei, and asked him and the scientists in his lab to start looking into the best methods of distillation separation. And on top of all of that, travelling at near light speed for that long will take its toll on the ship, I'm not sure how the gravity plating will hold up under that much strain for the extended duration," Jona explained.

Norita had been looking through the data as Jona explained everything. She nodded, "Alright then, let's set course. 2 months will give us enough time to figure out how to harvest it, and with any luck we won't lose too much of the methanol during distillation, so we can use it to fuel some of the ship's systems and machinery. It may be a rough ride, but we'll make it. Good work, Jona," she smiled at him. Jona returned the smile, but Norita knew Jona well enough to see through the guise. "What is it?" Norita asked.

"Nothing... I just, we've never cut it so close," he said with worry hanging in his voice, "The science division is also looking to perfect our way of purifying our urine recycling system, so there's less waste, just in case we have to extend our reserves." Jona fought back his fear and swallowed the lump in his throat.

Norita stood up from her chair, and placed her hand compassionately on Jona's shoulder, "A par for the course, I suppose. Sometimes I'm amazed we've survived so long in space, but then I remember, it's because we have a destiny, I can feel it in my bones."

Jona looked Norita in the eye and could see she meant every word she said. Norita was in her fifties and had lived through a few times of famine on the ship, as well as being caught in a deadly asteroid belt, which had pummeled and badly damaged a significant portion of the ship; ripping open parts, with many lives lost. She had seen tragedy and come through it on the other side. Her face was weathered, equally from smiles and frowns; Norita fully immersed herself into life, and it gave her an aura of wisdom. She was a strong leader, and as

Jona gazed into her deep brown eyes, he felt a sense of security wash over him.

"Thank you, ma'am," he said. They shared one last look of understanding, and then Jona took his leave from her office.

Once she was alone Norita allowed herself to feel the stress, then took a long inhale, held her breath, and then let it all out in one big exhale. Her first advisor had taught her this breathing technique to get through times of heightened anxiety, and she had found it always helped to settle her nerves. Norita looked at the pile of data pads on her desk, and then to the clock which read 2:15AM, and decided it was time to head back to her quarters.

Chapter 2: DRAUGHT

A month had passed since the water rationing had gone into effect, and it was beginning to affect morale. Nerves were frayed, anxiety high, and tempers thin. The council did its best with assurances that everything was well under control, and to quell any panic, but the pressure was building up, and it was palpable.

While the ship was travelling at full speed, the military pilots were grounded; there was no way for them to launch and get back to the ship without the Saisei slowing down. At first Freya was furious, but as week after week had passed by, she was simply bored and impatient. She hated the idea of her skills dulling. Raiden had an unshakable feeling, and he wasn't sure if it was good or bad, but it wouldn't leave him be.

The Omega Squad had been assigned as peaceful crowd control during the water rationing, to make sure thing didn't get out of hand. Raiden and Freya stood side by side at the entrance to the main doors leading into the concourse, the central hub of the ship where people came to trade, dine, drink, and take part in all sorts of social activities. The lack of water for bathing was starting to take its toll, as the stale scent of body odor lingered in the air.

Freya cracked her neck and stretched her back. They'd been standing in place for over 4 hours, and it was painful on her lower back. "This job's a joke," she muttered under her breath, watching the crowds go by, then looked over at Raiden and asked, "How long till we can leave?"

Raiden looked at his watch, "3 hours, 42 minutes," he replied flatly.

"Then I'm getting coffee, want one?" she asked.

Raiden nodded, "1 cream, no sugar," he told her.

"Yeah, yeah, I know. Give me your ration chip," she said holding out her hand. Raiden passed it to her, and she wrapped her fingers around it, "I'll be right back," Freya said, and walked over to the nearby café.

Raiden kept scanning the crowds with his eyes, but he was getting tired of the monotony. Day after day, week after week, it had all been the same, watching people go about their days. He looked over at Freya and saw her several customers back in the lineup at the café and sighed; the coffee couldn't come soon enough.

A few minutes later Raiden caught site of a large group of people making their way towards the very far end of the concourse a few hundred feet away. He saw a man standing up on top of a cafeteria table, waving his arms, clearly making some sort of speech to the large gathering that had formed around him. Raiden had a sinking feeling in the pit of his stomach and started to make his way over.

Picking up the coffees off the countertop, Freya turned around to see Raiden walking briskly away. She ran to catch up to him. "Hey!" she called, as she ran toward him. Raiden stopped and turned to see her. Freya stopped when she reached him, "What is it?" she asked. Raiden pointed, and she looked at the ever-growing crowd. "Oh, shit," she said, and put the coffees down on the nearest surface, "These better be here when we get back. Alright, let's go."

The man standing on the table was emphatic, and passionate, and as he expressed his views, and the crowd fed off his energy, "...This is how it begins. Rationing is the first step to subjugation. Power does not rise up in a mighty swoop, it comes slowly, with false promises, slipping in gradually until it's too late to get it out..." His speech was eloquent and was gathering fast endorsement from his onlookers. Hiroshi stood amongst the crowd, watching the man speak, and feeling the frenetic energy of the crowd rising. *Short-sighted stupidity will be the undoing of us all.* He thought.

Raiden and Freya were trying to make their way up to the man, but the crowd had become too dense with bodies, and they were having a hard time maneuvering closer. "Excuse me," Raiden said, pushing his way through the tight-knit bodies. They could both feel eyes on them; they stood out in their black military garb amongst the civilians. Animosity was growing as the impassioned speech continued, and the crowd was beginning to cheer the man on in agreement. People were starting to intentionally block Freya and Raiden from making their way up to the make-shift podium. Raiden clicked in on his comm badge, "Backup in the concourse, I repeat, immediate backup in concourse requested."

"...But they forget, the power is with the people! There is strength in numbers, and the civilian body has the most numbers! And we will be heard!" The man's speech came to a crescendo, and the people were rallying behind him. The mood was heated, and it felt like a riot could start at the drop of a hat. Raiden and Freya struggled to try to get to the man but were still forty feet away.

Suddenly a voice overcame the cheering, strong, calm, and clear, "Is it so easy to forget the government *represents* the people?" Hiroshi asked the man.

The buzz of the crowd lessened as all eyes sought to see who asked the question and longed to hear the outcome. The man on the table met Hiroshi's gaze, his eyes like daggers sizing Hiroshi up. After a moment, he grinned, still feeling righteous in his views, "That is the greatest illusion of them all."

Hiroshi stepped to the front of the crowd, "Our people have seen corrupted power first hand, unchecked, and answering to no one. This is not true of our current government. *We* elect in our officials, this is a democracy, *not* a dictatorship," Hiroshi said with confidence.

"We call it a democracy, but we still live with Imperial rule," the man bit back.

Hiroshi was becoming agitated; if there was one thing that annoyed him to his core, it was ignorance. "Imperial in title only," Hiroshi said, fighting back his urge to yell.

"And yet… we don't vote for who gets the ultimate title, do we?" the man said sternly, a terrifying finality to his voice. Hiroshi didn't know what to say, the man wasn't wrong in his statement, but his ideals were dangerous. His mind raced for something to say. Before Hiroshi could think of anything, Raiden and Freya finally busted through to the front of the crowd.

Raiden turned to address the crowd, "Folks, it's time to go home! Disperse immediately!"

Freya spoke directly to the man, "You're under arrest for public disturbance, get down off that table now!"

The man looked to the crowd, "They can silence the individual, but not the masses!" he yelled before Freya pulled him down off the table. The man purposefully went limp when Freya tugged him down, and as a result he fell and hit his forehead off the corner of a metal chair. The impact had cut him, and he bled profusely.

Freya and Raiden got the man up to his feet. Someone in the crowd saw the injury and screamed, "Militant brutality!" and the crowd roared with hate.

"Oh, shit…" Freya said under her breath.

The man stood there, laughing as blood trickled down his cheek, "You can't silence the people."

"It was an accident, we'll be taking this man to get immediate medical care," Raiden attempted to explain, but the crowd refused to hear him out. Before he could blink Raiden was hit in the face with an empty soda fountain cup, and while it didn't hurt, he recoiled from the shock.

"Fuck!" Freya let out, her fear taking over. The adrenaline was pumping, and tempers were flaring.

Darting eyes scanned the crowd as Raiden tried his best to analyze the situation and plan his next move. His mind was unfocused, he tried to fight back the urge to panic. A moment later a fog horn sounded behind them, and like a wave, it washed over the crowd and silenced them. A distant voice bellowed, "Cease and desist! The concourse is officially shut down for the rest of the day. Civilians have 20 minutes to vacate, shop keeps 1 hour. Anyone still here beyond those times will be immediately arrested and detained for questioning. Now, go!"

The people began to make their way towards the exits. Raiden and Freya turned around to see Captain Gin Yoshini, along with 8 other soldiers, including Koji, in tow. They both breathed a sigh of relief at the sight of their backup. Gin directed the soldiers to stand watch at the exits.

"How lucky for you," the man jived at Freya.

Freya gripped his arm firmly, "C'mon, let's get you to the medic..." she said, holding back her rage. One of the other soldiers accompanied her as she left the concourse with him.

Hiroshi watched as Freya took then man away, then turned to leave, but Raiden caught his attention before he did, "Hey, sir, thank you," Raiden said, extending his hand. Hiroshi felt a bit dazed from the whole situation, he stared at Raiden's hand for a moment, then took it and shook it.

"Just trying to be the voice of reason. It's Hiroshi, by the way."

Raiden smiled, "I'm Raiden, pleased to meet you. You helped diffuse a very tense situation, things could have gone much worse if you hadn't stepped in when you did. That said, be careful, with people like that... you just never know."

Hiroshi nodded in agreement, "Good advice." With that Hiroshi headed off.

Raiden walked up to Gin, who was meticulously keeping an eye on the crowds as they left. "Just in the nick of time," Raiden said, letting out a sigh.

"What in the hell happened?" Gin asked.

Raiden shook his head, "People are tense, and this guy's anti-government speech riled them up. I just… I just can't believe things got ugly that fast. If you hadn't come when you had…"

Gin grunted, "Yeah, well, you fly boys never think civilian security has its dangers, but an angry mob is nothing to snub your nose at. People are dangerous," he said in all seriousness, and Raiden knew he was right.

|

Closing the holding cell door behind her, Freya locked in the man, whose identity had come back as Niko Adai. Freya's hair was disheveled, and the stress still sat heavy on her. She felt shaken and took a moment to gather herself while she was alone in the hallway, before walking back out to the security post. Freya cracked her neck, and stepped into her power, as she approached the guard on duty. The guard looked up, and she gave him a nod, "Detainee number 13, Niko Adai, holding cell 9, under arrest for public disturbance and attempting to instigate a riot," she told him as he input it into the computer log.

He finished typing, "Got it, lieutenant."

Freya gave him a pat on the back, then started to walk away, "G'night, man."

Freya headed straight back to her quarters, and when she was alone, the pent-up fear overcame her. Tears welled up, and she felt like she couldn't breathe. Freya tore off her military jacket as she gasped for air, tears streaming down her face. She couldn't get the angry mob out of her head, the rage in their eyes, the angry shouts, surrounding them, trapping them in, there'd been nowhere to go. *What if...?* Her mind kept grasping at all the horrible possibilities of what could have been. She tried to push away the thoughts, but they latched on, and refused to budge.

Once Freya caught her breath she began to calm down. She caught a glimpse of her face in the mirror, blotchy red from crying, and was disgusted with feelings of anger and shame. She slapped herself, "Get yourself together!" she said vehemently. Freya viewed herself as one of the boys, strong and impervious; not a victim to her emotions. After a few moments she calmed herself down. *You're better than this...* she kept repeating to herself in her mind.

Pushing the feeling aside, Freya went over to the sink to splash cold water on her face. It was only when she got there did she remember the pipes were turned off for the water rationing. "Dammit!" she hollered and punched the metal wall. "Aw, fuck!" she recoiled as the sharp pain surged through her hand. She shook her hand then stuck it between her side and her left arm to apply pressure to it. "Sssst!" she cringed as the throbbing began.

After a few minutes she looked at her hand, the bruises were already forming, and the skin had split on her middle finger's knuckle. She shook it out some more, rolled her eyes at her own stupidity, and her gaze landed on her clock. It was 5:20PM and she's promised to meet Raiden for drinks. She grabbed a shirt, patted down her face, and headed out to the mess hall.

|

It was another late night for Dr. Seto Takei. All of his staff had already left for the night, and he sat alone in the lab, the light from his computer monitor shining bright on his face. He sipped a cup of green tea as he looked over today's data. Dr. Takei had a marvelous mind; he could analyze a situation in layers to see the big picture in a way few people ever could understand. His most difficult task in life was always conveying his conclusions, they were unorthodox, and left the average person unsure.

Seto remembered in his youth being disciplined in math class for not displaying the process of long division. But he didn't need the long-drawn-out path to get to the answer, his mind worked differently, although as a child he had no way of explaining it. *Ignorant small-minded fools. Being different is our greatest strength, being average is weak.* He thought, feeling the same agitation he did as a schoolboy being accused of cheating. *Cheating? Hmmp! I never needed to cheat.*

Trying to shake free of that memory, Seto attempted to refocus on his work. He drank deeply from his cup, and instantly felt more focused. The past few weeks had been very demanding, though that was what Seto lived for: a challenge. Late nights, tough problems, life and death stakes, it made him feel alive.

There was something about late nights in the lab, when the last of the scientists finally left, and the quiet set in, that Dr. Takei felt like he was fully in his element. His mind came alive at night, and he often got his best work done then. Without interruptions, he could let his mind run through all kinds of scenarios, through to their conclusions. During the day Seto found himself often coordinating the rest of his team, and while he enjoyed that work, his solitary time brought him the most joy.

Dr. Takei glanced at his agenda for the next day. He had a big meeting scheduled with Zavion, the head of engineering for the Saisei, at 8AM. Yesterday had been a great day as his team had finished the plans to implement the upgrades to the reclamation system for urine recycling back into usable water. The team had done such an incredible job on refining the techniques that that water percentage saved would go from 93% to 98%. The difficulty would come in making the modifications throughout the ship's infrastructure; at best it would take several years to retrofit the entire ship to make the upgrades, but that was a problem to deal with at tomorrow's meeting.

Seto had bigger more pressing problems on his mind; how to collect and distill the water from the asteroid they were heading to. The biggest issue was creating the drilling equipment to work under such extreme temperatures. So far, he was able to find methods of keeping the fuel and lubricating oils from freezing up to -200°, however that was a far cry from where he needed it to be. Thickening fluids, frozen fuel lines, cracks causing leakages, were just part of the problem. Keeping the battery operating under such extreme cold posed entirely new difficulties, and time was starting to run out.

A big yawn overcame Seto. He took off his glasses and rubbed his eyes; even the caffeinated tea wasn't strong enough to fight off this level of fatigue. He looked at his watch to see it was already past midnight. With his early morning meeting Seto decided to call it a night. He saved his project, then shut down his computer terminal. When he stood up from his chair he took a big stretch and yawned again. His footsteps echoed in the large empty lab as he made his way to the door, and when he left, the heavy door shut behind him sending a deep boom throughout the room.

Chapter 3: ARRIVAL

After 9 and a half weeks at top speed, the Saisei was finally closing in on the ice asteroid. They'd entered into the solar system 2 days ago and were just hours away from reaching the asteroid now. It couldn't come soon enough; tensions had been high on the ship since the incident in the concourse. The bridge crew were laser focused. Koi Goto, pilot in command of the Saisei, had been in the pilot's seat for the past 10 hours, and had no intention of leaving this close to their destination.

As Koi went to take a sip of his coffee, he picked up the cup to realize he'd already finished it off. "Damn," he muttered to himself. His intercom at his terminal then popped on.

"Pilot Goto?" Jona's voice came on.

Koi sighed, annoyed with Jona who'd be incessantly contacting him for his entire shift. *Does this guy ever take a break?* Koi wondered. He pressed the button to speak, "Yeah?"

The intercom crackled, "What's our ETA?" Jona asked.

Koi rolled his eyes having answered this several times over the last few hours, "Still on track to be there in about 3 hours," he said, not hiding his annoyance.

"Thank you," Jona's voice crackled, then the intercom beeped and turned off.

|

Dr. Takei and head engineer Zavion stood in the hanger bay finalizing the salvage equipment. It had been a major feat, challenging both theory and practice, to create safeguards against the drastic cold temperatures for the drill and excavation unit they'd be sending down to the planet. Between Zavion's mechanical expertise, and Seto's brilliant problem solving, they'd devised several new techniques to develop the modifications.

Using aerogel insulate, which could withstand absolute zero, −459.67°F, Dr. Takei had created insulation tubes for the fuel lines. This would prevent any cracks and leaks, as well as keep the fuel from solidifying in the tubes. The aerogel was used in many other areas of the motor to ensure heat retention.

More challenging would be ensuring the mechanisms would not seize up, and to keep the battery warm enough to run. Zavion had devised of a built-in heating system that they'd have running prior to launching, and which would have to remain operational for the duration of the trip. While it was an incredibly risky plan, it was the best option available. They could only hope the heating system would not give out from the extreme stress.

On the final approach to the asteroid they ran final tests to ensure everything was operating smoothly. "I'll need you to come and take a look at the distillation chamber when we're done here," Seto said to Zavion as he finished checking the backup generator to the heating system.

"Problems?" Zavion asked.

"Some sort of issue with the reflux drum, we're not getting pure separation in the final product," Seto explained.

Zavion nodded, "No problem, we'll get it fixed."

The two men enjoyed working together. Both of them were high achievers, both top in their fields, and highly revered for their skill and knowledge. Zavion was much more of a hands-on worker and learner, while Seto preferred to work things out in his mind, however when they collaborated often the grandiose creations in Seto's mind got to come to fruition in the physical world just as he envisioned them. Zavion's work was all too often extremely practical, lots of repairs, and the occasional replacement of broken-down parts in the ship. He reveled in the opportunity to do something that allowed him to use the full extent of his skills.

|

The bell rang signifying the end of the class period. "All right, that will be all for today," Hiroshi said, setting down his chalk. "As you all know we're about to come into orbit of the asteroid we've been travelling to for the past couple of months, and it should be quite the sight. Be sure to get to an observation port over the weekend to view it and make notes. On Monday we'll be discussing the asteroid, it's composition, and talk about the unique distillation system that our scientists have devised to be able to collect the ice and turn it into water by separating the methanol from it. Class dismissed," Hiroshi announced.

The students began to make their way out of the classroom. Suki, who'd been sitting at the back of the class, picked up her digital notepad and shoved it into her book bag. She walked down the steps from the top row of seating towards the front of the room; the classrooms on the ship had all been designed as lecture halls, and were often used after hours for theatre, lectures, and political debates during elections.

Suki walked up to Hiroshi's desk. He looked up at her, "Yes, Suki?" he asked.

"I just wanted to give you my essay," she said.

"That's not due until next week," he replied.

Suki shrugged, "I know, I just finished it early."

Hiroshi smiled, "I used to finish my homework early too, weekends are more fun when they're free."

Suki smiled, she always felt as though Hiroshi understood her. Suki grabbed out her digital work pad and clicked to send it to Hiroshi's. Instantly it popped up on his screen.

"Got it. Thanks Suki," he said.

"Thanks Mr. Kasai," Suki then turned and walked out of the classroom.

The passageways were littered with people vying for window space. The asteroid was now in viewing range, although it'd be another hour before it was visible in full detail. Suki disliked crowds, they made her uncomfortable, and after hearing the news about a near-riot breaking out in the concourse last month she was even more wary. Suki kept her head down and walked as fast as she could to get home.

When Suki finally got home, which had taken her nearly twice as long while maneuvering the crowded corridors, she opened the door only to hear her parents fighting. Suki quietly closed the door behind herself, trying to go unnoticed; her parents never argued, and certainly never yelled at each other that she'd ever heard. She could tell the voices were coming from the kitchen. Suki stood still in the entranceway and listened in.

"...That's absolutely crazy!" her mother yelled, "Have you lost your mind, Link?"

"If you would just listen," Link barked back.

"To what?" her mother interrupted, "Socialist propaganda?!"

Link huffed angrily, "Get your head out of your ass! Can you not see..."

Again, her mother cut him off, "No *you* get your head out of your ass! This isn't the time or the place for this, we live on a ship! You can't have that kind of government on a ship, it just wouldn't work!" she said emphatically.

"You just don't want to see it work!" Link yelled.

Suddenly Suki heard footsteps stomping towards her as her father stormed out of the kitchen. Suki froze momentarily, then grab the door handle, opened the door and closed it hard, then called, "I'm home!" just as her father walked into sight, from the kitchen into the living room.

Suki tried to pretend everything was normal and took her shoes off by the front door. Her father walked right past her and out the front door without saying a word. She could hear her mother sobbing in the kitchen. A sinking feeling of dread overcame Suki, she didn't know exactly what was going on, but she knew it was terribly wrong.

|

Norita sat in her office, waiting to be called to the bridge. She wanted to get some paperwork out of the way while she waited, but she couldn't focus her mind. She tried to push the worries and fear from her mind, but they kept barging their way back in. *What if the drill fails? What if we can't distill it well enough to drink it?* She kept asking herself; but there was no answer.

Last night she hadn't slept a wink. She'd tossed and turned all night and couldn't get her brain to quiet down. Painstakingly she'd looked at the alarm almost hourly throughout the night, until 5A.M. rolled around and she decided she'd had enough of just lying there without sleeping.

Picking up her third cup of coffee of the day, Norita slurped down the rest of it, trying to concentrate her fatigued mind. She set the empty cup down and let out a sigh. Her intercom buzzed on, "Empress, uh, I mean, Norita, we're on approach to the ice planet," Jona came over the speaker.

Norita clicked the button to respond, "Thanks Jona, I'll be right there." She let go of the intercom button and breathed deeply. "Here we go," she said to herself, hoping for the best. She stood from her desk and immediately left her office to go to the bridge.

|

It was absolutely breathtaking; as they approached the asteroid is seemed to have a blue-green aura emanating from it. The entire asteroid was a solid ball of ice, with deep chasms that ran so deep and so long that they were visible even before they'd entered orbit. The chasms looked like deep blue bands of ribbons by the way they'd formed in the ice. Varying hues of blue and white covered the asteroid's surface. It was littered with craters; clearly it had been hit by some significant comets over the years.

When Norita walked onto the bridge, she stopped in her tracks the second she saw the asteroid. "It's beautiful," she couldn't help but utter in awe.

Jona turned around at the sound her of voice to look at her, "It is," he agreed with her.

"We're about to enter geosynchronous orbit," Koi informed them, as he prepared to take the Saisei in.

|

Raiden, Koji, Masato, and Freya sat around a table in Koji's quarter's playing cards. Freya's foot was tapping the floor; she'd been impatient all day. This would be the first time in months they'd get out in their ships to fly. The ship-wide intercom came on, and after some static crackled away, Koi Goto came over the air, "Attention! Attention! We are entering the asteroid's orbit. Please be aware, watch your footing, and have something to stabilize yourself on as we disengage the neutrino field. Thank you." The static hung in the air for a moment before it was gone.

"Finally," Masato said.

"No kidding," Koji agreed, "this has been the longest 2 months of my life."

The intercom came on again, "Omega Squadron, report to flight deck B for pre-flight checks in 20 minutes," General Yamamoto's voice directed sternly.

Freya folder her cards, and popped up out of her chair, "Hell, yes," she cheered. The boys chuckled at her exuberance. Raiden, Koji and Masato set down their cards, and Koji quickly swept them all up, tapped them neatly into place and stuck the deck pack in its box.

Freya buttoned up her flight suit, and as she did, she glanced over at Raiden, "Race you around the asteroid."

Raiden looked at her and saw her big grin and competitive eyes glint at him. "Ha, OK. Loser buys drinks tonight," Raiden said, extending his hand.

Freya grabbed it and shook, "Deal!"

Masato walked over, "Hey, hey, I want in on that too!"

Koji laughed, "What the hell, I'm game." They all felt uplifted to finally get back out and fly.

|

As the Saisei entered into geosynchronous orbit, Hiroshi's quarters turned to face full view of the asteroid. Hiroshi stood in his living room, one hand pressed against the window, watching as the asteroid drew closer and closer. He studied the landscape of this foreign rock with curious eyes and wonderment. Ever since Hiroshi had been a boy his favorite times on the ship had been when they got close to celestial bodies. His curiosity and imagination were always piqued at those times, and it gave him a sense of being part of something much grander in the Universe.

After the Saisei settled into orbit, Hiroshi set up an easel by the window, and took out his cherished and rare pad of paper, propping it into place. The Saisei grew trees along with the food crops, both to preserve life forms from the homeworld, as well as to produce natural oxygen for the ship. Only when a tree was about to exceed its size for the environment it was in did they cut it down for resources like paper, and lumber.

Hiroshi had purchased his pad of paper, 100 handmade 20 by 20-inch pieces, 7 years ago, spending nearly half a year's salary to get it. He'd spent his childhood drawing on data pads, but after discovering his affection for history, he longed for the palpable experience of using real paper. When he first got home with the pad after he bought it, he'd opened it up and gently run his fingertips over the paper. The texture was exquisite, soft and smooth yet with subtle divots.

Hiroshi only ever took out his paper when there was something truly exceptional to capture. He kept his skills sharp with his data pad sketching, but there was nothing so therapeutic, so raw, so real, as using natural paper. The charcoal catching on the ridges, blending under the heat of his fingertip into perfect shades; it was like magic. He pulled out a tin, which held his charcoal, and he carefully pulled off the lid and picked out the piece he would use. Setting the tin aside, Hiroshi stood in front of the easel, and taking in the view, he touched the charcoal to the paper, and began to draw the asteroid.

|

When Raiden, Freya, Masato, and Koji arrived in the hangar bay, they got into formation with the rest of Omega Squadron. General Yamamoto came over moments later to address the squad, his eyes going straight to Masato and Koji, "Corporal Koji Akagi, Private Masato Ito, report to flight deck E, you two will be piloting and operating the drill on the asteroid. You will be briefed on the operations there. Dismissed." Koji and Masato saluted, and then immediately left.

Freya glanced at Raiden and mouthed, *What the hell?* Raiden shrugged and mouthed back, *No idea.* Takeo cleared his throat deliberately to draw their attention, "Eyes front soldiers!" he commanded. Freya and Raiden immediately snapped to attention and straightened their posture. "We will be escorting the drill team to the asteroid. Once everything is green lit and the drilling is underway, we will clear the asteroid by 50,000 kilometers for drill practice. We launch in one hour, go prep your ships. Dismissed," General Takeo Yamamoto said, then walked off.

Everyone headed towards their own ship for pre-flight checks. Freya ran up to Raiden, "How the hell did Masato and Koji get picked for the drill?!"

Raiden laughed, "Are you seriously jealous?"

Freya flushed, "What? I, no, I just… screw you," she shoved him playfully.

They laughed, then Raiden had a realization and looked at her, "You know what, I think I remember Koji saying he used to work in engineering before he enrolled in the military. I bet he's on board in case anything goes wrong."

Freya smiled and pointed at him, "See this, *this* is why I keep you around. You remember shit!" she winked. "Alright, see you in the skies," Freya said and walked off towards her ship.

Raiden watched her walk away, feeling euphoric about getting to fly again. He approached his ship, and it felt like it'd been a lifetime since he'd last stood there, and yet, it felt like it was just yesterday at the same time. *Time is funny like that…* Raiden thought. He walked around the outside of the ship, inspecting it. The streamlined metallic body was in pristine condition. He reached out and placed his hand on the ship, and the cool metal sent a shiver down his spine.

Once he was done with his exterior checks he climbed the ladder up into the cockpit and turned the ship on for a system check. The panel lit up, all the buttons glowing, and it made Raiden impatient for take-off. One by one he went through his checklist until he cleared all systems operational. He turned the engine off and looked at the time to see there was still 30 minutes until launch. Raiden sighed and leaned back in his pilot's seat, waiting for the time to pass by, one painfully slow minute after another.

|

In launch Bay E Masato and Koji were going over the mission parameters briefing with Dr. Takei and Zavion. "…and we'll be available on the comms' at all times," Zavion assured them.

"All tests have come back positive, we're not expecting any issues," Seto said.

Koji nodded, "Understood."

"Right then, let's get you ready to launch," Zavion said, and began walking towards the drill.

Masato and Koji took in the sight; the drill was enormous and took up the space of over half the launch bay. The large drill at the front of the craft was able to expand and contract, like a shutter, allowing them to open it to collect the materials they needed, which were then pulled into the largest part of the vessel; a massive storage compartment on the back which was over 80 percent of the ship. The cockpit sat resting on top, giving the pilot and co-pilot full view of their operating area.

Climbing up the ladder to get to the cockpit, Masato felt his nerves overcome him; he'd never had to pilot something so big. Koji's engineering skills meant he'd be in charge of the drilling, leaving Masato as their head pilot. While in open space the flight wouldn't be any different, however the idea of fitting this massive contraption out of the hanger bay doors was making him nervous. He swallowed the lump in his throat as he climbed into the cockpit.

Koji came in behind him, "This is amazing!" he exclaimed, "I can't believe they built this so fast... Man, in my days in engineering we never had projects like this. Ha, if I knew I'd have had the opportunity to do shit like this I might've never left!" He laughed.

"Yeah, yeah, old man, don't bust your gut," Masato said, trying to bury his fear with humor.

"Uhuh, *kid*, well don't take half the ship with you when you pull out," Koji jived back.

They both got in their seats, put their safety harnesses on, and began their internal systems check. After a few minutes they were green across the board and ready to launch. Masato flicked on the comm channel, "We're all systems go in here," he said.

"Roger that," a voice from flight control came back.

Orange lights in the hanger bay came on, signaling the opening of the exterior doors. While there was a force field preventing the suction from the harsh vacuum of space, it was still common practice for all personnel to evacuate the bay when the doors opened.

After 2 minutes the bay was cleared, and the outer doors opened up slowly, their pneumatic systems releasing the pressure as they went. The force field was holding at 100% integrity. Koji and Masato watched as the door cracked open and they could see it; space. The dark black blanket, sparking with distant stars, and the green-blue glow of the icy asteroid as it came into view. Both felt a sense of calm wash over them as they took in the sight; they were most at home in space.

Chapter 4: The Ice Asteroid

The drill had launched seamlessly from the hanger bay and hovered not far from the Saisei. Once they'd cleared the immediate vicinity of the ship hanger Bay B opened and Omega Squadron launched to join them. They got into a standard formation and began to make way towards the asteroid.

Norita watched from the command deck, as the ships disappeared toward the planet, with bated breath. It had all come down to this. General Takeo Yamamoto was on the command deck as well, overseeing his pilots. Jona hovered next to Norita, his nervous energy contagious.

"Jona, go check in with Dr. Takei, I would like an update on the distillation situation," Norita told him, grateful for the excuse to send him away.

Jona, looked at Norita, wanting to object so he could stay to watch, but he could think of no reason. "I… yes, yes of course," Jona said with a heaviness to his voice, and then left.

Immediately Norita breathed a sigh of relief when he'd left the room. She'd always been very empathetic, which had made her an excellent leader, but left her susceptible to the mood of those around her. She worked hard to stay focused.

Masato came in staticky over the radio, "Saisei, this is drill team, about to set down on the asteroid's surface."

Takeo clicked on the radio, "Slow and steady. Keep us apprised." Again, silence and waiting. Norita paced back and forth as she gazed out the window, the ships were out of view from this distance.

|

Masato let out a nervous breath and then took the ship in for a landing. Koji let down the landing gear, and Masato eased the ship down. The surface was horribly uneven, full of deep crevasses. It had taken them 10 minutes to finally find some ground they thought was suitable enough for landing. Masato eased the ship down slowly, and one by one he could feel the feet touch down on the surface. Once the ship had settled, Masato looked over at Koji who looked back and smiled, both feeling relieved.

"Nice job, kid," Koji said, unbuckling his harness, "I'm going to go prep the drill."

Masato nodded, "Need help?"

Koji shook his head, "Nah, take a break, you earned it."

Koji stood up and began to walk towards the back of the cockpit when suddenly the ship jolted forward sharply. Koji lost his footing and tumbled forward, smashing his shoulder into the front panel. "Urg!" Koji cringed as sharp shooting pains raced down his arm.

Masato's heart was racing as the ship tipped forward. He looked over at Koji who was trying to stand back up despite the steep angle the ship now sat at. "Koji, you OK?!" he asked, exasperated.

"I'll live," Koji grunted angrily. The ship creaked loudly as it settled into place. Both men held their breath as they waited to see if that was the end of it, and after a few moments, they breathed a sigh of relief.

Flicking on the radio, Masato reported in, "Saisei this is drill team. We have landed on the surface. Preparing to engage drill." Koji, nursing his shoulder, went to get the drill prepped.

A moment later he hard Takeo come back over the radio, "Excellent job drill team. Keep us updated with your progress."

"Yes, sir," Masato replied, then turned off the radio transmitter.

Unbuckling his harness, Masato went to check on Koji, "How's the arm?"

Koji kept working, "Arm's fine, but I think my shoulder's dislocated. Hurts like hell... feels like sandpaper in the joint, and I can't lift my arm."

Masato felt a pang of guilt for not landing the ship better, "Is there anything I can do?"

"Systems coming online... looking good," Koji said, focused on his work, then he looked at Masato, "Once we get the drill going I need you to pop my shoulder back in place."

Masato stared back dumbfounded, "I, uh, I've never..." he was at a loss for words.

Koji laughed, "Don't worry, I'll walk you through it, kid."

They continued to go through the drill prep sequence together. Everything was going according to plan. The ship's insulation was doing well to maintain heat. Masato had landed the ship on the daylight side of the planet, to help with the extreme temperatures while they tested everything out and got the drill up and running.

I

Omega Squadron engaged their neutrino emitters and took off en route to their designated training zone away from the asteroid. 10 minutes after the drill had safely landed on the planet they had been given the all a clear to break away from the planet for drill practice. Months overdue, Raiden was finally getting the chance to lead the team. They broke orbit and Raiden instructed the team on the maneuvers and flight plan he had in store for them once they were far enough away.

Takeo watched from the Saisei, between the window and the radar read out as Omega Squad flew out to get into position to carry out their drills. Once they were far enough out Raiden had the team cut their neutrino emitters and start the drills. General Yamamoto listened in on his earpiece as Raiden gave commands to the team and watched the response times pan out. The General was impressed with Raiden's command abilities; he'd always had a way with his comrades that made them respect him. Between that and Raiden's natural piloting skills, and intuitive strategic sense, it made him a natural leader.

Norita, pacing the command deck, walked up to Takeo and stood next to him. "How're the drills going, General?" she asked, trying to pass the time, and calm her nerves.

"Quite well," he replied simply.

Norita smiled, Takeo always treated her like a normal person, unintimidated by her title. She watched the radar screen intently. The dots representing the ships moved with precision, and unison. A moment later Norita's personal communicator beeped, and she clicked it on, "yes?" she said.

"It's Jona, I'm with Dr. Takei and Zavion," his mild-mannered voice was hard to hear over the static, "The distillation unit is ready. Dr. Takei has requested we have it moved into one of the docking bays for its first real test run with the first load that the drill brings back, in the event any harmful fumes get into the air the bay can easily be purged," Jona explained.

"Approved, you can get underway immediately," Norita replied.

General Yamamoto chimed in, "Bay D is empty."

Norita nodded at him, then spoke to Jona, "Jona, take the distillation device to bay D."

"Yes, ma'am. We're on it," Jona said.

Norita clicked off her communicator. "Thanks," she said, turning to Takeo.

Takeo simply nodded, "You're welcome."

"What the hell...?" Koi blurted out as he sat staring dumbfounded at his control panel. Norita and General Yamamoto immediately turned their attention to him.

"What is it?" Takeo asked.

"The exterior door to docking bay A is opening," Koi said, confused.

"There's nothing scheduled in bay A," Takeo said.

"I know," Koi said, "I'm trying to override it... shit, I'm locked out!"

Suddenly the emergency lights and siren came online. Yellow lights flashed along the way, and the loud *Bleep!* of the alarm sounded every 10 seconds. Norita clicked on her communicator, "Security, report!" she demanded.

A long 20 second passed and then, "...It's a coup! ..." the voice came in, along with the sound of gunshots. "...So many... outnumbered.... they're stealing the ships! ..." the distorted voice came fragmented.

"What the hell is going on?" Norita asked, trying to piece it together, and shot a glance at Takeo who had heard it all.

"They're launching!" Koi announced. Norita and Takeo rushed back over to the window and watched as ship after ship flew out from the Saisei. The General turned his attention to the radar, and it was clear the ships were headed towards the drill site on the asteroid below.

Takeo flipped on the radio, "Lieutenant Saito, come in!"

"Raiden here, go ahead," his voice came back over the comm.

"Ships are inbound on the drill site, you need to return with your squadron immediately to intercept them and protect the drill team," Takeo commanded.

"Yes sir," Raiden replied. Immediately they could see the course change of Omega Squadron as they turned about face to head back towards the drill site. Then Takeo contacted Koji and Masato to warn them of the potential threat that was headed their way.

"What in the world are they trying to do? Take the water for themselves? But why?" Norita said, thinking out loud. They stood in silence watching and waiting. Then Norita's eyes widened, "Jona and the science team, they're heading towards the docking bays!" Quickly Norita tapped on her communicator, "Jona, come in! ...Jona? Are you there? ...Jona?!"

There was nothing but static, and then, "Jona's unable to speak right now," an unfamiliar voice replied.

Norita's eyes shot up to meet Takeo's, "Who is this?" Norita demanded.

"Hahaha, you don't get to make demands anymore," the voice said, amused and yet entirely serious. Then the connection was cut, and everything went silent.

"Hello? Hello?! Dammit!" Norita said, exasperated.

After pacing for a moment Norita turned to Koi, "Can we lock down the entire docking area? Use the emergency port seals maybe?" she asked, trying to find the solution.

Koi shook his head, "Normally yes, but whoever did this had a plan, they've completely locked me out of the controls. I'm trying to get past their encryption, but it could take a while," he explained, still working away at his computer.

The constant pulse of the alarm was beginning to give Norita a headache, but she tried to push through it. Norita walked back over to Takeo who was anxiously watching the radar. Glancing at the screen Norita could see the rogue ships were just minutes away from the drill site. Omega Squadron was closing in, but at least twice the distance away. She looked up from the monitor and stared down at the asteroid, feeling a pit at the bottom of her stomach as she watched, helplessly.

Then it happened, in an instant, a bright blinding flash. Norita's jaw dropped, and she felt the air rush out of her lungs. The renegade ships had all fired on the drill, igniting the fuel assembly, which created a massive explosion as the drill exploded. "Holy hell!" Koi yelled, in shock. General Yamamoto watched stoically, suppressing the horror of it all to keep his mind straight.

Why would they blow it up? Norita's mind raced, unable to understand the destruction. *Who the hell did this? What the fuck do they want?* She felt rage overcome her.

"Don't let them get away!" Norita spat angrily.

General Yamamoto was already a step ahead, "Raiden, come in."

|

Speeding towards the asteroid and the drill site, the unexpected explosion of the drill nearly sent Omega Squad reeling off course. The blast wave from the explosion shook their ships violently as they continued, on course with their approach vector. Wide-eye Raiden stared ahead at the flames and the wreckage floating away. "Koji! Masato!" he gasped.

"Mother-fuckers!" Freya screamed in her cockpit. The explosion was horrific, tearing the drill to shreds. Bits of the ship began to float away; the asteroid's gravity was too low to hold them down. The methanol in the ice on the asteroid fueled the fire, lighting up the ground all around the drill site in a brilliant burst of blue and yellow flames. The attacking ships turned and fled, engaging their neutrino engines, to get away from Omega Squad. Raiden ordered his team to engage their own neutrino engines and to pursue at full speed.

|

Koji floated among the wreckage of the ship, disoriented and terrified. He'd been next to the front window of the pilot's cabin when the ship exploded, and the force of the blast had knocked out the window and shot him through the hole. Masato had been right next to the engine when it happened, and though it had been in the blink of an eye, Koji couldn't get the image of Masato's body being consumed by the flames out of his mind.

Straining to breathe, Koji tried to focus; the world around him spun out of control as his body was hurtling into space. He brought up his right arm in front of his face to access his suit's built-in computer panel, only to find the screen had been horribly smashed. He tried holding down the button to activate his radio signal, "Hello?!" he asked scared, hoping for a response. But none came.

|

Back on the Saisei all hell was breaking loose. Reports were pouring in from all over the ship, political officials were being rounded up, and dragged out of their homes. An all-out war between the security teams and the terrorists had broken out.

Norita tried to make sense of it, but it was all too chaotic.

"Takeo, we have to get this situation contained! The ships aside, I'm assuming this is all happening in the docking bays, so I don't want anyone able to come in or out of the area. If they've locked us out of the controls, then we need people down there barricading them in. It sounds like the security teams were overwhelmed, so I need you to get soldiers in place down there," Norita explained.

"Right," Takeo nodded in agreement. Turning on the comm, Takeo spoke, "Captain Yoshini, come in?" A long silence hung in the air. "Yoshini, do you read me?" Takeo asked. Again, a long silence followed.

Just as Takeo was about to change the frequency, Yoshini replied, "I'm here," the voice came in a whisper.

"What's your situation?" Takeo asked.

There was a pause, and then, "The barracks are being overrun... I'm hiding in my locker. They raided the armory, I... I think they're leaving. Whoever they are, they're organized... they're gone," Gin explained. Norita and Takeo looked at each other, their mutual concern overwhelming them now.

They listened to Gin as he walked around the barracks and explained what had happened. Most of the soldiers were at their posts, but Gin had been scheduled to a late shift, so he'd been sleeping when he'd awoken to hear the alarm going off, and a mass of encroaching footsteps. Immediately Gin had hidden and watched as it all unfolded. The terrorists were well armed with military weaponry. They had ransacked the barracks, and after a thorough search for anything usable they'd finally left. "… then they mentioned something about finishing their rounds. A couple of them were covered in blood, I think they might be shooting people," Gin finished.

Norita shook her head in disbelief. "Where's the rest of your team?" Takeo asked.

"Supposed to be on guard duty as well as some at the holding cells, but with everything going on I don't know for sure," Gin responded.

"Round up whoever you can. We believe the bulk of the terrorists are holed up in the docking bays. Make your way down there and report in, we need to get a clearer picture of what's happening. I'll be calling in Alpha and Beta Squads as well, we will retake control of this ship," Takeo instructed with conviction.

"Yes sir," Gin said.

|

Link led the rebellion's ships when they'd blown up the drill, and now on their escape vector. They hadn't anticipated such a narrow escape from Omega Squadron. The chase was getting more intense by the minute. Link instructed all of his pilots to max out their engines in an attempt to gain more distance, but Omega Squad wasn't afraid to pursue at the same alarming speeds. Now their engines were beginning to redline, and Link was feeling the pressure.

Link considered heading back to the Saisei, but he knew Omega Squadron would never let them get close. He wanted to turn his ships around to take out Omega Squad, but the pilots he commanded were much less skilled, and he was certain they'd all die in a head-on battle. His mind was racing.

Out of the corner of his eye Link noticed a large gas giant planet to his left in the distance. It would take over an hour to get there if they kept up near light-speed, but then they'd have a chance to lose the pursuant ships in the atmosphere, and then, they could form a surprise attack, and with any luck come out unscathed. It was their only chance. He gave the command, and they all changed course for the gas giant.

Immediately Omega Squadron changed their flight path to match, but Link expected as much. "Come get us," he said, watching the ships on his radar. Link had once been a military pilot, but he'd resigned his post when Suki was born; he wanted nothing more than to provide the best life possible for her. Though it'd been years since he'd been at the helm, it felt as if it'd only been a day. Link was born to fly, the ship was an extension of himself, and he could maneuver it effortlessly in any way he could imagine. His adrenaline was pumping, and for the first time in years, he felt alive.

|

"Lock them up over there, with the rest of them," Niko commanded. For the past hour Niko's insurgent men had been bringing the government officials into the hanger bay, locking them up as prisoners in the equipment room where all of the repair equipment for the ships were stored. Terrified, enraged, pleading; the officials came into the situation confused and overwhelmed. They didn't know why they were being taken, but panic and fear ran rampant among them.

Several of the insurgents approached Niko with Zavion, Dr. Takei, and Jona in tow, all of whom were handcuffed and disheveled. Blood dripped drown Zavion's chin from an obvious kerfuffle between him and one of Niko's men. "I found 'em walking down the hall. They said they were headed to work on the distillation processor," one of the men explained.

Niko nodded, "Thank you," he said to his men.

Niko looked Dr. Takei and Zavion up and down, then smiled, "The Saisei's lead scientist and head engineer, what a catch." Then his attention turned to Jona, and he frowned, "Put this one with the others," Niko said, disgust rang in his voice. Immediately one of Niko's men jumped to action and hauled Jona away.

Turning back to Seto and Zavion, Niko spoke jovially, "Well... do I ever have a job for you two." Zavion and Seto said nothing. "You'll reprogram the system, so I can control the Saisei from here." Niko explained, "Full control, we'll need a complete navigation system so that..."

Zavion cut him off, "Go to hell!" he spat.

"*Tsk, tsk, tsk!*" Niko began again, "Bad manners are unbecoming," his voice became flat. Then Niko waved over one of his men, and the man zapped Zavion with an electrified baton.

"Argh!" Zavion screamed, then fell to his knees, gasping for breath through the pain. Seto watched wide-eyed, horrified by the barbaric display of power.

"Now then," Niko started again, "the navigation system..."

|

Suki was beginning to panic. When the alarms had gone off, someone had engaged the emergency quarantine system, which had locked her and everyone else's quarters. She was trapped and alone. Not long after her father had left, her mother had gone to pursue him, and she hadn't returned.

After a long struggle with the door, Suki had given up on trying to open it. The locking system was mechanized, controlled by the main Saisei systems panel, and could only be opened from a main access panel. Suki paced in her living room, wracking her brain for a way to escape.

What the hell is going on? She wondered as she paced. She had seen fighter ships flying away from the asteroid, though she couldn't tell why or where they were going; her window didn't face the drill site. *Where the fuck did dad go? I hope mom's okay...* she thought to herself, worried. A nagging sinking feeling gripped at her. As she continued to pace, suddenly, she remembered her data pad...

|

Hiroshi had watched the entire thing from his quarters; the ships, the explosion, the chase, he was in shock and awe of it all. While he had no way of knowing for sure, he instinctively felt Niko had something to do with it. The way that Niko had spoken with such spiteful passion in the concourse about the political structure, it all made sense to him that Niko was behind this. He'd heard a commotion in the hallway not too long ago, and Councilor Uda's voice was as clear as day.

Merrick Uda lived two doors down from Hiroshi and had always been a pleasant neighbor. Merrick was someone who always led from the heart and had gotten into politics to make sure the voices of the minority were also heard. Hiroshi had great respected for him, and hoped he was OK.

Standing by the window, Hiroshi watched as the debris from the asteroid continued to slowly drift away into space, lit up by the sun. It was as beautiful as it was tragic. The ships had quickly disappeared out of view behind the asteroid after the explosion, and he wondered what was happening amongst them now.

Suddenly Hiroshi heard a faint *Bleep!* which drew him away from the window. He sought out the sound and found his data pad was blinking while it beeped. He turned it on and found a message from Suki on the screen: Are you there? Hiroshi wondered how the message had arrived, the communication channels had been shut off since the lockdown had gone into effect. He wrote back: Yes. How'd you get a message through? Where are you?

A few minutes passed, and then another message from Suki came in: I'm locked in my quarters alone. I set up a proxy signal, so it looks like regular ships systems talking to each other and I just piggybacked our signal into the military network. Do you know what's happening? Hiroshi shook his head and smiled. *Brilliant,* he thought.

Hiroshi began writing back: I'm locked in too. I don't know for sure, but I think it's some sort of coup. I heard one of the councilors being dragged from their quarters, and I haven't seen the fighter ships since they blew up the drill. Where are your parents?

A moment later Suki's reply came: They blew up the drill?! Why would they do that?! We all need water! And a coup? This is crazy. My parents had a big fight before this all happened, I don't know all of the details, but it was about politics. We need to get out and help. Do you know how to override the lockdown?

Mulling over the question, Hiroshi tried to think through the problem. He wasn't an engineer, or overly technically minded, but he knew the ships lockdown ran through electrical systems. The electronic computer interface is what allowed complete autonomy to run everything from the helm of the ship. But knowing the basic system set up didn't help Hiroshi in thinking about how to override it. He was unsure if the systems could be hacked into. While he was certain getting into the wall to access the wiring could manually open the doors, even if he had the tools to get in he wasn't sure he'd know what to do.

Resigned, he wrote back: The systems are electrical, and tied into the ships main computer, but I don't know how to access any of that. For now, it's safer to stay where you are. If anyone comes by your quarters, just hide. I'm sure help is on the way, we just have to wait it out. Hiroshi wrote, only half believing it.

Hiroshi tossed his data pad down on his couch, and then walked back over to the window, and stared at the asteroid. *What are we going to do?* He asked himself, but there was no answer. His mind raced, as if trying to piece a 100 puzzle pieces together while only holding 5 pieces, it was infuriating.

Chapter 5: Discovery

Norita and Takeo waited with bated breath. The General had managed to round up soldiers from all over the ship, got them organized, and was sending them in force down to the hanger bays to retake control of the ship. Norita kept checking the radar, but the ships had gone out of range. The lack of intel caused her anxiety to creep up. She continued to tell herself to let it go, but she couldn't seem to manage it; she was rattled.

They had closed the secondary door hatch with its manual lever lock that could only be opened and closed by hand from inside their room, and it had saved their lives. Not 30 minutes prior, a massive insurgent team had tried to storm the command center. With complete control over the computer systems they unlocked the outer door in under 30 seconds, much to Koi's dismay. The hatch, however, proved impenetrable.

The inner hatch had been designed using the old methods in submarines and major sailing vessels; made of ultra-thick steel, reinforced with polycarbonate, and it had been designed to create an airtight seal. It was bulletproof and had no method of entry from the exterior. To Norita's horror the insurgents attempted to blow the door up with some sort of pipe bomb, and despite a hefty explosion, the door held, though the shockwave had still been extensive and had sent Norita toppling to the floor. The men had given up trying to get in after that, at least for the time being, but the incident had left her feeling shaken.

After what had seemed an eternity, a voice came on over the radio, "This is Captain Yoshini, come in, over." Immediately General Yamamoto perked up and hurried over to the radio, Norita in tow, to respond. Koi, who'd been bent over his work station tirelessly trying to override the controls, sat up and leaned over to listen in.

"This is General Yamamoto, report," he said, eager to get information.

"I've made my way to the hanger bays. Most of the ship is quiet, everything is locked down. There are groups of the terrorists wandering the ship, how many, I'm not sure. Here in the bays I see about 100 of them, the majority in Bay A. They've taken hostages, they're locked up in a caged-in section of the bay where the parts and tools for ship maintenance are held, in Bay A. I gathered most of my team, 21 men, and have them getting in positions around Bay A," Gin explained.

"Excellent work, Captain," Takeo praised. The General felt immediately better now that he had a better idea of what was happening. "I've got more troops on headed your way. What's your exact position? I'll have them coordinate with you. Even with the backup you'll still be outnumbered, about 2 to 1, but with the element of surprise, I want you to subdue and dissolve this insurrection and free the hostages. You're to take all of these terrorists under arrest, disarm them, and have them return control of the ship's computer to the main helm. Understood?" Takeo directed.

"Understood, sir. My men and I in cover in the air duct by the left entrance to the bay," Gin responded.

"I'll relay that, expect reinforcements to arrive within 10 minutes. You have the authority to begin the operation as soon as they arrive," Takeo replied.

"Yes sir," Gin's voice came back, enlivened.

Norita looked to Takeo and smiled, "Good work."

|

Time had seemed as if it had suspended as Koji floated in space, and he wondered how long it had been. His shoulder pained him greatly; Masato had never had a chance to fix the dislocation. Koji felt light headed and fought to concentrate. *Did I hit my head?* He asked himself, unsure. Everything since the drill landed had seemed like a blur.

The trajectory of the blast had sent him hurtling towards the Saisei at first, though as the ship rotated in orbit as the asteroid rotated, it was slowly moving out of alignment with him. Koji had no idea how fast he was moving. At times he felt as if he was still, and at others, he could see his distance from the drill site on the asteroid was becoming greater and greater. *Am I going to die? No one knows I'm here... or do they? But the ships are gone... what the hell happened?* His mind was rapid-firing questions to which he had no answers.

Koji tried to turn his mind off, but the questions persisted. Fear gripped at him with the thought of dying alone in space. *I don't want to suffocate...* he thought, terrified by the idea. He wished his suit's computer had been operational, so he could check the O2 readouts. *How much is left?* He tried to think, but there were too many factors to know for certain.

I

Raiden watched as the enemy ships disappeared out of sight into the gas giant's atmosphere. Raiden checked his radar, but the ships weren't visible on it. *Must be a lot of radiation...* he thought. Raiden eased up on the throttle, and his squad did the same.

Freya came in on his headset, "Hey, we goin' in?" she asked.

Raiden hesitated before answering, "No. Could be a trap, we'd be going in blind." Taking a moment, he tried to think of the best next move. "Alright, Omega Squad, we're going to set up NET formation, so we have eyes on all possible angles. We're not going to risk an ambush, but we're not letting them get away either. We'll get into position, and then wait them out," Raiden instructed. "Freya, you and I will take the far side of the planet," he said, then instructed the rest on their positioning. "Alright everyone, move out!" Raiden commanded at the end, and all the pilots began to head towards their designated position.

"Race ya to the other side!" Freya's voice playfully said, and then Radian watched as her ship sped off.

"Hey!" he laughed as he watched her take her unfair lead, then sped after her.

"Can't be asleep at the helm, man!" Freya jived.

Raiden, focused on the race, didn't respond. He pulled in closer to the planet to use the force of the orbit to pull his ship around faster. It only took a moment before he was catapulted past Freya's ship, and with a good lead on her.

Checking his rearview, Raiden saw Freya following suit and catching up fast, so he pushed the engines harder. *They red-lined before, they can handle it*, he told himself. The engine light went off, but he ignored it, and pressed forward. Freya was doing the same, keeping pace not far behind, though Raiden was certain she wouldn't be able to get ahead now.

Navigation read that they were nearing the back end of the planet. Raiden gazed at his radar and saw his lead on Freya. He opened his mouth to tease Freya about not being able to beat him, but his jaw just dropped instead, and that's when he saw *it*. Staring forward in awe, Raiden marveled at the sight before him.

About 20,000 kilometers ahead of Raiden's ship he saw long curved silver-metallic arcing beams, massive in scale, entwined into what looked like a giant eye. The massive structure, 10 times the size of the Saisei, floated in space like a celestial being. In the center of it all light emitted from white particulates dancing in circles. The light from this solar system's sun lit up the entire structure, bathing in in golden light.

"Pull up!" Freya's voice screaming at him snapped Raiden back to reality. They were approaching the structure alarmingly fast. Freya pulled her ship up hard and immediately reduced speed. Raiden veered left, diving towards the planet's atmosphere, hoping the gravitational pull would help pull him far enough away to avoid a collision.

The engine light was blinking and this time it had gone too far. The alarm began to go off, and the engine stopped responding; the overheating finally taking its toll. "Fuck!" Raiden yelled, as his control panel went dark. Raiden's trajectory wasn't far enough over, and he could tell he was going to collide with the outermost ring of the structure. There wasn't enough time to let the engine rest for a restart either. His adrenaline was pumping, and his mind racing. With no other choice, he started preparing to eject, checking his space suit to make sure all of his seals were done up properly, and securing his helmet.

Fear overcame Raiden, he'd never had to eject before, and only had minimal training during basic spacewalks during his first year as a cadet. They were so far from the Saisei, he wondered if his homing beacon would work. *What if it malfunctions?* His mind ran through all of the worst-case scenarios. All the while the structure was getting bigger and bigger as the ship hurtled towards it.

WHAM! Without warning Freya ran her ship into Raiden's to push it out of the way. The unexpected hit gave Raiden whiplash. His unprepared body flung back head against his seat, and the weight of his helmet threw his head back hard, badly straining his neck. "Ouph!" Raiden belted involuntarily from the impact. The hit had been just enough to push his ship out of harm's way, and they sped past the side of the structure unscathed.

Both ships were fine, despite how intense the collision felt to the pilots, less for some scratched paint. Freya had impeccable control over her ship. She caught her breath as the exhilaration started to wear off. "You OK?" she asked.

It took a minute before Raiden replied, "I'll live..." his voice indicative of the pain he was in.

"Sorry for the surprise man, I saw your ship go dark, and the opportunity, and I went for it. If I hadn't..." she went to explain.

Raiden cut her off. "You saved me and the ship, no explanation necessary... though next time yell or something," he said. Freya laughed, glad her best friend was alive and safe.

Turning her attention to the mega-structure, Freya was enthralled. *What the hell is this thing?* She wondered. It was so massive in scale. Moreover, it was clearly developed by someone, or something. After all their years alone in space, they finally had proof of other forms of intelligent life. Freya wondered if that was good or bad. *How could anything bad make something so beautiful...* she thought. It was ethereal.

Raiden's engines started back up, and his ship lit up, grabbing Freya's attention. "Good, you're alive," she said.

"Ha, yeah not dead in the water. Not yet anyway," Raiden's jovial voice replied.

Freya's smile faded as she turned her attention to the structure, "This thing... what do you think it is? Hell, my proximity sensors didn't go off, did yours?" she asked.

"I have no idea what it is, and no mine didn't go off either," Raiden replied.

"Shit, must be made of something weird," Freya said, staring at the arcing metal.

"Turn on your scanners, let's see what we can find out, but don't get too close. We don't know what it does," Raiden warned.

Freya and Raiden started flying around the massive structure, scanning everything they could. Their imaginations ran away with them as they wondered what the monolithic structure was for, and who could have built such a thing. Freya imagined it might be a weapon, the energy at the center of the structure deadly. She shuttered at the thought of the devastation something so big could cause; if it was a weapon it could obliterate an entire planet.

Hours later they were only done scanning roughly a third of the structure. Freya shifted uncomfortably in her seat, her left butt cheek had gone numb. *I'd give anything for some coffee,* she thought, he energy waning. Thirst and hunger were beginning to take their toll. She looked over at her emergency rations kit and considered opening it, despite how tasteless and unpalatable she remembered that the dense protein was, her rumbling stomach convinced her it would be delicious. Her parched mouth and dry lips demanded satisfaction.

Freya reached over to grab the emergency rations when, all of the sudden, she noticed movement on her radar screen. She looked up to see ships emerging from the planet's atmosphere. "Shit! Raiden, we've got company!" she leaned back hard into her seat and changed course.

Raiden saw them coming, and he could feel a cold sweat break out all over his body, "Omega Squad, this is Raiden, close in on my position. We have incoming hostiles, repeat, incoming hostiles on my position!" Raiden matched Freya's position, and primed his guns. "Don't be a hero Freya," he said.

"Yeah, yeah. You be careful too," she said, trying to disguise the worry in her voice. Raiden smiled, in their roundabout way, though they never talked about it, they cared one another, and he could feel it in her inflection. Raiden watched, and waited, laser-focused as the ships came on approach.

Trying different comm frequencies, Raiden tried to make contact with the renegade ships, "This is Lieutenant Raiden Saito, Omega Squad leader. You are to surrender and return to the Saisei immediately, failure to comply will result in the use of force." No reply, only static, so Raiden moved on to the next frequency.

The ships were closing in fast, in a V formation. Freya took a deep breath and prepared herself for action. She saw the first of the Omega Squad reinforcements circle around the side of the gas giant, but they wouldn't be of any use to them for some time. For now, it was up to her and Raiden to subdue to the insurrection forces.

The first volley of shots was fired from Link's ship, the head of the V formation, and seconds later, the rest of the insurgent ships fired. A wide spread of bullets rushed toward Freya and Raiden. Immediately they both went into evasive maneuvers.

"Shit! Guess it's on... Freya, open fire!" Raiden commanded, his heart thumping hard in his chest. "All ships, open fire!" he relayed to the rest of the enclosing Omega Squadron pilots. Freya went full throttle towards the insurgents, gunning at Link's ship. The V formation broke, and all of the ships scattered, swarming like flies. Raiden flew into the frenzy cautiously, still worried about his engines. He kept his eyes open and his senses alert. There was a lot happening all at once, and one wrong move could mean the difference between life and death.

Bullets flew in continuous streams, so Freya and Raiden did their best to use confusing tactics and flight patterns to avoid being hit. They both knew they just needed to buy enough time until the rest of their squad could join the fight. While they aimed to disable the enemy ships, more importantly, they tried to stay elusive to avoid being taken down themselves.

When Freya and Raiden had been cadets they'd both constantly tried new flight maneuvers and made up their own duo moves. They were competitive, both wanting to be the best, and yet highly innovative as a team. Their skills were unmatched by any of the other cadets.

One duo they'd created was called the *infinity,* where each of them flew around the other, each creating a horizontal S that combined formed the infinity symbol ∞. It was a risky move, both ships came in alarmingly close contact in the center of the infinity, but it also kept them in a perpetual dodge, and was excellent for disorienting onlookers. "Freya, infinity!" Raiden instructed.

Freya grinned wide, "Oh, hell yeah!" she cheered, and got her ship in position.

Several of the insurgent ships were rushing at them from the front, guns blazing, while another was positioning themselves to attack from the rear. Meanwhile Link was organizing a pincer attack with three other ships; the direct attack was just a distraction. Link knew his pilots would be hard pressed to succeed if they had to face all of Omega Squad all at once, and that their best chance was to pick away at them. Now that the other ships were closing in, taking out these two before the other's arrived was his only hope.

"Freya, now!" Raiden commanded, the approaching ships hail of bullets seconds away from taking them down. Raiden pulled hard to the right and started the maneuver, arcing upwards, and accelerating as fast as he felt the ship could take it. The intense force on his body from the sudden high speeds made him wonder why they added gravity plating to the small fighter ships, but then he shook his head and forced his thoughts to refocus on the perilous task at hand.

At the top of the arc Raiden always felt a sense of fear, even as a so-called fearless cadet, although he'd never admit it to Freya. Every time, right before he plunged his ship down to create the near-miss of the two ships meeting in the center of the infinity, his heart leapt into his throat. They'd done this maneuver countless times since its creation, and Raiden knew Freya was an extraordinary pilot, but even so, no matter what he told himself, the vision of colliding in a lethal explosion always played through his mind.

Fighting through the all-too-familiar fear, Raiden took the plunge. Cascades of bullets were flying at them from all angles. Freya and Raiden fired back as best they could while flying their risky ploy. Somehow Raiden managed to check his radar in the midst of it all, the closest of his squad were about 3 minutes away still. *C'mon, hurry up!* He thought, worried they may come too late. Sweat dripped down his face.

Then the pass came. Freya's ship passed under Raiden's, just a few feet away from each other, at breakneck speeds. While it only lasted for less than a second, time felt like it had slowed to a near halt. Freya reveled in the danger, it made her feel alive. The euphoric endorphin rush it gave her made her feel like she could take on the entire insurgency herself.

Narrowing her vision, the dangerous pass over, Freya focused on taking perfect aim. She targeted one of the ships trying to circle overhead, aiming just ahead of the cockpit to disable the navigation system, she fired. The ship veered right to dodge, but not in time, and the bullets shredded through the O2 cylinder and gas tank, exploding the ship into a flying fireball that surged past Freya's ship.

Freya's eyes bulged at the near miss as the ship whizzed past hers, and she let out a shaky exhale. After taking a second to regroup Freya noticed that there were 2 ships coming at her from the side. It was Link and another insurgent, speeding up, and putting their pincer attack into action. She was about to turn her ship to face them, when she saw there was another ship closing in from behind. "Fuck!" she yelled, feeling trapped, and abruptly shot the nose of her ship down and tried to speed away.

The other ships were in full pursuit of Freya. Raiden watched as Freya broke formation and then saw the ships enclosing on her, their barrages barely missing. Just as Raiden was about to go help, he saw 2 ships on approach towards him; the other half of the pincer attack. "Slimy bastards!" Raiden grunted through his teeth. There was no time to think, he immediately set into pulling the nose of his ship straight up and pushed the ship's speed to its limits.

He did a full circle and pulled in behind both ships, then fired before they had a chance to escape.

He managed to disable the first ship, but the second ship had only taken superficial damage, and was coming around to counterattack. Raiden rushed to try and match the pilots' flight path in order to stay behind him and to avoid having to dodge the guns. Continuously firing, Raiden was hoping for a hit.

Meanwhile, Freya was in the fight for her life. All three ships were enclosing on her. She accelerated, trying to gain some distance, but they were quick to adapt. *Fuck... there's too many... I can't... Wait!* Freya felt a sense of empowerment wash over her. She may have been outgunned, but she had more piloting skill than the entire insurgency put together. "Let's play..." she muttered under her breath and bit her lip. Changing her heading, she began to fly right towards the nearest arc of the mega-structure, her pursuers not far behind.

Something about a challenge enlivened her. It was the rush that she found herself so easily addicted too. It was almost sensuous; the power trip, the complete and utter control, and the risk of it all. One wrong move and she'd be dead. She accelerated even more.

Freya was in the *zone*. It was as if she had access to her sixth sense, she felt almost out of body, and had complete awareness of everything; her ship, their ships, the swaths of bullets, the distance to the structure, everything. She could feel the rise and fall of her chest as the air came in and out, and it felt slow, even though everything was happening so fast.

Around or through?... Through, she thought. She was less than 30 seconds away from a collision with the large arc she was speeding at. It would be safer to make a wide birth and go around all of the entwining arcs, but that would also be easier for the insurgents too. Zigzagging in and out of the arches was a master pilots game at these speeds, and Freya was ready for the test.

Just a couple seconds away from running full speed into the metal arc, Freya pulled hard left, narrowly missing it, and then sharp right, maneuvering through the arcs. One of the insurgents followed closely, with much less precision, catching his wing on the metal arc which savagely ripped it off and left him spinning out of control towards the gas giant. The second panicked after seeing the first not make it, and froze up, crashing directly into the arc in a massive ball of fire that was quickly snuffed out by the vacuum of space.

Link had intended to follow Freya, his skills reasonably sharp, but the explosion had thrown off his concentration, and he had involuntarily pulled right instead of left, and was now going towards the center of the mega-structure. As he neared the center, the particles sped up, and then a miraculous burst of colors occurred, and the sky blurred into a vortex that distorted the view of the stars. Link tried to pull away, but it was too late, the vortex pulled him in, and then it disappeared as abruptly as it had begun. Link was gone, and the small particles in the center began to innocently dance around again just as they had before.

Raiden had watched it all in horrified-awe. *What in the world?!* He couldn't make sense of it. Seconds after the vortex disappeared he heard a terrified voice come over his headset, "I surrender!" it screamed, strained with fear. The ship he'd been struggling with slowed down and powered off.

"Freya, are you alright?!" Raiden asked. Silence. "Freya?!" he felt his heart sink into the pit of his stomach. *Shit, oh, shit! Was she pulled in too?!* He feared the worst.

"...Did you ...ucking see that?! Tha... ship just poof.... gone!" Freya's voice suddenly came in, distorted in static. Raiden let out a sigh of relief.

"Yeah, no shit I saw that! Fuck, I was starting to think you were a part of it..." Raiden replied, still feeling his uneasiness at the thought of losing Freya.

"It was close, that vortex opened up right next to me. What the hell was it?" she asked, not expecting an answer, the static clearing up in the signal.

"Hell if I know, but my scanner was running when it happened. We'll see what the science team can figure out back at the Saisei," Raiden said, then, "Oh my god, the Saisei, the insurrection, we need to get back!"

The rest of Omega Squad had just arrived. Comm chatter took off as everyone incredulously gave their account of the vortex incident. Raiden did his best to calm them down and get them organized. He had one of the ships tow the surrendered ship back. They scanned for the ship that had lost its wing in its assault against Freya, but it had disappeared into the gas giant, and they could not find it. After giving up their search they set their course back to the Saisei at top speed.

Chapter 6: Control

The battle to reclaim the ship had turned into an all-out fire-fight in the flight bay. Captain Gin Yoshini had led the infiltration team. Strategically they'd enclosed on Bay A, and on Gin's command, they had all entered simultaneously, surrounding the insurgent troops. Before Gin had had time to call for a surrender, Niko had screamed at his unprepared men to attack. The peaceful surrender Gin had hoped for had turned into an assault within seconds. He commanded the men and women he led to run for cover and to fire at will.

The precision shooting of the military troops gave them an edge, but the sheer numbers of the insurgents had kept them in a powerful position. Niko was fearless, gripped with the feeling of righteousness, he bellowed his freedom speech through the Bay A speaker system. His voice rang above the deafening gunfire that echoed horribly off the metal walls.

Zavion and Dr. Takei had been out in the center of the room, under gunpoint, at work on the navigation system computer when the assault had begun. The man who had kept them under watch ran off to join in the fight. Defenseless and out in the open, they had decided to run to the far corner of the room and dove behind a stack of storage crates.

Shots fired were out of control, and the imprisoned diplomats found themselves dodging stray bullets that came in between the cage's bars. "Get down!" Merrick Uda had yelled, after he had narrowly missed being hit. The petrified politicians were frozen in place, they'd never seen such violence. Once Merrick was on the floor and realized only a handful of the others had listened, he yelled again, with a sense of authority ringing in his voice, "If you want to live, get on the damn floor!" The sheer shock of the tone of his voice got the attention of the others, and they quickly made their way to the floor.

There were many casualties on both sides, however all in all the military forces were succeeding at suppressing the uprising; and Niko knew it. His mind was racing, seeking a solution. Niko was unwilling to lose, to let his ideals die and kowtow to imperial government, let alone to rot in prison indefinitely for treason. Niko had been near the entrance to the storage unit where they kept the prisoners when the assault had begun and had locked himself in the large wrap around station next to it. This was where Bay A was controlled from, anything from the electronic locks of the storage unit, to mechanic maintenance scheduling, to the ship launches, was done from here.

After careful thought Niko knew there was no way escape. While eccentric, Niko was not willing to die for nothing, and the idea of living to fight another day, regrouping stronger, was the first thought that had crossed his mind as the situation became dire. But that wasn't an option. Every exit was covered, and the enemy would certainly gun him down the second that he made an attempt to get away. *If only there was a way to distract them… an explosion… Oh!* It was suddenly so clear.

Niko, on his knees, keeping his head down, sat up to access the bay's computer system. He cycled through the systems quickly until he found what he was looking for and activated the launch sequence, overriding the safety features, he disabled the outer force field, and opened the exterior door. The Bay A pneumatic door clunked loudly, the yellow lights lit up, and the door began to open. The very second the most minute gap in the exterior door occurred, the incredibly strong pull of the vacuum of space began to pull everyone and everything towards it. The fire-fight immediately ceased; everyone was now fighting desperately to survive.

Survival instinct kicked in before Gin even had time to fully realize what was happening. The second the yellow lights popped on he stopped firing, and ran full tilt, with no regard for being shot at, towards the nearest Bay A exit. He was 10 feet from the door when he began to feel the intense pull of space. Gin dropped to the floor, knowing full well there wasn't enough time for him to make it to the exit now. He pulled his rifle's shoulder holster off from around his neck, and deftly looped it through the metal grating on the floor. Once it was through he wrapped it multiple times around his right hand, and then held on for dear life.

Private Rei Davis, a petite woman, had watched Gin use the floor grates to hold on, and while she had dropped her rifle, her delicate fingertips were tiny enough to fit between the slats in the floor. She was holding on with great difficulty, but she was determined to live. Fear gripped at her, and she closed her eyes, wishing to be anywhere else.

The suction worsened exponentially as the door continued to open. Soldiers and insurgents alike tried to run, but they were no match against the force pulling on them, dragging them helplessly towards a grim death. That's when the screaming began. Horrified men and women struggled, grasping to hold onto anything to stop themselves from being pulled out into open space, but there wasn't much in the bay to grasp.

Seto and Zavion behind the storage crates were right next to the exterior door. The creates were secured to the floor with a ballistic fiber net that had been bolted down at the corners. They had grabbed onto it immediately, interlacing their hands behind the weave. As the suction became worse they found their bodies lifting up off the floor.

The diplomatic prisoners were pulled unceremoniously into a pile against the steel bars. The pain was excruciating, but no one could move. Jona had been next to the metal bars before the doors had opened, leaving him at the bottom of the pile of all the bodies. He was being crushed by the immense weight and was unable to breathe under the intense pressure of all of the bodies. The cold metal bars the dug into his side. He desperately tried to speak, to cry for help, relief, anything, but he couldn't make a sound.

Hovering in the air, gripping tightly and watching horrified, Gin saw, as one by one, the soldiers and insurgents were pulled out into space. Guns and debris flew out too. An unfastened storage crate slid screeching across the metal floor towards the outer door. It was on a direct path to hit Private Rei Davis. "Hey!" Gin had screamed to get her attention. Private Davis looked up and saw the massive heavy crate scraping against the floor coming like a freight train towards her.

Like a dear in the headlights, she froze, petrified, and seconds later it hit her, severing her fingers at the second knuckle. Even above all the other noise Gin heard the high-pitched anguished scream when it hit her. Her body was violently sucked out into space, blood spray and her fingers followed, and then the crate. Gin vomited violently.

While it hadn't been long, it had felt like an eternity. Whether it was the adrenaline, or the lack of oxygen, Gin didn't know, but seconds felt like minutes. The dizziness was beginning to set in, and Gin knew he would lose consciousness soon. He wanted to loop his hand around the holster again, but his arms felt numb. Then the blackness came.

Niko was about to lose consciousness as well. While the control room was walled in, it still shared ventilation with the Bay A, and the oxygen had been sucked out. Niko wanted to give it more time, to ensure his safety, but he knew if he didn't do it now he might pass out, and then he'd very likely die. With great difficulty concentrating, Niko accessed the computer to turn on the outer forcefield and shut the exterior door.

Instantly the suction stopped. Gin, Seto, and Zavion dropped down hard onto the floor, all of them unconscious. Oxygen was now being fed back into the room, but it was a slow process to fill such a massive space. Niko fought the bitter fatigue and took his opportunity to escape.

|

Beep! Koji heard the low oxygen indicator in his ear. Instinctively he lifted his arm to check the read-out, only to see the broken screen. "Shit..." he muttered. *It beeps when... 15% left? 5%? Fuck... I don't remember... Oh cock, shit, piss, I'm going to fuckin' die out here!* Koji, panic-ridden, began to hyperventilate. He had drifted further from the Saisei. He focused his eyes on it longingly. Then he squinted; the bodies and debris from Bay A were just becoming visible as tiny specs in the distance.

I'm seeing things... Koji thought. *Hallucinating, great... oxygen must be really low... And I'm starving. I'd give anything for some food. A big bowl of spicy peanut noodles...* Koji's belly rumbled at the thought. Koji blinked hard, but he still saw the specs in the distance, and they were moving, and getting bigger. *Is it real?* He questioned, unsure of himself, and of his mind.

Koji floated there, staring ahead with wonder. After a minute the large crate that had been sucked out from the bay was close enough for his eyes to make out. *It IS real!* He thought, momentarily delighted that he wasn't hallucinating. Then a sinking crushing feeling swept over him, *What the hell happened?* Koji tried to make sense of it. The attack on the drill, the ships flying off, and now the debris from the Saisei. *Is it all related? It must be... too odd to be a coincidence.*

Why would they vent out the hangar bay? Koji wondered. It seemed careless that they'd forgotten to tie down a crate before doing it. *Was there something going on? A Fire? Contamination of some sort?* There were too many possibilities for Koji to know.

He looked up, squinting, trying to get a better look at the smaller debris. A chill ran down his spine as the realization his him: he was looking at a person. Then he saw another, and another. Instantly he was reminded of his first day in pilot training when

General Yamamoto had been going over safety basics with them...

"...More than anything, you must remember to check your suit before every use and be extra careful when clipping in your helmet. Ask a fellow pilot to check your helmet seals if you're ever unsure. When the body is exposed to space, you must immediately exhale any oxygen from your lungs, or they will explode. The rest of the oxygen in your body will expand, and your body will bloat to approximately twice its regular size. Any moisture on the body instantly evaporates, meaning the surfaces of your tongue and eyes will boil. Without oxygen, you will lose consciousness within 15 seconds, and within 90 seconds, you'll be dead from asphyxiation..."

Koji shuttered remembering the grim details of exposure, and retched, but nothing came out. A cold sweat broke out all over his body, and Koji could feel the *thump!* Of every beat of his heart. He couldn't imagine the fear, the utter lack of control, or how it must have felt for all of those people now floating in space. *Those 15 seconds must have felt like foreve*r... he thought, fighting the lump in his throat.

|

"What the hell is going on down there?!" Norita demanded, her nerves frayed. There had been no response from the soldiers infiltrating Bay A for over 10 minutes, and their computers had shown them that the outer door had opened and that the forcefield had gone offline. General Yamamoto had continuously been trying to make radio contact, to no avail. Koi kept his head down, focused on his work, determined not to come under Norita's line of fire.

"Well?" Norita asked again, her voice low, and guttural.

Takeo stood up straight and faced her, unafraid and not in the mood to placate, "You know as much as I do. If you have nothing helpful to say, sit down, and keep quiet, so I can handle this."

Norita stood there, shocked. No one had ever spoken so bluntly to her before. While all her life Norita had always asked everyone to treat her like anyone else, no one had ever really done so. While she was overall a level-headed and practical woman, she found herself insulted by Takeo's slight. Just as she was about to retaliate, she reminded herself that this wasn't about her, that there was much more at stake than her ego, and to simply breathe. Biting her tongue, she turned her back to Takeo and walked over to the back wall and leaned against it. She focused on her deep breathing, trying to find her center, though she swore she was breathing out fire.

Takeo had seen the glint in Norita's eye, and he'd wondered if he'd gone too far. She was, after all, the Empress. After Norita had walked away, Takeo let out a silent sigh of relief, and returned to the radio, "Gin?... Gin, report!" There was nothing but dead air. "Anyone from Alpha squad, come in!... Beta squad, what's happening down there?" Still dead air.

The sound of Norita's footsteps approaching stole Takeo's attention. "Is there anyone we can send down there to see what's happening?" she asked, no edge to her voice.

Takeo sighed, "No, everyone's already down there..." The silence lingered.

"Oh my god!" Norita gasped.

"What?" Koi asked, the fatigue putting his nerves on edge. But Norita said nothing, and simply stood there as if paralyzed. Takeo caught her gaze and followed it; looking out the window he saw what she was looking at and was at a loss for words. The body of one of his soldiers from Bay A was floating past, then another, and another, then a civilian, and

Takeo wondered if it was an insurgent or an unlucky bystander.

"Well, now we know why the force field went down, the only question is, which side did it..." General Yamamoto said grimly.

"What in the hell?!" Koi said, enraged. *If only I'd had control of MY ship this never would have happened! Why didn't we have better safeguards? How could they do this...* he thought, the guilt panging.

Norita began to weep, feeling trapped and utterly defeated, "This is a nightmare..." she said almost inaudibly.

Then out of the silence, "...hello? ...repeat, this is... a squa... in..." the extremely distorted voice was barely audible above the static.

Takeo shot a hopeful look to Norita, who looked back at him with disbelief in her teary eyes. Takeo clicked in the radio then responded, "Repeat last transmission!" Again, an almost undecipherable message. Takeo waited a moment, despite his impatience, and then asked again for the transmission to be repeated.

"Command, this is Omega Squad, retur... base... reporting in," Raiden's voice was finally distinguishable above the static.

"Good to hear your voice," Takeo said, his relief evident, "report, where are you?"

"Approximately 15 minutes out from the ice asteroid, 50 or so away from the Saisei. The gas giant has been interfering with our comms, we detected high levels of radiation. All Omega pilots returning safely, we have one enemy ship surrendered we're towing back. All other enemy ships were destroyed, except for one..." Raiden explained in great detail about the megastructure they'd found and what had happened to the ship that had flown to close to the center.

Takeo, Norita, and Koi listened, not believing their ears. Norita was brimming with questions, but there were more immediate problems at hand. "General, have them sweep the debris, collect anything valuable, try to collect our people for... last rights, and then immediately dock and investigate Bay A," she instructed. Takeo nodded, glad to see Norita had regained her composure and sharp mind, which he had always respected.

Takeo began to relay the orders, "Come as quickly as possible, we're dealing with a terrorist situation and need all hands aboard. Change trajectory by 1-degree starboard. On your return vector you'll come into a debris field not far from the ship, run active scans and collect all valuables and bodies..." Before Takeo could continue, Raiden's distressed voice cut him off.

"Bodies, sir?! Did I hear that correctly?"

"You did, Lieutenant. Once you've collected all you can dock in Bay E, and immediately proceed to Bay A to investigate. The terrorist cell was held up in Bay A, but we've lost contact with our troops for over 30 minutes. The safeties were overridden, the outer hatch opened, and the force field was lowered. That's all we know," Takeo explained.

"Roger that, we're on our way, sir," Raiden said, trying to keep his composure in the face of the morbid news.

"Cavalry is on the way," Takeo said, trying to break the tension, but no laughed.

"It'll be over an hour before they dock, at least," Norita said, wringing her hands, "Koi, how's overriding going?"

"Slow, but I have some minor systems back, lighting, hydroponics bay atmosphere control, that sort of thing," Koi said wiping the sleep from his eyes. *How long have I been awake now? 28, 29 hours?* Koi's mind was beginning to wander, too tired to concentrate. Chills and cramping had swept over him from time to time.

"Koi," Norita said, snapping him back to attention.

"Hmm?" he asked.

"I need you to focus on getting control over the Bay E outer door. We need to be able to remotely access it to let Omega Squad in, roughly one hour from now, OK?" she asked, seeing how tired Koi was.

Koi nodded and then turned back to face his computer which just seemed to blur in front of his eyes. *Focus, damn you!* he demanded of his eyes. Koi worried about being able to gain access in time, and Norita could sense the man's anxiety. "Let me bring you some coffee," Norita said, happy for the excuse to do something, and needing a cup just as badly herself.

|

Hiroshi began to feel the weight of his eyelids. Things had been quiet for hours now, no footsteps in the halls, just silence. He had continued to communicate to Suki, for updates, but now there was nothing left to say. They were both trapped, all attempts to escape had been futile. All that was left was to wait. *Wait for what?* Hiroshi wondered.

He contemplated sleeping, there was nothing else to do, and yet, his survival instincts, ingrained from some millennia of evolution, told him not to. *Don't sleep… but you might as well rest,* he reasoned. Hiroshi sat down on the floor cross-legged, facing his window with the great view of the asteroid and the stars, and placed his hands on his knees. Letting out a long exhale, Hiroshi closed his eyes, and began to meditate.

|

The flight back to the Saisei was a solemn one. Raiden had relayed the orders from command to his squad, and after the initial shock, no one had spoken. They were on approach to the Saisei, and Raiden broke the silence, "Active scans on, everyone," he said, switching on his own. The rest of the team confirmed, and Raiden felt a pit knot up in his stomach, knowing what lay in store for them.

A few minutes later his computer began relaying feedback from the scans. Metals, polymers, biomatter, and a live life sign. Raiden squinted at his screen, "It can't be?" He said, looking across the debris field. All of the bodies he could see had no space suits on. "Freya, I need you over here. I'm picking up a life sign," Raiden said while rebooting his scanner.

"A live one? Shit, on my way," she said and changed course. Freya's scanner picked up the exact same reading. "Someone's out there, man," Freya said, shaking her head.

Raiden put his radio on a wideband frequency, "Hello? Is anyone out there? This is Lieutenant Saito, do you copy?" he said, then waited. There was no response. "Must be unconscious," Raiden said, letting out a sigh, feeling the stress and pressure of having to work quickly.

"Guess we're going to have to narrow in on their location," Freya said.

"I'm here!" Koji was screaming at the top of his lungs. He'd seen the ships closing in, and when he'd heard Raiden's voice in his ear his heart had nearly skipped a beat. Immediately, Koji had begun talking back to Raiden, only to remember that he had no way of turning on his headset with his busted control panel. Panic set in, swallowing him, and he began to hyperventilate again. Rescue was so close, and yet, if they couldn't find him, he'd be just as dead.

Bleep! Bleep! Bleep! Koji's O2 alarm began sounding continuously, which only added to his anxiety. "Fuck!" he cried, his voice hoarse from the dehydration, and riddled with fear. Koji waved his arm and legs and looked as if he was doing jumping jacks while suspended in the air, but in the vastness of space the movement was imperceivable.

The ships were following a standard search pattern. Koji was further away from the rest of the debris, and he wondered if they'd even be able to find him. Then the lightheadedness began to set in. The oxygen reserves were dangerously low, and Koji knew he didn't have much longer before he'd pass out.

Koji tried to focus, but it was getting harder to keep his eyes open. He wanted to breathe slowly, but he couldn't stop gasping. The ships were headed his way, but then, they turned. Time was running out, and Koji was getting desperate; that's when the idea struck him to use the O2 tank as propellant. *You've got, what? Minutes left anyways... They aren't close to finding you, you're too far from everything else. If you can get any sort of distance, maybe you'll show up on the radar, or maybe they'll see you, it's your only chance!* he reasoned with himself. The fear was palpable.

Pushing through his unease and sense of dread, Koji grabbed hold of the tube that fed the oxygen into his helmet with his good arm, then stared at the ships, waiting for them to face him. *You've only got one chance...* he thought and swallowed hard. The ships were beginning to turn his way, and he felt his nervous system revolt in a shiver. *Now! Now! C'mon!* "Now!" he yelled and yanked the tube out with all of his strength. It came loose, and while he aimed the tube behind himself in an attempt to propel forward, he simply ended up spinning in circles. Each time he swung around to face the solar system's star it nearly blinded him.

The immediate oxygen deprivation hit hard, and Koji fought the encroaching darkness, trying to stay awake. The spinning slowed to a stop and the tank was entirely emptied. Koji desperately tried to look for the ships, but he was facing the opposite direction. Alone, floating in the abyss of space, Koji slipped into blackness.

"Did you see that?" Freya asked, "Something flashing?"

"No, but check it out," Raiden replied.

Freya broke her search course to go and investigate. Halfway there, she saw the body in the spacesuit floating, vital signs fading. "Raiden, found 'em!" Freya called out and rushed to get her ship aligned beneath the body. She double checked that her helmet was locked on properly, then opened the top hatch of her fighter ship's cockpit entrance, and ever so carefully flew up until the body had landed in the back seat.

Freya closed the hatch and re-pressurized the cabin. Crawling out of her pilot's chair, she made her way into the back seat, and pulled off the helmet of her rescue to discover it was Koji. "Holy shit, you're alive!" she blurted out, still remembering the intensity of the drill explosion. Koji was pale, his lips blue. She checked his pulse to discover he didn't have one. "No! Aw, fuck..."

Freya scrambled to grab her first aid kit and unzipped it as fast as she could with shaky hands. She pulled out the bandages and gauze, and finally got to the medications below. She found the large needle sealed up in an anti-contamination plastic bag, that was prefilled with adrenaline, as well as a loose piece of rubber.

She set the needle and the rubber piece down on the pilot's seat then as quickly as she could, unfastened the top of Koji's spacesuit from the bottom, and pulled the top half off over Koji's head. Then she removed her own helmet, and the gloves of her suit, to be able to work with the needle properly.

Once she'd set aside the top of his spacesuit, and her helmet, in the foot space where she'd been kneeling, Freya straddled Koji's lap, the tight quarters leaving little other option. Quickly tearing off Koji's uniform shirt underneath, exposing his left arm, Freya grabbed the needle again and held it between her teeth, and held the rubber band in her hand. Thinking back to her first aid training, Freya tried to remember practicing on the cadaver, but this felt much different. Grabbing his left arm, she tied the elastic around his bicep and then slapped the crevasse of his elbow to raise the veins.

Line it up carefully, insert quickly, and try not to collapse the vein... she reminded herself. Freya took the needle in her hand and then took a deep breath. Lining it up, she plunged the needle with as much precision as she could muster into his vein and push the needle's plunger down. Koji shot up mere seconds later, so fast that he head-butted Freya, which sent her reeling backward. "Ouff!" Freya hit the back of her pilot's seat hard.

Koji sat up straight wide-eyed and panting. His heart felt like it was trying to escape from his chest, beating faster and stronger than ever before. Freya leaned forward, nursing her throbbing and bruised forehead. "You OK?" Freya asked, wincing through the pain. Koji didn't answer, the discomfort of the adrenaline coursed through him and made his body feel incredibly strange. Freya just sat there, waiting for his response.

After a few moments Koji got his breathing under control, although he still felt the intensity of his heart. His eyes met Freya's, and while he couldn't muster words, he nodded at her. Freya nodded back, squeezed his hand, and then grabbed her helmet and climbed back into the pilot's seat.

Once Freya put her helmet back on all she could hear was Raiden frantically trying to raise her on the comm. "I'm here, I'm here!" she said, trying to get him to calm down. "You won't believe it," she smiled and shook her head, "It was Koji." There was dead air for a moment.

"How?" Raiden finally asked.

"Don't know, he wasn't breathing and didn't have a pulse, but I gave him a shot of adrenaline and he's pulling through but in no mood to talk," Freya explained.

"Understood. Good work," Raiden said, meaning it.

The ships quickly finished scavenging the debris field and then headed back to the Saisei. "We're going in blind," Raiden began to prepare Omega Squad, "so we're going in with weapons hot. Be careful, there's been more than enough loss of life today. Stay in contact, be vigilant, and let's re-take the ship!"

A resounding "Yes, sir!" came back. Raiden squeezed his hands on the steering.

|

Koi had worked his magic and had managed to override the controls with time to spare. Docking had gone smoothly for Omega Squadron, despite the dark. Emergency lighting made it exceedingly difficult to see in the large docking bay, but Omega Squad had practiced many drills over the years and could nearly dock blind. The soldiers had gotten out to explore hesitantly, only to find that no one else was in there with them. Once Raiden had cleared the hallway outside of Bay E, Freya had gone back for Koji, to escort him to the infirmary.

"I'll be fine, I'll be fine!" Koji protested. "It's dangerous, they need you," he insisted.

Freya sighed, feeling torn. Koji was in rough shape, but stable as far as she could tell, and her squad was in a potentially very dangerous situation. Despite her desire to join her squad, she knew what Raiden had ordered, and she felt the importance of verifying her friend's health. Through all his objections, Freya managed to coax Koji into coming with her, partially through force.

Once Koji was out of the ship and standing upright with the gravity plating pulling down on him, fatigue hit him, and he leaned on Freya for support. They made their way up to the bay doors that led into the corridor, where Raiden was keeping watch. Raiden smiled at Koji, "You're one lucky S.O.B. my friend."

Koji let out a laugh, then cringed as it sent a shooting pain from his shoulder into his chest, "I've seen better days," he muttered.

"How's everyone doing?" Freya asked, dying to know.

"All reports showing the other bays are vacant so far," Raiden said simply, but his guard was up.

Freya nodded, "OK, we're off. You call me if things change," she said firmly.

Raiden nodded. Freya and Koji set off down the hall, and Raiden watched them until they had vanished out of sight, and then set off in the opposite direction.

One by one they scoured each docking bay, clearing them. Finally, they arrived at the far end at the final bay, Bay A. Raiden hit the switch and opened the door. At first glance it had looked like all of the others. Then Raiden spotted someone lying on the floor, he signaled his soldiers to keep watch and provide cover, and then he made his way cautiously into the bay and over to the body.

Raiden first checked for a pulse, and found a strong one, then he flipped the body over. "Gin!" Raiden exclaimed, seeing the man's face. Gin was unconscious, but the movement had begun to bring him out of his stupor. "Gin, it's me, Raiden," he said, trying to help the man to focus. Gin squinted, his head foggy, as he tried to get his bearings.

"Help!" a cry came from across the room. Raiden looked up and saw the locked in councilors. Merrick was waving them over.

"Ken," Raiden called one of his men over, Private Ken Adama, who had just joined the squad this past year.

"Yes?" Ken asked as he approached.

"Keep an eye on Gin here while we help the others," Raiden said.

Ken nodded, "Yes, sir!"

Raiden took 3 other soldiers and went over to the storage area. As they got closer they could see 3 people lying on the ground, unmoving. Several of the councilors were in tears, others pacing. "Unlock the gate," Raiden said, and one of his men hurried inside the control room and used the computer to release the locks.

Merrick stepped forward to greet Raiden, "It's good to see some friendly faces, we have some injured in here," he said, extending his hand. Raiden took it, and Merrick shook firmly. Merrick's gaze fell to the 3 people on the floor, Jona was one of them, "They're dead," he said flatly.

Raiden looked at the bodies, but saw no wounds, "What happened?" he asked.

"Crushed to death... the poor bastards," Merrick shook his head.

"I'm sorry," Raiden said, the words feeling somehow inadequate. "Let's get you out of here," Raiden continued, "Councilor...?"

"Uda, Merrick Uda," Merrick said.

"Pleasure sir. Let's get everyone to the infirmary. The halls and other bays have been cleared for safe passage," Raiden informed him.

Merrick sighed, "Yeah, of course it's safe, crazy bastard killed them all..."

Raiden furrowed his brow, "What do you mean?"

Merrick explained that while the insurgents were losing the battle, there had still been many of them fighting when the Niko had opened the exterior door. "...I saw the bastard do it," Merrick said, pointing to the control room, showing Raiden his field of view.

Raiden shook his head in disgust at the news, "We'll get him. I'll need to interview you later, once we've helped everyone."

Merrick nodded, "Of course."

Raiden began to address all of the government officials, "Alright, we're going to be evacuating the..."

Before Raiden could get another word out he heard footsteps on the metal floor to his left. Raiden readied his gun and he spun around, only to see Dr. Seto Takei and Zavion walk out from behind some storage crates looking groggy. Seto froze when he saw the gun pointed at them and stared at Raiden wide-eyed. Raiden lowered his gun, "More survivors, good, are you two OK?" he asked, happy to see friendly faces.

"OK is a matter of opinion," Seto snipped, his patience gone.

"We're fine," Zavion chimed in.

Ken knelt down next to Gin to help him stand up. Gin's head was swimming, and he wondered if he'd gotten a concussion when he'd lost consciousness. Everything was foggy, he tried to remember, but it came back in pieces. Holding on, staring at the floor, seeing the bodies fly out the door, the screams, the crate, "Davis!" Gin blurted out, the sprung to his feet, fueled by newfound energy.

Gin pushed past Private Ken Adama, and ran forward, towards the outer door, to where Private Davis had been holding on. Gin collapsed on his knees, overcome with grief and anger. *I should've done something!* His mind screamed. He felt shame in his fear and his inaction. Tears blinded him, and the snot and thick saliva made it hard to breathe. He sat there, breaths heaving, in a well of self-pity. His eyes drifted ahead, seeing all and nothing at once.

Ken came up slowly behind him, "It's OK, you're safe now."

Ken tried to help Gin back up, but Gin just pulled his arm away. As he blinked out the tears, his eyes focused, and he saw something sparkle, barely visible, 10 feet ahead stuck under one of the grates. Gin scrambled to his feet and dashed ahead. When he got to the grate he crammed his fingers between the slats, with great difficulty, and tried to pull free the shiny object. After several failed attempts Gin finally grabbed hold to pull it up and out.

The second he saw what it was Gin dropped it and vomited bitter bile. Ken ran up to see what was happening. A delicate silver nail polish, with gold fleck that sparkled even in the dim light, decorated the nail of Davis' severed finger which lay on the floor.

|

Freya and Koji made their way slowly through the halls. Fatigue nagged at Koji, and he had a hard time walking. He finally felt his heart rate returning to normal, and as the adrenaline wore off, so did his ability to concentrate. The pain in his dislocated shoulder had become more acute and ignoring the stabbing grinding pain of it was now impossible for him to do.

The hallways felt eerie in their silence. The Saisei had always been a ship filled with boisterous life. Over a million people inhabited the massive ship, and there was never any calm within the passageways. Like busy bees in a hive, the residents of the Saisei were always going here and there, as they lived their lives. Freya felt an involuntary shiver ripple up her spine, and throughout her body, raising goosebumps on her skin.

"You OK?" Koji asked, feeling her quiver.

"Yeah, just a shiver," Freya replied.

They kept quiet and alert as they made their way through the ship. Koji was struggling more and more, and Freya was having a hard time supporting him. "We're almost there," Freya told him, but Koji was barely awake.

Freya was losing her grip on him and they lurched forward, and she tried to ease him to the floor before dropping him. She sat him up against the wall and crouched down in front of him, then tapped his cheek. "Hey, hey, stay with me," she said, trying to get his attention. Freya snapped her fingers in front of his face, "C'mon Koji! Hey!" she tried again, but Koji's head just rolled back; he was unresponsive.

Freya let out a sigh and then felt the cold metal of a pistol barrel on the back of her neck. Her eyes bulged, and she held her breath. "Arms up," Niko's all too familiar voice said. Freya's rifle was hanging by her side from her shoulder holster, and her eyes couldn't help but fall on it. *You'll be dead before you touch it...* she told herself, quelling her impulse, and raised her arms up.

"Now stand up slowly," Niko said, his calm unnerving. Freya begrudgingly did as she was told, clenching her jaw to deal with the anger. Once she was fully erect, Niko spoke again, "Good. Now, don't move. I'm going to take your rifle, and if I even think you're going to try anything, you'll be dead before you know it. Understood?"

Fighting every urge in her body to turn around and choke the man to death, Freya answered, "Yes."

Keeping the pistol pressed up at the base of Freya's skull, Niko took the rifle in his other hand and began to pull it up over Freya's extended arm. *Think dammit...* Freya's mind raced. She knew if she didn't think of something Niko would take them as hostages, or just shoot them and leave.

As Niko's gaze was focused upward, Koji gazed up and met Freya's eyes, and nodded at her ever so slightly. Freya winked back to let him know she'd seen him. Then Koji took the opportunity to kick Niko in the shin with all of his strength, and he could feel the bone break under the weight of his boot. "Urk!" Niko yelped in agony. Simultaneously, as Koji made his move, Freya ducked her head down, and snatched the rifle free of Niko's grip. Niko, shocked, fell backward and squeezed his pistol's trigger, firing a shot that hit the wall 3 feet to Freya's left.

Before Niko could take stock of what had happened, he had the barrel of Freya's rifle pointed right between his eyes. "Don't fucking move!" Freya yelled at him, "Toss the pistol over there," she said pointing next to Koji. Niko nodded, staring into her eyes unafraid. Niko arced his arm as if to throw the gun, but as he flung his arm forward he didn't let go, and instead held onto the pistol, and when his arm was fully extended he took a pop shot at Freya, hitting her left bicep.

"Ahh!" Freya screamed when the bullet hit, the pain intense. The shot sent her reeling back. She'd seen Niko make his move a split second too late to avoid being hit. She squeezed down and the trigger immediately, and a spray of bullets tore through Niko's head and chest. The wall behind Niko was painted in a spray of crimson blood. He was dead instantly.

Freya stumbled back against the wall and slid down to the floor next to Koji. Everything happened so fast, she just stared forward at Niko's body, waiting for her mind to catch up. Koji was up on his knees next to her quickly to check on her, "Gotta check that wound, I'm going to pull off your flight jacket, OK?" he told her.

Absently she nodded. Koji carefully took her jacket off and looked at the gunshot wound. "Through and through, you're good. Just need some stitches. But you're bleeding pretty good here," he said. Koji took off his belt and put it around Freya's arm above the gunshot wound and did it up tight to slow down the bleeding. "That'll help," he said.

Freya stared at him for a moment before she spoke, "You're OK?" she said, bewildered.

"My shoulder hurts like hell and I'm tired as fuck, but yeah, I'm OK. Sorry for the show, but I heard something while we were walking, and I didn't want to give it away. I thought the ruse was the best bet, if we needed it," he explained.

Freya grinned, "Crafty son of a bitch."

They both laughed. "C'mon, your turn to lean on me," Koji said, helping her to her feet.

|

A few hours later the ship had been cleared of hostiles. A few insurgents had been arrested, and Dr. Takei had restored command controls to the bridge. The ship was taken out of lockdown, and the residents cautiously, in a solemn quiet with the events of the day still fresh, made their way about the ship. Norita had made a ship-wide announcement once she was able, and had explained the uprising, the destruction of the drill, and the unfortunate loss of life. There would be a mass funeral held in two days.

Norita relieved Koi of duty, insisting he get some rest, and despite his protests, he finally complied and let someone else take the helm. Norita wished for her bed as well, the day had been too long, and sleep had been too scarce the night before, but she was too riled up to sleep.

"Takeo, I want to come with you to debrief the pilots," Norita said.

General Takeo Yamamoto nodded, "Let's go."

They made their way through the corridors. Few people were out and about, most had stayed holed up in their homes even after the lockdown had been lifted. Those who were out walked with their eyes on the ground. Norita felt unnerved as well but kept her head up; she knew she was their leader, and she had to set the right example.

The barracks beds were sparsely filled, too many had died that day. Some soldiers laid in bed, trying to sleep, but sleep wouldn't come. When Norita and General Yamamoto had entered everyone snapped to attention, stood up and saluted. Takeo saluted them back. Norita smiled and nodded to them and felt a tinge of guilt for waking them.

Takeo led Norita through the hall and down to the officers' quarters. They arrived in front of one of the doors, **RAIDEN SAITO**, listed as the occupant. Takeo rapped on the door but there was no response. "Hello?" he said, loud enough to be heard on the other side, but still no reply. Without skipping a beat Takeo took off further down the hall, at the room labeled for **GIN YOSHINI**. The door was open, and he walked in. Norita followed two steps behind.

In the room Raiden sat by Gin's bedside. Gin was curled into a ball and openly sobbing. Raiden looked up and saw the General, and the Empress, and shot up to his feet to salute.

"At ease, soldier," Takeo said.

Raiden relaxed, "Good to see you, sir."

Takeo tilted his head toward the hall, indicating for Raiden to follow. Takeo, Raiden, and Norita went into the hall, and stood just outside the door. "How is he?" Takeo asked.

Raiden shrugged, "He's been hysterical for hours. He was raving and shouting until he finally exhausted himself. He's been laying in there like that for the past 30 minutes. Med bay is full up, and he's not hurt, so they can't do anything."

"I'll arrange for a therapist," Norita said.

Raiden bowed gratefully, "Thank you. That man... he's seen too much death."

"I know you must be exhausted, but while things are fresh, we should debrief you," Takeo said compassionately.

"Of course, General Yamamoto," Raiden nodded, "Doubt I could sleep anyway."

Takeo led the way through the corridors to his office. In General Yamamoto's office the three sat around Takeo's desk. The office was sparsely decorated, there was a metal desk, 3 metal chairs, a metal bookshelf, a metal filing cabinet, and several awards and certificates on the walls. The room was otherwise barren. The metal furniture against the metal walls made everything blend into a monotone grey-blue haze. Takeo pulled a recording devise from his drawer and set it on his desk, then clicked it on.

"So, tell us exactly what happened," Takeo said to Raiden.

Raiden rubbed the sleep from his eyes and began to recant the entire events from the flight, from when they'd launched, to when they'd docked. Norita leaned back in her chair and hung onto every word. "...I thought the Saisei was big, but this *thing*, it was absolutely massive in scale. I've never heard of the Saisei finding anything like this structure, this *eye*." Raiden shook his head.

"That's because we never have," Norita said. "The Saisei hasn't ever found any trace of anything made by any non-human sentient life before at all," she added.

"And after the flash you described, was the insurgent ship destroyed?" Takeo asked.

"No, it was just gone," Raiden said, remembering the experience vividly.

Takeo nodded, "Alright, we've got the flight records and scans downloading, and we'll have them analyzed in depth to learn more. You've had a long day, get some sleep, solider. Dismissed," Takeo said.

"Thank you, sir," Raiden stood and saluted, then left.

Norita and Takeo sat in silence for a moment. "What do you make of it?" Norita finally asked, breaking the silence.

Takeo shrugged, "I'm too tired to think."

Norita let out a half-hearted laugh, "Ha, yeah, I suppose I am too... Let's finish these debriefings in the morning, everyone's too tired now. It will still be fresh enough in the morning."

"Aye, aye, ma'am," Takeo said, half smiling.

Norita stood up, and walked to the door, then turned to face him, "Good work today. You really pulled through for us."

"I was just doing my job," the General said modestly.

"You kept a cool head in a stressful situation... I don't think I'd have been able to cope without you. Thank you," Norita said sincerely. Takeo looked her in the eye and they shared a moment of understanding before Norita left.

Chapter 7: Mourning

The next day was filled with grief. As the officials sorted through the wreckage of the uprising, they began identifying the dead, and the families began to be officially notified. Norita was shocked when the news arrived that Jona had died. The detained surviving insurgents, of which there were few, divulged the names of their accomplices. Lists were formed of the insurgents' families and friends who would need to be questioned.

Late in the afternoon, a knock came to Suki's door. Suki answered the door to find a soldier in formal uniform standing before her, "May I help you?" she asked.

"Are you Ms. Suki Rose?" The soldier asked.

"Yes," Suki answered, feeling confused.

"May I come in?" he asked. Suki shrugged and then welcomed him in.

They took a seat in the living room. Suki sat cross-legged on the couch and crossed her arms. "What's this all about?" she asked. She was beginning to worry, *Shit! am I in trouble for hacking the data pads on the military channels? How'd they find out?*

The soldier sat up straight and looked her in the eye. "I'm sorry to inform you miss, that your mother was found dead this morning," he said.

"What?!" Suki blurted out.

It didn't feel real. She thought her mother had been out looking for her father. She had so many questions, but her voice wouldn't work, and her eyes welled up with tears.

"I'm so sorry for your loss. As for your father..." before he could continue Suki perked up.

"You found my dad?!"

The solider took a moment before he spoke, seeing the hopeful look in her eyes he could do nothing but sigh, "Your father was identified as the leader the aerial attack on the drill site. We currently don't know if he's alive or dead. He's wanted for treason and murder."

Suki shook her head, "Oh my god," she choked up.

After a moment she managed to swallow the sticky saliva that had formed in her mouth, and got out a question, "What happened... happened to my mom?"

"It seems she was caught in a crossfire. I'm sorry," he said. "The funeral for all of our lost, including your mother, will take place tomorrow at 2 pm, in the atrium," he explained, "We will need to see you to discuss your father at a later date. You'll receive summons once it's been determined."

His words fell on deaf ears, as Suki had withdrawn within herself. She nodded absently. He said a few more things, which she didn't hear, and then saw himself out. Suki crumpled into a ball and cried bitterly, having never felt so alone in her entire life.

|

The hospital staff was all working overtime to deal with the casualties. On top of the wounded soldiers and insurgents, civilian injury and illness during the lockdown had soared. Freya and Koji had been in observation overnight. Koji's dislocated shoulder had been reset, and his arm set in a sling. They'd given him an IV to replenish his fluids, and oxygen to strengthen his heart. Freya's bullet wound had been disinfected and stitched up. While she hadn't lost enough blood for a transfusion, she had been exhausted from losing as much as she had and was ordered to bed rest for the next 48hrs.

By late afternoon both had been discharged from the hospital with doctor's orders to rest. The beds were needed, and they were just well enough to go. The two walked slowly, both feeling their fatigue acutely, as they made their way back to the barracks. Overnight they had talked, and laughed, to take each other's minds off of what had happened. Koji didn't want to have to think about being stuck in space, how hard it was to breathe, the pain in his chest as his lungs as he'd desperately searched for air, and then the darkness... it was too much.

"What do you think it was?" Koji asked.

"Psst, hell if I know. I'm just glad I didn't get sucked in. If it's a weapon, then it literally vaporized the ship. There was nothing, and I mean *nothing*, left," Freya explained. They'd talked about the massive construct she and Omega Squadron had found the day before. Koji had been awestruck when she first told him about it.

They arrived at the barracks and went their separate ways, both longing to crawl into bed. When Freya got to her private quarters she found a letter pinned to her door. She opened it to find summons to see General Yamamoto in 2 days' time for debriefing. The idea of it just made her feel that much more exhausted.

Freya went in her room, changed into a fresh pair of underwear and a tank top, and crawled under the blankets. Her arm throbbed where the bullet had gone through. Her eyes gazed at the clock, but she couldn't take her pain medication for another three and a half hours. She sighed and tried to get comfortable. Her mind rambled when she closed her eyes. After an hour of struggle, she finally drifted into an unrestful sleep.

|

The rest of the day seemed to pass in a haze for the entire ship. The next day felt sobering; the reality of everything that had happened had caught up. In the morning the preparations for the mass funeral were well underway. Norita was practicing her speech in her office, but her mind was elsewhere. It was going to take at least 2 months to build a new drill, and then there was the mega-structure. Her curiosity was nagging at her. She had hoped for some feedback from the scientific department about the scans that the pilots had taken, but as of yet, there was nothing. She tried to refocus on her speech.

Time marched on faster than she had realized. Norita glanced up at the clock and realized she needed to get ready to head to the atrium. A sadness swelled in her chest; Jona would have been there to guide her and keep her stay on schedule if he was still alive. At times Jona had annoyed her with his precision and seeming lack of humor, however, he'd always been there for her. In his own strange way, he'd been a friend, and his absence began to feel more real.

Death is such a funny thing... Norita thought. *Every time, it's like it's not real. How can someone just not be there anymore? I don't know...* It had felt the same when her grandparents had passed, and when her own mother and father had died. The reality of the loss just didn't sink in immediately. Norita wondered if everyone felt this way about death. *Probably not, some people seem to melt into grief immediately... When mother told me that her father had died, I felt nothing. It just seemed bizarre. I don't think I cried until a week later... C'mon, enough.* Norita tried to pull herself out of her thoughts, she had to be ready to address her people.

|

The atrium was over capacity. They had expected a massive turnout, but it seemed the entire ship wished to come and pay their respects. In a last-minute change of plans, the committee in charge of the funeral made an announcement, asking only friends and family who had lost loved ones to stay for the official services. With that request came the promise to broadcast the services live for the rest of the ship, and to allow others to pay their respects after the initial group had left. It was a logistical nightmare.

Even after some people had filed out of the atrium it still felt alarmingly claustrophobic. Suki pushed her way through the bodies, overheated and overwhelmed, to the front of the room where the dead lay in the pods which they'd be released into space in after the services. For many, only a photograph took place of bodies which had been lost to space, or which were too mangled for viewing.

When Suki had finally made it to the front of the room, she felt her heartbeat pick up in speed. There were so many dead. She began to look through them all one by one, trying to find her mother's body. It seemed like an endless task, and anxiety began to creep over her. *What if I can't find her? What if I don't get to say goodbye?* She tried to fight off her urge to panic.

The ushers had begun to try and quiet and organize the large crowd. There was only enough seating for less than a quarter of the attendees. While it hadn't been particularly loud, the buzz of chatter, and the crying whimpers of grievers had created a constant drone. The soldiers were all organized at the far right of the room, all in official dress uniforms. Raiden, Freya, and Koji were in the front row.

I have to find her! Sudden guilt panged Suki as she angrily wondered why she hadn't come to the atrium earlier to see her mother. She hadn't slept the night before, and when morning came she still felt numb. Running frantically to find her mother now, her last chance to see her, the finality had finally sunk in.

Tears blinded Suki's vision, and she felt utterly lost and alone in the world. Just when she thought she couldn't take it anymore, she felt a gentle hand on her shoulder. She turned around to see Hiroshi standing there. She opened her mouth to ask what he was doing there, but all that came out were sobs, and she found herself throwing her arms around him. Hiroshi gently stroked her hair and Suki let out her tears. Patiently and unwaveringly Hiroshi held her and waited until she was ready to speak.

After she'd exhausted herself, and the tears had slowed down, she took a step back. "I'm, I'm sorry, I don't know..." she tried to apologize.

"There's nothing to say. Today is a dark day for us all," Hiroshi said compassionately.

Suki forced a smile that lasted less than a second. "What are you doing here?" she asked.

"An old friend of mine died, he was in the army. We hadn't really talked in years," Hiroshi sighed, "but we were close growing up."

Suki nodded, "I'm sorry."

"Me too. I saw your mother's name in the casualty list," Hiroshi said, then felt like nothing he could say could adequately convey condolences, so he said nothing.

Suki swallowed hard, "I'm trying to find her," her voice trailed off weakly.

"She came into the school not long ago, I remember her face, let me help."

"Yes," Suki said, though she had wanted to say *thank you*.

As quickly as they could they made their way through the seemingly endless rows of bodies. Most of the attendees in the atrium had made their way back into the mass of the crowd. Suki felt torn, "Should we just join the crowd? They're starting soon..." she said, feeling defeated.

Hiroshi stopped her and looked her in the eye, "There are some things in life you need to do that mean breaking away from the crowd. You have to walk your own path, even when everyone else is acting like a sheep. You follow your heart; we're going to find your mother so you can say goodbye, even if that means we're the only ones walking around when the Empress herself is giving a speech," he told her with conviction.

A sudden feeling of empowerment and self-determination swept over Suki. The rigidity of school, and rules, and conformity, especially on the close quarters of the ship, had shaped her entire life. Now as Suki was on the brink of adulthood, and for the first time in her life, with real clarity, rules and norms all suddenly felt subjective. With a new-found sense of self, Suki looked at Hiroshi, "Let's find her."

|

Freya fought off the urge to slouch in her seat. She hated being in the front row to be scrutinized by all, just as much as she loved being revered for being the best. It was a catch 22 for her.

Funerals made her uncomfortable, which made her want to make jokes to lighten the mood. But today of all days, in front of the eyes of the entire ship, not mourning the loss of one, but the devastation of so many, Freya bit her tongue. She bounced her right heel up and down nervously, her frenetic energy having nowhere else to go.

She'd been whispering to Koji and Raiden up until the ushers had begun to hush the crowd. She crossed her good arm under her sling-held arm and gave a long exhale. Koji noticed Freya's leg bouncing up and down and set his palm on her knee gently. She hadn't noticed the bouncing and stopped once he had touched her. She looked up at him. He silently mouthed, "It's OK" and she smiled and nodded.

Raiden was lost in his own thoughts. He had had to help move the bodies of the dead councilors and unloaded some of the ships which had collected some of the soldiers and insurgents who had been sucked out into space. The feeling of their cold, limp, heavy bodies was still fresh.

As he gazed out across the sea of coffins he wondered which ones contained the ones he'd moved. Some of them had died with looks of horror or agony of their faces, and the sight had etched itself into his mind. It was something he knew he could never forget.

His gaze lowered after some time, and he noticed Koji's hand on Freya's thigh. He felt an instant twinge of jealousy and a flash of anger that rippled through his body. Raiden turned his head to the side and looked away, *what the hell is wrong with me?*

He and Freya had always been close friends and nothing more. Both had dated and had sexual trysts with other people over the years, though nothing had lasted long. But Raiden had never really felt jealous about Freya being with anyone before. *Does that even mean anything? Freya and Koji have always just been friends... Even if it does, so what?* Raiden asked himself, glancing back at Koji's hand. But he couldn't shake off the feeling.

|

A make-shift podium had been set up in front of the rows of the dead. Norita, escorted by several guards, made her way to the stage. The low murmurs dissipated until all that could be heard were the gentle cries people were trying to suppress. Cameras and audio equipment had been quickly set up to capture the services, which would be broadcast live across the ship, and recorded for posterity.

When Norita stepped in front of the podium she felt all eyes on her. She was used to the limelight, having spent her entire life addressing her people, but never before had she felt vulnerable in front of them. Norita set her data pad with her addressment speech down in front of herself, and then took a moment to look upon all of the faces in the crowd.

"It is with a heavy heart that I stand here before you today," Norita began, and then took a moment to find her center. "This tragedy affects us all. We of the Saisei, we nomads of the stars, stand as one. Everyone has lost a relative, a friend, a neighbor, a co-worker, or a familiar face among us. We, the people of the Saisei, are lesser for these losses.

"With death comes many questions: Where do we go? Is there an afterlife? Are we reborn? Why did this have to happen? To these uncertainties, there are no definite answers. It becomes all too easy to fall into anger and blame. However, evil begets evil, and hate and blame will only bring about more sorrow.

"It is in these trying times that it is hard to see the light, and yet it's the most important time to look for it. While death brings with it this undeniable feeling of being alone in the universe, we are not alone. We are as one. Together we grieve, and together we will overcome. We will find the light once again," the crowd hung onto Norita's every word.

|

The broadcast played in the background of the lab while Dr. Takei worked fastidiously. He hardly noticed it was on. He was the only one in the lab; apart from the necessary ship's functions staff, the day had been declared a day of mourning, so everyone was either at home or at the funeral. Seto never took day's off, though he did take breaks. His passion was in his work, and he felt incomplete if he did not put his mind to work each day. There was satisfaction in the learning and overcoming of challenges.

The past couple of days he had felt quite tired. The stress from the near-death experience in Bay A had aged him. Ha hadn't been able to sleep the past couple of nights without waking up gasping for breath. The fear of suffocating to death was all too real.

The terror of mortality had made itself clear that day. While he had held on for his life next to Zavion, as the intense suction of space had tried to claim their bodies, time seemed suspended. Though he knew it couldn't have been long, it seemed like an eternity as they hung on for dear life, and then, slowly, the desperation crept in. Once the oxygen had all been sucked out of the massive hangar, and his lungs longed for air, he felt the rapid beat of his heart and a warm flush wash over his whole being. His chest began to ache, and he felt ill and dizzy. Panic struck like a lightning bolt, and then, after what seemed for forever, darkness consumed him.

Seto shook his head, trying to forget. But the thoughts kept coming back terribly frequently. He was having a hard time concentrating, and so he stood from his seat and stretched, and then walked over to the far end of the room and out the door into a small waiting room, where he made himself some much-needed coffee.

A few minutes later Zavion walked through the main doors of the lab, "Seto, you in here?" he called out, but there was no response. He carried a data pad in his hand. One of the computer terminals began to flash a blue light and make a gentle *BING!* sound, so he walked over to it. He looked at the screen to see that it had completed processing a large data stream and was displaying a long dense readout of information. Most of it was beyond

Zavion's understanding at a glance, but the metallurgic reading caught his eyes.

Zavion's eyes widened, and his jaw dropped. This analysis stated that there were billions and billions of tons of rhodium, platinum, iridium, and palladium, in the mega-structure. "Unbelievable..." Zavion heard himself say. These rare metals were all highly sought after, their conductivity incredible for a whole variety of uses. In all the years the Saisei had been in space, they'd only found a few small deposits of each.

The possibilities this meant overtook Zavion's mind, so much so that he didn't ever hear Dr. Takei walk up next to him. "Hey," Seto said, setting down his coffee on the desk. Zavion flinched, his mind coming back to the present moment. "Sorry," Seto chuckled, "Didn't mean to startle you."

"No, it's alright, I just... This is incredible!" Zavion said pointing at the computer screen.

Seto gazed at the screen, "Of course it finished while I was away," he sighed. Throughout his life, Seto had always had his projects seem to finish while he wasn't there to see it happen. He sat down in his chair and propped up his head in his hand and began to take in the massive amount of data, "Let's have a look, here."

Dr. Takei took in the information bit by bit. Zavion stared at the screen, impatiently waiting, wishing he understood more of the analysis readout. Seto picked up his coffee to take a sip, his eyes never leaving the screen. Before the cup reaching his lips, his arm stopped, and he sat up straight in his seat. Seto set down the cup and pointed to what he was looking at.

"You see that?" Seto asked emphatically.

"Yes?" Zavion said, unsure what it meant.

"This is just miraculous..." Seto said awe-struck.

"What? What's it mean?" Zavion asked.

Seto turned to face him, "It's a wormhole."

Chapter 8: New Possibilities

Norita had retired to her office after finishing her speech. The heavy oppressive grief she'd felt from the crowd when she'd entered the atrium seemed as if it had become a little less heavy by the time she'd left. Her father had always told her that it's up to a leader to set the tone for the people. That was something she had taken to heart and had consistently tried to implement in her leadership strategies.

While she was happy to leave everyone more uplifted than she'd found them, her own grief still felt all too real. The bodies would be launched out into space shortly. She stood up from her desk and walked over to her window and looked out into the deep black of space. She stood barefoot on the floor, and the cold metal felt blissful. Her feet were sore from her high heels.

Her intercom clicked on, "Miss Hiroshu?" the timid voice of her secretary came on.

"I thought I said I didn't want to be disturbed?" Norita said, struggling not to sound as grouchy as she felt.

"I, I know, I'm sorry ma'am, but Dr. Takei insisted it was urgent you come to the lab right away," her secretary replied.

"Alright, tell him I'm on my way," Norita reluctantly replied.

"Yes, ma'am."

Norita put her hand on the glass of her window. The cold from it was soothing and permeated through her skin. She closed her eyes and took a moment to breathe deeply. "Goodbye, Jona..."

|

General Yamamoto was already in the lab, standing around the computer with Dr. Takei and Zavion, by the time Norita arrived. She walked swiftly across the room, the heels of her shoes clicking and resounding in the large room as she made her way. The large screen on the far wall lit up and Seto displayed the readings from his computer on it. Norita stared up at the screen as she walked toward them. She had always loved science in school and had thought she'd have loved to be a scientist. *In another life,* she told herself. "This is the data from the mega-structure?" she asked as she walked up to them.

"Yes!" Seto excitedly replied. He was practically inhaling the data, in awe, and eager to share the discoveries. He'd coerced Zavion into recording everything as he explained it, so they could more rapidly move through deciphering it all. "The massive energy output, the light the pilots saw in the center of the structure, it's a wormhole!" Seto explained to Norita, his eyes lit up like a child's.

Norita didn't know what to say for a moment. "I thought wormholes were just theoretical?" she finally managed.

"They were," Seto said, grinning from ear to ear, "Now we have proof! And this data shows that the structure is an anchor. Wormholes theoretically would jump to alternative destinations, instead of having one fixed spot. If this has an anchor on the other end as well then, well, it's a stable passageway."

Zavion, Takeo, and Norita stayed silent as they took in the information. *Who the hell could build this thing? What's on the other side... could we ever get back? Does it matter? There's nothing here for us...* "I want to know what's on the other side," Norita finally said.

"I'll arrange for one of our pilots to go through for a test run," Takeo said.

Norita nodded, "As soon as possible. There might be water on the other side."

|

The Saisei set course for the mega-structure the next day. Debriefings and interrogating the insurgents kept Takeo and Norita busy during the trip. Bit by bit they pieced the puzzle together and found themselves with a greater picture of what had happened. The general unrest stirred in her people left Norita feeling somewhat dejected. She reminded herself that it was impossible to please everyone.

They'd dismissed their last interviewee and had summoned Gin Yoshini to come in next. In addition to taking his statement, General Yamamoto had a medal of valor to present him with for his pivotal role and bravery during the crisis. The minutes passed by as they waited for him. After 15 minutes the General had tried to raise him on the intercom again, but there was no reply.

"Must be on his way," Norita had said.

Another 10 minutes went by and he had still not come. Another attempt on the intercom, and again no response. Takeo and Norita decided to go and find him. After checking the mess hall and the training center, they made their way to his quarters.

When they reached his room, Takeo knocked on the door which hadn't fully been closed and cracked open from the tapping. Takeo pushed the door further open to check for Gin, and that's when he saw the crimson red twinkling on the floor under the bedroom light.

"Oh my god!" Norita had gasped, raising her hand to her mouth in shock.

Gin was laying on the bed unconscious, his arms dropped down of the side of the bed, his wrist slit, and a massive pool of blood had formed on the floor beneath. His skin was incredibly pale. Takeo dashed over to him to check for a pulse.

"He's alive!" Takeo announced.

Norita ran over to the intercom on the wall to call for help, "We need a medical team down here now!" she yelled, unable to take her eyes off of the massive amount of blood on the floor.

"Right away," a voice replied.

She looked around and saw a t-shirt tossed over one of the chairs. Norita grabbed it and dashed over to Gin and Takeo. "Here, tie it around his wrist. It'll help slow down the bleeding," she said holding it out to Takeo. Takeo took it and carefully pulled it snuggly around Gin's arm, then tied it around his wrist.

They waited in silence until a paramedic team arrived. The whole thing felt surreal as Norita watched them come is and hastily remove Gin. After they'd gone, the overwhelming blood pool was still there pulling her attention, smelling sickeningly metallic; she ran to the toilet to throw up.

|

Hiroshi was in his quarters, working on his art. School had been let out for the remainder of the week, and he was glad, for he wanted to finish the asteroid sketch while the image was still fresh in his mind. He'd taken photographs to work from, but there was something about the experience of being there, the feeling of it, that couldn't be captured working from a photo alone. Skillfully his nimble fingers worked with the charcoal. Perfect forms of figures, light and shadow, came to life on the paper.

|

Freya and Koji were sitting in the mess hall playing cards, each with their good arm. Until their injuries healed they were both on restricted duty and had time to spare. Both had given their statements earlier to Takeo and Norita and felt exhausted from having to relive it all; though neither would admit it.

"Why do you think the empress was there?" Freya asked.

Koji shrugged, "No idea. If I had to guess she's pissed about the whole thing."

Freya laughed, "The Empress is pissed? That just sounds wrong to say out loud man, haha! But maybe you're right."

Koji smiled, "I know, but think about it, there's been no civil unrest on the Saisei ever, and now she's in control and the people have an uprising? Fuck, I'd be pissed."

As Koji reached for his beer mug Freya peeked up at him, pretending to look at her hand of cards. She took in everything about him with her eyes, his sharp jawline, the crystal blue of his eyes, his dark brown-black hair with the few pale grey hairs peppered in. He was ruggedly handsome. Even after a fresh shave, with his dark hair, he looked like he had the outline of his beard, and it was incredibly attractive. *How have I never seen him like this before?* She wondered.

Freya set down her cards on the table and stood up, "Come on," she told him.

Koji pulled the beer away from his lips, "What?" he asked confused.

She bit her lip, "Come on, and I'll show you."

They hastily left the mess hall, and Freya led Koji down the corridors to her quarters. Once the door was shut Freya pulled Koji in close and kissed him passionately. Koji was surprised but he went along with it. He pressed his body into hers, and she could feel him getting hard through his pants. She felt swept away by the moment, lust or love, she didn't care.

Freya let her jacket slide off onto the floor and tried to pull off her tank top with her good arm. It was a struggle, the arm brace got in the way. Koji helped her with his good arm and they laughed as they kissed and undressed each other. After some struggle her shirt was off, "You'll have to help me too," he said between kisses. She helped him get his shirt off with equal struggle around his sling, but the struggle just made it more fun for them.

With relative ease, Freya one-handedly undid the simple clasp of her bra and then let Koji pull it off. Her breasts were creamy white, her pink nipples hard in the cold air. She pushed her chest against his and the warmth of his body permeated into her.

As they fussed with undoing each other's pants with one hand, Freya slid around the side of Koji's face, her soft cheek rubbing against his rough face. She bit down playfully on his ear lobe, and he let out an almost inaudible gasp as a shudder went through his body.

Once they were fully undressed they made their way over to Freya's bed. She playfully, yet with force, pushed him down on the mattress, and climbed on top of him. She leaned forward and kissed his stomach, and then took his hard cock in her mouth to wet it. "Mmm," Koji watched her. After a moment Freya sat back up, and with some struggle only having one hand to work with, she took him and slid him inside of her.

Freya slowly began to ride him, bracing her good arm against the wall for support. Koji lay his hand on her hip to guide her, and following her rhythm, thrust up into her. As he watched her on top of him, he remembered her sitting on his lap in her ship when he'd come back to consciousness after she'd revived him. The thought made his heart race, the intensely uncomfortable feeling of the adrenaline all too easy to recall. He closed his eyes, trying to shake the thought. She could feel his body tense up. Freya looked at Koji's face and could see the distress.

"You OK?" she asked.

He reopened his eyes, "Yeah, just..." he sighed unable to find the words, "it's..."

Freya leaned forward, pressing her body against his, setting her head next to his, and whispered gently in his ear, "I know, I get it. Just stay with me, all that matters is right here, right now. Be here with me."

Koji ran his hand up her body, all the way to behind her head, and pulled her in to kiss her deeply. He felt vibrantly alive and safe with her. When Freya pulled away after their kiss, Koji had her help him take his sling off. Once it was off, despite the pain in his shoulder, Koji lifted Freya and flipped her on her back.

Freya grinned, impressed and even more aroused by his strength. He rode her deeply, his hips a powerhouse, which took her to a state of inexplicable ecstasy. When she orgasmed, her spasms brought him to climax too, and they shared the fleeting moment of bliss together.

|

Suki found herself unable to sleep since the insurgency. The day of the funeral, with Hiroshi's help, she had found her mother among the dead. She still wasn't sure how she felt about it, but in many ways, she wished she hadn't seen her. Her body was there, but without the soul, the body felt meaningless. A remnant of what once was. She remembered reaching out to touch her mother's cheek, but it was lifeless and cold. That was no longer her mother.

When the bodies had been launched in their pods out into space, she had watched them go and felt nothing. After seeing her mother, they were all just bodies. This wasn't goodbye to everyone, because they had already left. She felt unsure how to process these new feelings; this new level of understanding was as enlightening as it was discomforting.

Sitting in her room, Suki found herself just staring out her window into space. She had a million thoughts, and yet her head felt empty. She felt as if she had been thrust into adulthood without any warning. While she was graduating from school in the coming months, the sudden unexpected changes in her life rested responsibility heavy on her shoulders.

More than anything Suki wondered about her father. How could he have done what he did? Was he still alive? She wanted answers, but there were none to be had. She sighed and tried to think of other things, but it always came back to her father and a gnawing need to know.

|

General Yamamoto sat in his office, waiting for the call to tell him when they were nearing the mega-structure. He'd finished the rest of the debriefings without Norita and was organizing the files. He remembered how shaken Norita had been when they'd found Gin, and he couldn't blame her, it was horrific. The medical team quickly had come and taken him away on a gurney. After that, standing there, blood everywhere, the room had felt eerie. He remembered feeling bad having to order several soldiers to clean up the room.

His boots and uniform had been bloodied as well. He'd parted ways with Norita outside of Gin's quarters and had headed back to his private quarters to change and shower. Due to the biohazard of getting another person's blood on himself, he'd been granted permission to shower, albeit briefly, and it was blissful. The water had felt incredibly cleansing after months of sponge bathing.

Takeo refocused his mind to concentrate on his work. He had always had a very sharp mind, and it had helped him to power through getting many things done. As he continued to organize and add his notes to the audio logs, his curiosity about the mega-structure grew. It held innumerable possibilities and risks. His instinct was to prepare. *Prepare for what?* He asked himself. *Everything...*

The comm system clicked on, "General Yamamoto?" Koi's voice came through.

"Yes?" Takeo asked.

"We're nearing the gas giant, it won't be long now. ETA 1 hour," Koi informed.

"Thanks," Takeo replied, "Back on the bridge already, heh?"

Koi laughed, "Can't keep me away. See you in a bit." The comm clicked off.

Takeo hurriedly finished organizing the data entries, and then uploaded them into the main computer hub for safety. He set down his data pad and called Raiden. "General, what can I do f... you?" Raiden's voice came in, slightly distorted from the planet's radiation.

"Meet me on the bridge," Takeo instructed.

"Yes, sir!" came Raiden's prompt reply. The General stood from his desk, straightened his uniform, and walked out the door.

|

Everyone on the bridge fell silent when the megastructure came into view. They were awe-struck. Dr. Seto Takei watched in wonder, with keen fascination. "Remarkable," Seto finally said, breaking the silence.

Raiden felt just as amazed seeing it for the second time as he had the first. He had thought his memory of it was over embellished but the reality of seeing it again proved otherwise. It was truly massive, it's presence humbling.

Koi's eyes were glued forward on it as he flew the ship in closer. He could hardly bring himself to blink. Norita walked past him and got right up to the window, "It truly is colossal," she said, taking it in.

Takeo stood next to Raiden, and he spoke quietly while the others marveled at the gigantic structure, "Raiden, your scans helped Dr. Takei determine that the energy you saw, the bright light, it's a wormhole."

"A wormhole, sir?" Raiden asked.

"Yes. The doctor described it like a short cut from one point in space to another. He believes this structure is some sort of anchor to keep it in place, apparently, otherwise the two ends can jump to varying locations," the General did his best to relay the information as he understood it.

"Wow..." Raiden said, thinking about what that could mean for them.

"Raiden, we need someone to test it. To go through and make sure the other side is safe, and that it too is anchored, so that we can get back. With the drill destroyed, and water supplies bottoming out if there's any chance of attaining water on the other side we need it. We have no idea what to expect... it may even be a one-way trip," Takeo explained.

"I understand, sir. I'll do it," Raiden said without a second thought. This was the discovery of a lifetime and despite the fear of the unknown Raiden's curiosity demanded he go.

General Yamamoto looked Raiden in the eye and saw his conviction. "Alright then, thank you," Takeo said.

Takeo turned to face the rest of the room, and raised his voice, pulling the others out of their reverie, "Lieutenant Saito will be our test pilot for the wormhole," he announced. The others turned around to face them. "Doctor Takei, would you please brief him on what to expect?" General Yamamoto asked.

Seto nodded and walked closer to them, "Up until now wormholes have been purely theoretical. To be completely honest, we don't know what to expect. From theory alone, it's presumed to be like a galactic highway, so we suspect once you enter the corridor of the wormhole that you will be accelerated through the wormhole to the other side. How long that will take and what you'll experience in transit is impossible to say. You'll need to run scans for us during your time in the wormhole for us to understand the science behind this phenomenon. We've set up your ship to send us a feedback relay as you go."

"Understood," Raiden said, nodding at the doctor.

"The head engineer has been reinforcing your ship, you'll have a better chance of withstanding intense gravimetric forces. We're taking every precaution. There's no way to know if we'll have communications capabilities at such a great distance. Presumably, if the wormhole is open, it may work as a conduit for communications as well, however, that is just an educated guess. In the face of the unknown, well..." Seto stared out the window, "You'll know once you're in there."

Norita approached Raiden and extended her hand, "You're a brave man, and on behalf of everyone abroad the Saisei, I thank you." Raiden took her hand and they firmly shook. He was at a loss for words.

"Come on," Takeo said to Raiden, "Let's get down to the hangar bay."

Chapter 9: The Wormhole

A dedicated crew was tending to Raiden's ship when they entered Bay C. As soon as they walked into the hangar Raiden felt a twinge of panic set it, but he pushed it to the back of his mind and ignored it. He'd expected the ship would have looked bulkier, but in fact, it looked sleeker in design with the new upgrades. Zavion was overseeing the final touches.

"I wish I had advice for you, but I don't," General Yamamoto said with a heavy sigh, "But you've seen this first hand. Better than any of us, you know what to expect."

Raiden bobbed his head in agreement, "I think as long as I head straight for the center I'll be fine."

The ship-wide speakers clicked on and a lengthy announcement was made, explaining the mega-structure and the flight test they were about to attempt, encouraging people to find a window to watch the incredible event, along with a shout out to Raiden for safe tidings. When the announcement shut off Raiden shivered. Something about hearing it all, knowing it was now expected by the entire ship, felt unnerving. Again, he tried to push away his worry to focus on the mission and to remind himself of the incredible possibilities that lay in store if he succeeded.

|

Freya was lying in bed, wide awake with her thoughts, next to Koji as he gently snored, when the announcement came on. She jumped out of bed as soon as she'd heard Raiden got to pilot the flight, and hurriedly started getting dressed. Her abrupt departure from the bed had woken Koji up.

Groggily he looked up at her and saw her struggling to do up the button on her pants with one hand. "Everything OK?" he asked.

"How'd you sleep through that? There was an announcement. That thing we found, it's a fucking wormhole! Raiden's manning the first flight through," she finally managed to hook the button on her pants. Koji sat there silently taking it in.

"Where are you going?" he finally asked.

"They're prepping for launch, I'm gonna go see him off," she said. Freya finished pulling her jacket on, and quickly straightened her hair, "Stay as long as you want. I'll see you later," she said and hurried out the door.

|

Beep! … Beep! … Beep! The gentle beeping of the medical monitoring equipment sounded harsh to Gin's sensitive ears as he awoke. *Where am I?* he wondered, feeling weak. The white of the room blended together to his unfocused eyes; white walls, white beds, white sheets, doctors and nurses in white uniforms, it was veritably a sea of white. As his eyes focused things and people began to take shape, and hues of grey and other colors broke up the monotony of the room.

Gin went to lift his hand up to rub his face, only to find his arms were tied down. A sense of panic swept over him. His mind felt foggy and confusion ran rampant in his brain. The beeping of his heart rate monitor and the off-rhythm beeping of other patients' machines, the *whoosh* of nearby ventilators, the incessant murmuring, and patients crying out, all blended into a horrendous cacophony. Gin felt a throbbing headache coming on.

Just as Gin was about to cry out for help a nurse walked up next to him. "You're awake," the young man said, "I'll get your doctor."

Not wanting to be alone, Gin went to grab the nurse, but the restraints held him back, "Wait!" he cried out, his voice strained and hoarse from his parched throat.

The nurse turned around, "It's OK, you're safe here." Gin exhaled slowly and nodded, and the nurse took off.

A few minutes later the doctor arrived, and Gin was taken aback by her beauty. She was tall, with thick black hair tied up into a messy bun with a digital data-pad pen stuck through it. She wore glasses, and her eyes were almost violet in color. Her pale skin accentuated the pink of her lips.

"Hello Gin, how are we doing today?" she asked, looking down at him. The bright ceiling light behind her head made a halo, and he thought she looked like an angel.

"I... uh..." he was at a loss for words.

"Don't worry. I know it must be confusing to be waking up in a different place and not being able to move much. You're in the hospital. I'm your doctor, I've been looking after you. My name is Xena Nakamura. You were found unconscious and near death. Do you remember what happened?" she asked in a soothing tone.

"I...," he thought for a moment. As he tried to remember he felt an acute pain in his wrists and looked down at the bandaging. Then it came back to him, the knife, the cutting, the incredible dark red of his blood, how good it had felt to feel anything, and how beautiful he thought it looked until the darkness had consumed him. "I tried to kill myself..." he said.

Xena gently nodded, "Yes. Do you want to tell me what happened?"

Gin lowered his gaze, *What am I supposed to say? That it's all I've been able to think about since Rei died... How the hell would she know what it's like to watch someone die? To find your comrades fucking severed finger? Shit, she trusted me...*

Gin felt a swell of nausea as his private war raged within his mind. His saliva thickened in the wake of his emotional turmoil. He let out a whimpering sigh, and a single tear escaped and rolled down his cheek.

Touching his arm compassionately, Gin felt comforted by the heat from Xena's hand. "It's alright, we don't have to talk now. Try to get some rest. I'll have someone come by to check in on you shortly and bring you some food," she said, sincere care in her voice. Gin gently rocked his head up and down in acknowledgment, and then she left.

|

Freya entered Bay C and quickly looked around for Raiden. She saw him standing next to Ken, the two of them staring at the ship. She called, "Hey!" as she ran up to them. Raiden and Ken both turned to see her approach.

"Oh, hey Lieutenant," Ken said as he saw her.

Raiden smiled, "Hi, Freya. How's the arm?"

She looked down at her arm, "Hurts like hell but it's healing. Lucky you or I'd 've got this flight," she teased.

Raiden chuckled, "Yeah, yeah."

"That thing is seriously a wormhole though? Wow," she said shaking her head, "I know it's been a while but watch out for Link on the other side, could be an ambush waiting, never know, right?"

Raiden nodded, "Agreed."

"I gotta get going, my patrol shift starts soon. See ya," Ken excused himself.

"Come to the mess for cards tomorrow," Freya hollered after him. Ken turned and gave a thumbs up, as he continued to head out of the hangar.

Freya found herself distracted by the ship, and Raiden stared at it too, it looked immaculate. "You lucky son of a bitch," she said, pulling her gaze back to him. "Seriously though," she continued, "you earned this."

Raiden held her eyes with his, Freya was rarely serious, and he felt at a loss for what to do. "Thank you," he finally said and hugged her.

"So, when do you launch?" Freya asked.

"Within the hour, just waiting for the green light from the powers that be," Raiden replied, trying to hide his anxiety.

"The discovery of a lifetime... Be safe though, I mean it. When that wormhole opened before, the power behind it, it's just... well, it was intense," Freya grabbed his hand and held it firmly, "Don't die out there." Her eyes searched his.

"I'll come back, I promise," he said, and squeezed her hand reassuringly.

"OK, well, I'm going to go find a place to watch from. Don't fuck it up, alright?" Freya grinned, back to her regular self.

Raiden couldn't help but laugh, "Yeah, I won't."

Freya gave him another quick hug and then walked off. Raiden watched her leave, wondering if it was the last time he'd ever see her.

|

Hiroshi sat in his living room, staring out the window, waiting patiently yet attentively for the wormhole to open. He had been in total awe when the mega-structure had first come into view. He had expected it to be big, but this was truly beyond comprehension in terms of humanities building capabilities. It was clearly made by intelligent beings, and he wondered if those who had created this were nearby watching the Saisei. It was impossible to tell the age of the structure, for space was an immaculate preserver.

The camera app on his data pad was open and ready to capture the miraculous event when it happened. Of all the things Hiroshi had ever drawn, he was never so excited as he was to capture this. He wondered just what the aperture would look like when the wormhole opened.

The week off from teaching, while filled with its own challenges, had been a welcome reprieve.

Hiroshi loved teaching and seeing his students excel, but the artist in him felt nourished to have the time to think and dream and work on projects. *If only it hadn't come at the cost of so many lives...* he thought, feeling some guilt for his time to luxuriate. *No, that's not your fault. Just an unfortunate reality,* he told himself.

Just then he saw the small ship launching from the Saisei come in to view as it headed toward the mega-structure. Hiroshi stood up and quickly made his way up to the window. He steadied his hands and began to make micro-adjustments to get the perfect framing with his data pad to capture the photograph.

It took several minutes for the ship to make its way across the chasm of space to get to the megastructure. Hiroshi waited patiently, his eyes flitting up between the window and the data pad as he watched. As the ship approached the center of the structure suddenly there was a tiny flick of light and then a brilliant blaze of colors erupted in the center of the structure. Hiroshi was temporarily stunned by the brilliance of it, and then furiously began taking photographs as quickly as he could click.

|

At the mouth of the wormhole, Raiden's ship hovered, his thrusters in full reverse to fight being pulled in. He started up all of the scanning equipment, barely able to take his eyes away from the wormhole for more than a second at a time. The colors rippled, like light in a prism. Like a snake, the wormhole moved, as if to dance.

"All systems go," he spoke into the mic in his helmet.

"Godspeed," Takeo's voice came back.

Raiden swallowed hard. He took the reverse thrusters offline and was instantly was sucked in and swallowed by the worm hole. Inside the wormhole he could feel the intense turbulence of the ride. Sheering forces tugged at the ship. He checked his readings and was alarmed and nearly in disbelief at the extreme faster than light speeds he was traveling at.

Time was seemingly suspended in this corridor of light and as suddenly as it had begun it abruptly ended. Darkness appeared at the end of the tunnel and Raiden found himself to be suddenly in open space again. He breathed heavy, his heart racing.

Once Raiden had regained control of his faculties he began to look around. Behind him there was another mega-structure, however, the gas giant wasn't there next to it. He was somewhere else. *It really worked,* he thought, overwhelmed. The wormhole had closed behind him.

"Saisei, are you there? ... Saisei, come in?" there was no reply, as was expected. He thought about going back immediately to relay that the flight had been a success, but his curiosity nagged at him.

He'd arrived in a binary star system, bathed in brilliant light. Immediately he saw many other wormhole anchors. *Amazing! This must be some sort of transportation hub,* he thought. The limitless ability for the Saisei to acquire resources now had him nearly jumping out of his seat for joy. More than that, perhaps now they could finally find a planet to colonize and make their home.

Off in the distance, there was a stunning planet, massive in size, with lush greenery and the unmistakable deep blue of water. Several moons circled around it. In all his years in space, he'd never seen anything quite so beautiful. Raiden set a course to the planet to take a better look, *Might as well bring back some data on it,* he justified.

Raiden placed the ship on auto-pilot and watched the astrometric data as it came in, as well as the view. There was nothing recognizable about the placement of the stars. He began to wonder how far the wormhole had taken him.

His eyes moved bit by bit across the expanse of space. There were several other planets in orbit much further from the two suns. While none of the others could support life, the data coming in showed high levels of mineral deposits.

The telephoto lens on Raiden's ship was taking 360-degree photos at regular intervals. He pulled up the first batch on the screen and began to scroll through them. He came up to the planet he'd set course for. It was even more glorious up close with the suns creating a halo around it from behind.

That's when he noticed on the dark side of the planet that he faced, there were little white dots scattered about. Raiden looked up from the photo and squinted at the planet, but it was still too far away for his eyes to see anything. He cycled through the photos to find the newest capture of the planet. And there it was, unmistakable: those little specs were city lights, clear signs of civilization.

"Oh my god," Raiden couldn't help but blurt out. There was *the* proof. *We're really not alone...*

Raiden sat there in disbelief for a moment and then disengaged the auto-pilot. While the mega-structure of the wormhole anchor was immaculate, and clearly made by intelligent life, its origins seemed so distant. This planet right before him now, clearly teeming with intelligent alien life, was a whole other story. He stared at the planet, debating what to do. *I should go back to the Saisei,* he finally decided.

Just as he was about to turn the ship around to go back to the wormhole, an elegant white stream-lined ship, crested around the planet, heading towards him. Raiden knew he should feel afraid, but he felt no fear. The ship was coming straight toward him, and the idea of flying away, the logical choice he knew he should take, felt wrong.

An incoming transmission came in on his comm system. The voice was feminine, serene yet strong, but the words incomprehensible.

"I'm sorry, I don't understand what you're saying," he replied.

Another transmission of equally impossible to understand words came through.

Again, Raiden responded, "I can't make any sense of what you are trying to tell me."

On the third transmission from the white ship, one word, *follow,* came in amongst the alien language. Raiden sat up straight in his seat, "Did you say 'follow'?!" he asked in disbelief. Back and forth they sent transmissions and each time more and more words came back in English until finally, they were speaking perfectly.

"Thank you for your patience. Our computer algorithms needed more samples of your speech to properly process your language. I am Xan, captain of this ship. Welcome to the Bastion," her voice came through clear as day.

Raiden was in stunned silence for a moment, *Is this really happening?* "I… you're welcome. I'm Lieutenant Raiden Saito, pleasure to meet you. What's the 'Bastion'?"

"I'll show you. Follow us," Xan's voice said.

He watched as her ship took an arc to turn around, bathed in the light from the suns, swathing it in gold. Her ship then stood still, waiting for him to catch up. Raiden considered making a break to get back to the wormhole, but he couldn't help but set course to follow Xan's ship. As he got close to Xan's ship to follow, his sensors suddenly picked up what seemed to be infinite comm chatter on more channels than he could count.

Xan's ship came to life and began to make way around the curvature of the planet, with Raiden following closely behind. As they came about, Raiden couldn't believe his eyes. A gigantic structure, a space station beyond all comprehension, lay behind the planet. Countless ships, some that looked like Xan's, and many others of wildly varying designs, darted to-and-fro. He also could see off in the distance several other wormhole anchors, *This truly is a waystation. I wonder how far these wormholes go?* Raiden pondered.

A large freighter passed them by, on course to one of the far away wormholes. Incoming and outgoing ships came frequently. Xan had them on a direct course to dock with the massive space station.

The comm crackled, and Xan came on, "This is the Bastion. It's a galactic hub of all intelligent species. You've been cleared for docking with us, in docking section V, 56th port. It will be the port to the left of my ship's port, so just stay close and follow me in."

"I will," Raiden said.

The Bastion was of incredible design. A massive cylindrical centerpiece, one end bulbous that then shrunk down to a smaller pointed end like a teardrop. The entire station was supported by an outer ring. From the outer ring, large rectangular portions of the station hung as they gently rotated around the central cylinder. The entirety of the station glowed and twinkled from the light of the suns, like a massive city hovering in space. Xan's ship led Raiden to the far end of the central cylinder, the end that was narrow and held the opening for the ships entering and exiting. He followed her in.

Chapter 10: First Contact

When they entered into the Bastion Raiden nearly felt his heart stop. It was spectacular. A warm glowing light bathed everything. The docks were near the mouth of the entrance, and beyond that was a sea of greenery and buildings on all sides. The circular design of the centerpiece of the Bastion, spinning in gentle harmony, kept gravity in perfect balance. It was utterly astounding.

Raiden docked his small ship with ease and then exited the cabin. After closing the hatch, he turned around to see Xan walking towards him. She was elegant, at least 6 feet tall, hairless, her skin a deep indigo blue, and yet slightly mimetic of her surroundings. For all of her differences, she was incredibly human; 2 eyes, 2 ears, 2 arms, 2 legs, and similar torso. Her uniform was pearlescent white, just like her ship.

"Hello, Raiden, I am Xan," she said, with a smile, and slowly closed and opened her eyes.

Raiden smiled, and slightly bowed, feeling awkward and unsure of his actions. The docking area was vibrant. Many different species walked around, some humanoid, some so different that Raiden had a hard time imagining they were real. His eyes moved from one being to another as they passed by.

Xan turned to see what he was looking at, "This is your first time meeting new species?" she asked.

"Yes," Raiden said, nodding and wide-eyed.

"It is an honor to welcome you to our galactic hub," she said.

"Thanks," Raiden replied, still distracted by all of the sights.

Xan approached Raiden and extended her hand. In her palm laid a small white metallic device, not much larger than the head of a pin. Raiden reached out and picked it up, "What is it?"

Xan pointed to the base of her left ear, "We use these to decipher languages. On our ship, our computers have allowed us to communicate seamlessly in the interim. As you can see we have many guests that come to visit us at the Bastion. This device is injected by the ear and will be able to translate all discussion into your native tongue. Any doctor on our station can do your injection. For it to translate perfectly, a download of your complete language database would be beneficial to all," Xan explained.

Raiden stared at the minuscule device in awe, "That's amazing..."

"Are you the only one of your kind?" she asked.

"What?" Raiden said, taken off guard by the question, "Oh, no, haha! No, not at all. My race is called *human*. We have a large ship with over a million aboard. In fact, I should go back to tell my people about this place... Do you, I mean, can we get water here? Our ship is running dangerously low."

Xan nodded, "Barter and trade keep this station alive, you'll want to head to the commerce district to find a supplier."

Relief swept over Raiden's face, "Thank you!"

He couldn't explain it, but he felt at ease telling Xan the truth. There was something about her calm nature that nurtured trust. He felt safe confiding in her and asking for her help.

"Of course. As a new species on the station, you'll need to register through customs and submit to a complete physical examination. With so many species aboard with varying health requirements, it's standard procedure, for your wellbeing, as well as everyone else's aboard. Please keep your space suit on until directed otherwise," she told him.

"Oh, OK… I guess that makes sense," he said, trying to imagine the incredibly complicated logistics of running a station like this. "I should return, to fetch my ship," he began saying, feeling some anxiety at the idea of a physical examination by an alien.

Xan smiled, "There's no need. I'll arrange for a convoy to escort them to the station."

Raiden smiled meekly. He trusted Xan, but he was beginning to feel trapped. *Why didn't I go right back through the wormhole after I got here? I'm so stupid! Now what…* He was sure he could leave if he pressed the matter, but this was first contact. What procedure was there? He had no clue, he was no diplomat. This impression would be ever-lasting. Swallowing his nerves, he looked to Xan, "Where do I go for this exam?"

|

The entirety of the inhabitants aboard the Saisei waited with bated breath. It had been nearly two hours since Raiden had passed through the wormhole. Several communications had been sent out, but no reply had come. The data had transmitted back to them during Raiden's voyage through the wormhole up until it had closed, which hadn't been long.

Norita paced the deck of the bridge. The unease of waiting was all too familiar. The lack of sleep, the responsibilities, the draught; it all weighed heavily on her and was starting to take its toll.

Takeo Yamamoto had excused himself a half hour prior, to tend to work while they waited for the wormhole to reopen. The last 30 minutes had dragged on into what had stretched into an eternity for her. Norita clicked on her comm badge, "Doctor Takei, come in."

"Yes?" Dr. Takei responded.

"Have there been any changes to the wormhole composition?" she asked.

"No," he said curtly. Norita sighed, tired of waiting. "But," Seto continued, "the data we collected is nearly finished processing."

"I'll be right there," Norita said, relieved to have something to take her mind off of everything. "Koi, notify me if anything happens," she said as she headed for the door.

Koi, whose mind had wandered off, snapped to attention, "Yes, yes of course." Norita smiled and nodded at him, and then walked out the door. After the door had closed behind her Koi slouched back into his seat.

|

Seto was leaning over his computer when Norita found him in the lab. Busy scientists were bustling about, deciphering information as it came in. Seto was totally absorbed in what he was reading. Norita leaned down to see the screen and her closeness startled him, "Oh, uh, you made it quickly," he said, trying to regain composure.

"My curiosity begged haste. Tell me what you've learned," she said, her eyes scanning the screen.

"Much of it we're still putting together. The wormhole seems to generate a sort of electromagnetic field, and the anchor appears to work much like a lightning rod. From what we can tell, in the few seconds the wormhole was open, Lieutenant Saito's ship traveled hundreds of millions of kilometers," Seto explained.

"That far?!" Norita asked in disbelief.

Seto bobbed his head, "Yes. Theoretically, a wormhole has no limits in distance. At least not as far as we know."

"Astounding," Norita said, meaning it. "Any ideas as to why the ship hasn't returned?" she asked, looking down at him.

Seto shrugged, "Any number of reasons. The ship may have been damaged or destroyed, the pilot could have blacked out or suffered some sort of unexpected side effect from the abnormal means of travel, time could be slower on the other side..."

"What do you mean 'time could be slower on the other side?'" Norita asked, confused.

"The theory of relativity," Seto said.

Norita stared at him, trying to figure out what he meant, with no luck, "I'm sorry, I'm lost."

Seto tried to hide his amusement at her lack of understanding, "Time dilation. Time isn't consistent across the Universe. Time isn't a constant, even though in our day to day lives it appears to be. It's a variable. Our concept of time is based on our experience on our own home planet, which we've since adopted as our concept of time to live by aboard this ship.

"The theory states that 2 observers can experience time differently, either due to varying velocity, or their relative position to a gravity field. Gravity fields shift as we travel through space, based on our distance to celestial bodies and their own gravimetric pull. While we only left our home plant a little over 200 years ago, 10,000 years could have passed back there where our planet used to be, for all we know. So, while we've been waiting a few hours, it's possible Lieutenant Saito has only been over there for a few minutes,"

"Wow..." Norita said, taking it all in.

"Just a possibility. As I said, there's many reasons he could have not come back through," Seto said and returned to analyzing his screen.

Norita had a sinking feeling in her stomach. "Thanks, I'll let you get back to work," she said, and then started to walk toward the door. The many unknowns did not sit well with her.

|

"I'd like to apply to be a military pilot," Suki said, standing in front of the desk in the recruitment office. It was vacant less for her and the single officer who sat behind the desk. The man looked her up and down skeptically.

"How old are you?" he asked.

"Seventeen," Suki told him.

"Minimum age is 18," he replied.

"Yeah, I know. I'm not expecting to see the inside of a cockpit anytime soon. My 18th birthday is next month, and I'm ahead in my classes so I'm graduating early. I just want to get a head start, go over the materials, then I'll fill out the paperwork next month," she said, a stern seriousness to her voice.

The officer stared her in the eye. She had conviction behind her actions, not something he saw as often as he'd like in applicants. "You sure you want to be a pilot?" he asked.

"Yes," she answered.

"Why?"

Suki took a moment to try to find the right words, "I... I like order. I like rules that make sense, and I like a challenge. I'm a quick study, and I've always wanted to fly. Computers, technical code, it's always just come naturally. It's a good fit for me," she said. What she left out was that getting her own ship would enable her to track down her father. *And then… and then what? I don't know… Does he know Link is my dad?* she wondered nervously.

"If you're good with tech you should look into becoming a military technology expert," he said bluntly.

Suki felt caught off guard by the suggestion, "Oh, uh… maybe. But, no, I really want to fly."

He subtly nodded his head, "Alright. Wait here, I'm going to grab you the basic training manual to look over."

"Thank you," she said and meant it.

The officer stood up from his desk and disappeared into a small office closet in the back of the room. Suki looked around the room. There were recruitment posters on the wall, some medals and plaques commemorating outstanding soldiers, and several large cabinets lined the far wall. Overall it was subtle, clean, orderly, and minimalistic; just the way she liked it.

A few minutes later the officer returned with several data chips. When he reached the desk, he extended his hand and the chips to Suki, "There's the introductory military manual, and I also grabbed you the pilots' handbook for you to look over. And this," he held up the third one, "the technical experts' introduction, just in case you change your mind."

She took the chips, then looked him in the eye, "Thanks. Really, thank you."

"You're welcome," he smiled. Suki turned around to walk away, but before she left he called out to her, "Hey, what day is your birthday?"

Suki spun around to face him, "October 12th."

"OK, I'll make sure I'm in that day. I'm Officer Kaito Amari," he said with a smile.

She smiled back, "Suki Rose," she said and held up the data chips in her hand, "Thank you again. See you next month." And with that, she turned around and left.

Kaito sat down in the desk chair. It had been a quiet week for recruitments. *And why wouldn't it be? Who wants to sign up when so many soldiers just got spaced,* he thought and shuddered at the thought of getting sucked out into space to suffocate to death.

It had been an off-duty day for Kaito when the insurrection occurred. He'd been visiting a friend in the civilian sector for the first time in months for a poker game and had wound up being locked in his friend's quarters the entire time. He knew it had to have been divine intervention for it to have happened that day. In any other situation, any other day, Kaito would have been one of the soldiers that had gone down to the docking bay and vented into space for an early death.

Since the insurrection Kaito had been on edge and unable to sleep at all. *Survivor's guilt?* He wondered. *Yes, I do feel guilty...* so many of his brethren had died that day. And Gin had always been a good friend to him. Word had already spread about Gin's attempt on his own life, and Kaito had felt utterly shocked when word had finally come to him about it.

Kaito had known Gin for years. They often worked together in the military branches with civilian relations. On the Saisei, the military governed day to day aspects such as policing and civilian safety. The simplification of one organization supervising the ship prevented potential conflict and provided a simplistic means to protect and serve the people.

Kaito stared at the clock. It was mid-afternoon, and he doubted anyone else would come by the recruitment office that day. His body felt tired and sore from sitting all day. Normally he didn't mind desk duty shifts, but in the absence of work, the time crept by slowly.

His mind felt sluggish as if his thoughts had to be found in a thick fog. Kaito had always been able to sleep well, and now for the first time, he finally understood what insomniacs suffered through. He felt a great deal of empathy for them. He leaned back in his seat, rested his eyes, and before he knew it he had drifted off into a much-needed sleep.

|

Freya, with her arms crossed, stood in front of the large window in the atrium that faced the wormhole anchor. The atrium was otherwise empty. Since the mass funeral, and people paying their respects shortly thereafter, no one had wanted to spend time in the space that had held so much sadness.

Hours before Freya had watched Raiden go through the wormhole in a flash and had expected to see him pop right back. But he didn't. She hadn't averted her gaze in the several hours he'd been away. *He's coming back, I can feel it...* she kept telling herself, trying to allay the worry and anxiety she felt in the pit of her stomach. Stoically she waited for her friend to return. She was so focused on the anchor and her own thoughts that she didn't hear Koji approaching.

"There you are," he said with relief resonating in his voice and he walked up behind her.

Freya flinched and looked over her shoulder to see him standing right next to her, "Fuck!" she blurted out, her heart speeding away.

Koji couldn't help but laugh, "Sorry, didn't mean to scare you. I was looking for you everywhere."

"Why?" she asked curtly, an edge of annoyance to her tone.

Koji squinted questionably at her, "Are you OK?"

Freya rolled her eyes and then turned back to look out the window, "I'm fine. Now did you need something?"

Sighing heavily Koji, "I guess not," he said, then started to walk away.

"Wait," Freya said, turning around to grab his arm. "Sorry, look... it's just. Raiden's like a brother, we grew up together and... I'm worried."

Koji took her in his arms, "Why didn't you just tell me?"

"Because," she started to say, resting her head on his chest she felt his warmth and heard his strong heartbeat and felt safe, "I don't know. I just don't talk about these kinds of things."

"Heh, yeah you are kind of a hard-ass," Koji chuckled.

"What?!" Freya tried to push him back playfully, but he held her tight, and they both began to laugh. The break in the tension made her feel infinitely better, if only for the briefest of moments. Freya finally wrestled free of Koji's hold and then grabbed him in a headlock, "Thought you had me didn't ya?" she said cockily.

"I let you go," he said confidently.

"Oh, like hell you did!" she said and squeezed tight around his neck.

The restriction, the struggle to breathe, and the panic set in fast, "Right, OK, OK, you win," he wheezed.

Freya released her grip and Koji backed away and collapsed down with his hands on his knees catching his breath. A tremor of terror had rippled through him. He knew in his logical mind that it was just the post-traumatic stress syndrome reaction from the near-death experience in space, and yet he couldn't suppress the feeling of overwhelm.

"You're fuckin' merciless," he coughed, red-faced from the lack of oxygen.

Freya walked toward him, but he backed up, "Koji, I'm sorry, I didn't mean to…"

"You never *mean to*, you just don't think!" he spat, heaving and trembling.

Taking a deep breath Freya bit her tongue. She was always one to be quick to anger, ready to fight, but she knew more than anyone what he'd been through. "You're right," she simply said, and let the silence hang in the air.

Koji regained his composure after focusing on taking deep cleansing breathes like that doctor had shown him. He stood up straight and stared at Freya, his eyes no longer bearing anger, but instead seeking forgiveness. "I…" he started to speak but didn't know what to say.

Freya shook her head, "It's alright, I know."

He smiled meekly at her, and she smiled back. Before either of them could say another word the bright flash of the wormhole opening drew both of their attention. They ran over to the window. Freya's heart leaped, and for a split second, she felt relief, which was instantly swept away by fear.

The ship coming through the wormhole wasn't Raiden's ship, it was iridescent white, glimmering from the refractive light of the wormhole. Koji felt his heart skip a beat, "What the hell is that?"

"I don't fuckin' know..." Freya said, feeling the hairs on the back of her neck raise up. *What the hell happened to Raiden on the other side?* Freya wondered fretfully. The Saisei's emergency lighting went off and the siren sounded. Koji couldn't take his eyes off of the ship. With difficulty, Freya dragged herself away from the window, and tugged on Koji's arm, "Common, we gotta go."

|

Koi sat frozen in his chair, staring out the window at the approaching white ship. Minutes later Norita walked onto the bridge and stopped dead in her tracks when she saw the ship. "Unbelievable," she muttered to herself. Koi heard her and turned around in his chair, he went to speak but no words came out. Norita noticed him looking at her, "Have they done anything?"

Koi shook his head, "No, just a steady slow approach vector."

"Who else did you call up?" she asked.

"General Yamamoto and Dr. Takei, I didn't know who else to call," he said, feeling lost.

"That's good," she said.

They waited in silence, watching as the ship slowly got closer and closer. After another minute had gone by Dr. Takei walked onto the bridge, "Remarkable!" he said looking at the ship with a smile on his face. He ignored Norita and Koi and walked straight over to the computer terminal in the far corner.

"Doctor, what do we know?" Norita asked as she walked over to him.

"That we're not alone in the Universe," he said without looking up.

Norita, annoyed, was about to ask what else when she realized how monumental that statement was in and of itself. She looked back out the window at the ship with a new sense of wonder. Her leadership position had put her into a defensive mode, a feeling of the need to protect her people from the unknown. Now she wasn't so sure.

"Empress, we've got an incoming transmission from the ship," Koi said, stunned.

"Put it through," Norita said.

Koi did as she beckoned, and put the transmission on through the bridge's comm. The fear Norita had felt melted away instantaneously when the serene voice began to speak, "I am Captain Venu, and on behalf of the Bastion Conclave, I welcome you to the cultural hub of our Galaxy."

After a moment of revered silence, Norita turned to Koi, "Call the council into session immediately!"

|

It had been a heated discussion in the council chambers. Fear of the unknown ran deep with many, while desperation for salvation fueled others. After 30 minutes of uninterrupted debate, it had all but turned into a screaming match.

"They don't seem hostile," one said.

"It's a trap!" another yelled

"Our pilot never came back!" another chimed in.

"We have to go, we'll die here without water!" yet another insisted.

Norita stood up at the table and raised her hand, beckoning silence. "Please," she began, "we're all afraid. No, we don't know these aliens or their intentions, but I do not perceive them to be a threat to us. We do need water, desperately, and the likelihood of getting another drill built before we completely drain our stores is low. I don't see any other choice. We need to trust them and go through the wormhole. The decision is final," Norita said.

An uproarious burst of agreeing and disagreeing diplomats spewing their opinions overtook the room. Norita quickly made her way out. The hallway was serenely quiet by comparison and Norita was grateful for the reprieve from the incessant bickering.

Councilor Merrick Uda followed had her out, "Well played."

She turned to look at him, "I doubt many in that room would agree."

Merrick shrugged, "No matter. You did what needed to be done. Good job," he said and then walked away.

Norita watched Merrick as he walked off, and thought, *I hope you're right.*

Chapter 11: The Bastion

It had been 2 days since the Saisei had docked at the Bastion. Due to the massive size of the Saisei passenger manifest a rotation schedule had been put in place for visitation, so as to not overwhelm the Bastions customs terminal with incoming personnel. Norita and Takeo had been granted diplomatic privileges and were provided with accommodations in the consulate branch of the ship.

The room they'd been given was eloquently furnished with beautiful furniture, incredible plants, and provided them with a computer terminal that accessed an immense data base of combined knowledge from all of the species that formed the Conclave government. It had been a lot to take in in such a short time.

Norita stood leaning on the balcony railing; their room overlooked the winding walkways down below, which were surrounded by greenery, and a waterway that stretched the entirety of the wing of the ship, which was over a hundred miles long. An artificial sky created the complete illusion of being on a planet. She inhaled deeply; she'd never smelled such crisp air, not even when she'd been in the hydroponics bay on the Saisei.

How can this be real? She asked, in awe of it all, and squeezed her hands on the cool metal railing to affirm it wasn't a dream. *Who could have built something of this scope? It looks similar to the wormhole anchors. I wish Xan had been able to talk longer...*

When Norita had boarded the station, Xan had been there to greet her, and answered a few questions while guiding her to her assigned quarters. *Why didn't I ask more questions?* She wondered and sighed. This incredible place had brought up more questions in her than it had answered.

"You should see this," Takeo said, sitting behind the computer, reading intently.

Drawing her attention away from the people that wandered around below, she looked over to Takeo. "What is it?" she asked, then added, "it's incredible they created translations so fast for us."

"Agreed. I'm glad Dr. Takei is handling the information exchange, he works fast. Though I think he'd benefit from this database more than we do," Takeo chuckled.

Norita couldn't help but smirk, "Oh I bet he's had them patch it to the Saisei's central computer hub; he's probably reading all of this at night instead of sleeping."

"True enough," Takeo smiled and nodded in agreement.

Norita walked around the desk and stood behind Takeo, leaning on the edge of the desk to view the computer screen. He sat back in the chair and waited while she read. "This is incredible," she said after several moments, "I sure as hell hope Dr. Takei downloaded all of this."

The data included the complete informative breakdown of all species that lived aboard or had dealings with, the Bastion. Sociological, economical, religious, biological, historical, political; every piece of information one could ask for was available at a click.

"We can get to know our neighbors better," Takeo said.

"I'll take it," Norita said, enthralled with the find.

The Conclave had set an appointment to meet with Norita for 3 days after their arrival. She had brought General Yamamoto aboard for protection, as well as to get his opinion. After all that they'd been through she'd come to trust him implicitly.

The first day aboard the Bastion they'd cautiously explored the wing of the ship they'd been assigned to, the consulate wing. It was massive in scope, and it made Norita wonder how anyone could conceive of such a place, let alone build it. There were so many aspects of the ship to be maintained, it seemed a logistical impossibility, and yet everything was running in perfect harmony. *Zavion would have an aneurysm just trying to fathom how to handle this ship,* she remembered thinking.

After a few hours of walking down the many pathways, they had stopped for lunch. Both felt a nervousness in wondering what might appear on their plates. Their waiter scanned their DNA before providing them with menu's, explaining that their digital system removed anything potentially hazardous and optimized ideal nutrition meals for each species at the top of the list.

After lunch, they had continued to walk until they came to a recreational area. Green grass had been spread out, benches for seating, and various trees, flowers, and bushes had been landscaped in a perfect zen-like fashion.

"It's perfect," Takeo had said, as he sat down on the bench next to Norita.

They sat for nearly an hour, marveling at the station and the passers-by. Occasionally a member of the Saisei would wander by, too enraptured by the sights to even notice Norita or Takeo. As they sat on the bench watching everyone go about their business, they couldn't help but note the incredible variances in the many forms of sentient life aboard the station. Some looked majestic, some small, some large, some like their idea of a monster out of a nightmare, however, there seemed to be complete order among them. Bastion security personnel were scattered around everywhere they had attended, but no incident had occurred in all of the hours they had been out exploring the station.

They'd considered another stroll on the second day, but both Takeo and Norita were anxiously waiting for their meeting with the council the next day and found themselves uncertain of what to do with themselves. And so, without a decision they had holed themselves up in their quarters, ordered in food, and spent the day discussing what might happen the next day at the Conclave.

Now midway through the afternoon, the database Takeo had found had breathed new life into them; the distraction easing their nervous minds. Takeo scrolled slowly through the database, while Norita stood next to him reading along.

"How in the world do they keep all of this straight?" Takeo said after some time.

Norita shook her head, "Hard to say. Although I suppose if this was normal, growing up with all of these other species around, I suppose they'd learn it early on. It seemed from their reaction to us like we're the first new species to arrive at the station in a while."

"That makes sense... but still," Takeo let out a deep breath.

"I know what you mean... Oh hey, that looks like Xan. *Ethlana*, I guess that must be the name of their race," Norita said, tapping the screen.

"Yeah, it does. Says here their homeworld is in a nearby system... holy hell, their natural life cycle is 700 years! ...They were the first specifies to find the Bastion about 3,000 years ago, but they didn't build it," he said.

"I thought for sure they'd built it," she replied.

"I thought so too, they seem to be the predominant species aboard. I wonder if anyone knows who constructed this, it doesn't seem to say..." Takeo's words trailed off for a moment as he continued searching. "It seems they call the wormhole anchors *Heaven's Eyes*," he said, then again Takeo got quiet while he continued reading.

"3,000 years ago, this place is ancient, and yet it looks new... It's remarkable. I hope the Conclave can answer some of these questions tomorrow, I think I'm more confused now than I was before," Norita chuckled, though she felt slightly unnerved.

Before Takeo could say another word, a knock came at the door. Norita and Takeo shot each other a look, wondering who might be coming by, but neither knew. Takeo stood up from the chair, and briskly walked over to the door, and hit the switch to open it to find Raiden standing there.

"It's you," Takeo said, surprised.

Raiden stared blankly at him for a moment, "Uh, yeah, it *is* me. Is this a bad time?"

"No, no, come in," Takeo said, standing aside to let Raiden by.

Raiden entered the room and then bowed to Norita, "Pleasure to see you again, Empress."

Takeo closed the door and walked back over to the desk to sit down, "I was expecting to hear from you sooner once we'd boarded the station."

"As was I. We were beginning to think we'd never see you again," Norita smiled, "I'm glad you're OK. When you didn't come back through the wormhole... well, let's just say we were all very concerned."

"I'm sorry, everything happened so fast, and well..."

"Please," Norita shook her head, "there's no need to explain."

"Right. Well, after I arrived on the Bastion I went to the merchant's wing, and after some tiresome negotiations the past couple of days, I've secured enough water to fully resupply the Saisei. I just need your permission to provide the goods I offered in exchange," Raiden extended a data pad to Norita which she took and read over closely.

After a few moments Norita placed her thumb on the data pad to transmit her signature to the digital form, and handed the data pad back to Raiden, "That's quite some deal you made. You know, you'd have quite a promising future in politics."

He took the pad back and slipped it into the inner pocket of his jacket, "Thanks ma'am, but I think I prefer the skies."

"Good work, Lieutenant. I knew you were the right person for the job," Takeo said, pride ringing in his voice.

"Thank you, General," Raiden said, feeling elated. "Well, I'm going to head back to get this handed to the broker authorities."

"Take a day to enjoy the Bastion before you head back to the Saisei, but then I want a full report. And send off a transmission to Dr. Takei about where your ship docked, he's eager to get his hands on the flight records from the scanner," General Yamamoto instructed.

"Right away sir, and thank you," Raiden said with a smile.

Takeo curtly nodded, and then Raiden bowed quickly and left. Norita slowly meandered over to a small sofa-like piece of furniture and sat down. "I can't believe the water crisis is finally behind us," she said, feeling as if the weight of the world had finally been lifted off of her shoulders.

"He's a good soldier," Takeo said.

"Yes... he is."

|

Freya had been sitting in a decontamination chamber for over 20 minutes. The room was dark, and time felt like it was moving slowly. The customs procedures had been swift up until this point. Beyond the docks, to get into any of the inner sanctums of the Bastion, everyone from every ship was required to go through this sterilization process. As a new species aboard the ship, while data was being fully complied about their biology and possible transmittable diseases, bacteria, and viruses, each member of the Saisei was subjected to a full 30-minute decontamination for safety.

As soon as the Saisei had docked with the Bastion Freya had applied for shore leave in hopes of finding Raiden. The list had already become extensive by the time their ship had docked and she'd been forced to wait. Now minutes away from getting to explore the station, each second ticked by slower and slower.

The room was all metal, with a metal bench bolted against one wall. An intricate system of air purifiers and filtration systems was integrated into a triple protected ventilation shaft that vented directly out into space. The room had top of the line sensors and scanners that could extract medical data on every species down to the subatomic particles.

Freya sat on the bench with her back against the cool metal of the wall. She let her head tilt back to lean against the wall as well, and felt the cold permeate her scalp. It was strangely soothing. She rested her eyes shut and let out a deep breath. A split second later she heard a loud *BEEP!* and she snapped to attention. The decontamination procedure was finally over. The inner door, leading into the Bastion, had electronically unlocked.

Standing up from the bench, Freya promptly walked over to the door and pushed it open. *Finally*, she thought, exiting the chamber. After a long walk down a stark white corridor, she came to an opening, which led into the main body of the station. Her impatience dissolved entirely as she entered, marveling at all of the wonders.

Much like at the docks of the Bastion an array of different aliens walked about the promenade. But unlike the docks which, although well maintained were somewhat dirty from the many travelers, congested, and had an overpowering smell of fuel from the frequenting ships, inside the inner sanctum of the Bastion was a paradise. Trees lined the walkways, the air was pure and fragrant, a welcoming warm light mimicking a sun lit up the entirety of the central Bastion, and the walkways were all unbelievably clean. Amongst the shops, living spaces, and other buildings were vast amounts of greenery.

In this central part of the Bastion, gravity was caused by centrifugal forces; the circular center was always spinning. The curve of the ship was gentle, giving the near appearance of a flat surface to walk upon. When Freya looked up to see where her ceiling would be, she found that she was simply staring across to the other side of the interior of this section of the Bastion where aliens, upside down from her perspective, went about their business.

Science had never been her strong suit, so Freya didn't even try to fathom how all of this was possible. After several people pushed past her to get down the pathway she'd just come up from, Freya snapped out of her trance, and moved to get out of the way. She walked up to the nearest guard rail, overlooking a small pond full of aquatic life, and took in the sights, entranced.

"Freya?" a voice called from behind.

Freya turned around to see Raiden standing behind her, "Raiden!" she nearly yelled once she laid her eyes on him and then she ran over to tackle him with a hug.

"Haha, shit! Nice to see you too," he laughed, catching his breath after she knocked the wind out of him.

She let go and then punched him hard in the arm, "You scared the shit out of me, man! Fuck..." she shook her head.

"Ouch!" he recoiled, holding his arm.

"Don't you ever pull that shit again, OK? Disappearing like that... I thought you weren't coming back," she said.

"Well damn, maybe I shouldn't come back," he said pointing at his arm.

"Oh baby, get over it. So, tell me already, what happened?" she insisted.

"I can't right now," he said, holding up a data chip, "I'm on duty, I have to get this to our ship."

"Oh," Freya said, trying not to sound as disheartened as she felt.

"Tomorrow?" he asked.

"Yeah, that'd be great," she smiled.

"Keep your comm open, I'll let you know when I'm back aboard," he said, and began to walk off.

"See ya," she said and watched him leave.

Tomorrow... what am I going to do today? She asked herself, looking around. Without any plans, she began walking aimlessly down the nearest pathway.

|

After a long walk through the central structure of the Bastion, Hiroshi had found himself drawn to checking out the *Ecological Wing* of the station. Extending from the main structure of the bastion were 5 *Wings*, each dedicated to a major function of the Bastion. With the alarmingly large size of the Bastion, it had made sense to do so, to cut down on travel times for people needing to conduct their affairs with others in the same field. The 5 wings were *Business, Ecological, Politics & Law, Entertainment,* and *Military.*

Each wing had restaurants, living quarters, businesses, and picturesque greenery, making each wing its own livable space. The main central structure of the Bastion was for those who'd taken up a more permanent residence; those who worked solely aboard the ship, maintenance workers, engineers, cleaning staff, among the plethora of people needed to run the shops and inns. It was a perfect orchestra.

Hiroshi sat down to eat in a delectable café after the scent had beckoned him in. Like everything else on the Bastion, it was perfectly situated for the best view. There was wall to ceiling windows in the café which made up the entirety of one wall, which overlooked a field of berry bushes in full bloom.

After a long look at the menu, Hiroshi decided to be adventurous, and asked the server, a tall alien with tan colored reptilian-like skin, a short tail, and black eyes, to bring him what his favorites were. His waiter had smiled, clearly ecstatic to get to share his culinary picks. As Hiroshi waited for his food and drink he leaned back in his chair. His feet had begun to throb from all of the walking. *I guess I need to exercise more,* he thought to himself as he caught his breath.

He'd brought his camera with him to capture as many sights on the Bastion as he could. He'd longed to bring his pad of paper to capture an artistic rendition of the station, but with such a short time allotted on the Bastion, he knew he'd be better off exploring and focusing on his art later. He reviewed some of his photos while he waited for his food to come, just as astounded by them now as when he'd taken them. After a few moments, he set the camera down and took in the sights, sounds, and smells around himself.

The café was full, and bustling with energy, and yet he felt serene. He stared out the window into the field of bushes and noticed a small furry creature eating leaves off of one of the plants. He quickly picked up his camera and took a photo of it. *One amazing sight after another*, he thought, feeling incredibly grateful.

His waiter returned with a small tray of delights; there was a cup filled with a hot liquid with an earthy smell, a dense pastry-like desert, and a bowl filled with what looked like tiny rocks. Hiroshi leaned over the table to look at them all, then looked up at his server, "Thank you,"

A smile pasted on his face, his server beamed, "You're welcome," and walked away.

First Hiroshi took a sip of the hot drink. It tasted earthy, just like it smelled, like a sort of white herbal tea. The earthy flavor gave way to a sweet almost vanilla like after taste, that was quite satisfying. The hot drink was quite refreshing.

Next, he wanted to try the pastry. He'd been given a utensil, similar to a spoon, but flat and rectangular, which he scooped into the pastry with. The pastry gave way, in the same way gelatin does when cut. He lifted the utensil to his nose to smell the pastry, which had a warm aroma, similar to nutmeg. When he took the bite into his mouth a vast array of flavors exploded that his mind tried to explain with familiar foods; citrus, and cinnamon, hazel, and peach. Hiroshi closed his eyes and savored the experience. *For all the space between us, there is so much similarity across this huge galaxy*, Hiroshi thought.

Unable to pull away, he finished the pastry off. Last he looked to the small bowl of rock-like food. He picked one up from the dish and it felt just as hard as it looked. *How the hell do I eat this?* He wondered. He looked around for his waiter, hoping to ask, but he was nowhere to be seen. After a moment of indecision, Hiroshi finally decided to just pop it in his mouth.

The hard rock-like food rolled on his tongue, the edges sharp, making it tantalizing to the senses. He rolled it around in his mouth, and as his saliva came in contact with it, the rock ever so slowly began to dissolve, creating a syrup consistency that tasted almost like a mulberry. The rich flavor was incredible. After the first had finished dissolving he found himself grabbing another.

His server came by the table, "How is everything?"

"Delicious!" Hiroshi exclaimed through a thick mouthful of syrup.

The server smiled, "These have always been my favorites, ever since I was a boy. They're made from those berries out there in the fields," he said pointing out the large window.

"They're marvelous, thank you for recommending them. Would you like one?" Hiroshi asked, holding up the bowl.

Happily, his server took one, and then went back about his business, clearing off a nearby table. Hiroshi rested in his chair feeling very content. *Food always seems to be a Universal pathway to sharing,* he thought, almost laughing at his overly obvious observation. *I better stop eating these, must be a sugar high,* he thought feeling giddy. He gulped down the rest of his beverage, left a hefty tip on the table, and thank strolled out of the café.

Hiroshi found the energy aboard the station to be calming, *is it the plants or the people?* He questions. *Both? Probably...* He enjoyed watching the interactions of the various aliens as much as he loved the scenery. As newcomers every one of the Saisei passengers coming aboard the Bastion had an access link to the Bastion's database, allowing them to scan unfamiliar plants and other species to learn basic information about each. *I'm going to have to integrate this into my next lesson,* he thought joyously, as he read about the various aliens and plants he passed by.

A strange bird flew out of a tree that Hiroshi was walking past and then it perched on the railing next to where he was standing. The bird was bright red in the body, with blue and black feathers around its head and tail and had a jagged orange beak. Hiroshi stopped and scanned the bird. The scanner pulled up the information. The bird was called a *Jusu* and came from the homeworld of the *Kikari*, the planet *Grast*.

The Kikari were a massive alien species, 8 feet in stature, broad, and appeared tough as nails. Hiroshi had seen several while he had been walking around the station and their faces reminded him of photo's he'd seen of Rhino's faces from the history files on the Saisei; images from before they'd gone extinct on his home world so many centuries ago. The Kikari walked tall and proud and appeared easy to anger. The data entries he read had indicated they still operated in a tribal political structure on their own planet.

The Jusu birds were used by the Kikari hunting parties to distract their prey. The Jusu's favorite food was the *Qas* berry, which was the mulberry-like fruit Hiroshi had seen in the fields outside of the café. Despite its dynamic appearance the bird was a herbivore and known to be friendly. Hiroshi held out his hand to the bird. The bird inspected his hand and after a moment stepped onto his index finger. "Well hello there," Hiroshi said and smiled.

"Hey!" a deep guttural voice said powerfully from behind Hiroshi.

Hiroshi froze, the hair on the back of his neck up, as he felt the blood drain from his face. Hiroshi went to speak, but he couldn't. He let out a shaky exhale and turned around to see two male Kikaris standing behind him. He stood there staring at them.

"You found my Jusu, thank you," the one to the left said, his voice still booming and intimidating.

"Ah, yes," Hiroshi said and extended his hand with the Jusu on it toward the Kikari. The Jusu finished preened and then flew and landed on the Kikari's shoulder.

"Thank you, human," the same one said. The other Kikari, standing on the right, had his arms crossed, and looked at Hiroshi with what he assumed to be a hostile stare.

"Y, you're welcome. You know I'm human?" he couldn't help but asked, surprised after such a short time that others would take the time to recognize a new addition to this massive array of species.

"Of course," the Kikari said, and gave a deep belly laugh that Hiroshi thought could be easily mistaken for a growl. "Those Ethlana practically throw a parade when a new contact is made. Everyone on the station knows who you are."

"Oh," Hiroshi said, surprised.

"Thanks again, human," The Kikari said and began walking away, his silent compadre walking off behind him without a word.

Hiroshi took a moment to take a deep breath. He felt his heart begin to beat again, and the fear subsided. *Shit, they're huge...* he thought. *Get yourself together, they were nothing but nice... well, the one was. But still... how easily could they have killed me?* He shuddered.

Once he regained his composure Hiroshi began walking leisurely down the pathway again, taking in the sights, and snapping photos. But now his mind was preoccupied. *Xenophobia must be an issue. It doesn't seem to be but... I wonder if their data base talks about wars? Not all first contacts must go as smoothly as ours. Though those Ethlana, there's something incredibly soothing about being near them... I wonder if it's a biochemical reaction? Either way, I'm glad they're the ones we ran into...*

After a few hours of meandering down many pathways, through lovely landscaped areas, the artificial sky began to turn, mimicking a sunset. *Remarkable...* Hiroshi thought, overcome by the beauty of it. *If only we'd had such thought and consideration in the crafting on the Saisei. They knew it would be a generational life-ship for humanity and yet... I shouldn't complain, they were working against time. It's a miracle they pulled off building it at all with all the seismic activity they logged. They needed a ship to function, for over a million people, and they made it happen. It's lasted for centuries at that, kept us alive, but still... how many sunsets have I actually seen with my own eyes in my life? 3? Yes... just the 3. This may be simulated, but it's utterly...* his mind was at a loss for words to describe it.

He stood there, in stillness, staring straight up watching the sky change. It was mesmerizing. Even the feeling of radial heat from the artificial placement of the sun in the sky felt as real as standing on a planet. Hiroshi pulled up his camera to take several photographs, and then just allowed himself to enjoy it. Hiroshi spotted a nearby bench in his peripheral vision, walked over to it, and sat down. He sat there for over an hour watching as the sky changed from light blues to fuchsia pinks, pale greens, and a golden spread of yellow and orange hues, until finally it gave way to the starscape of night.

Chapter 12: The Conclave

Norita tossed and turned all night. No matter how she moved her body felt uncomfortable, and her mind was wide awake. General Yamamoto was in a deep sleep in the other bed, his snoring exasperating her insomnia. *I might as well just give up trying to sleep,* she thought feeling frustrated.

She laid awake wrestling with sleep that refused to come for the rest of the night. When daylight finally came she felt dread. *They better have something like coffee on this station,* she thought, wondering how in the world she'd be able to concentrate during her meeting with the Conclave.

With Takeo still sleeping soundly, Norita quietly got dressed and walked over to the balcony to take in the view, and to do some stretching. Her father had taught her that waking up the body helped to wake up the mind. *Daddy, you always knew what to do...* Norita's father had raised her by himself, all while smoothly running the ship.

Her mother had died when she was an infant, and her dad hadn't remarried after her loss. From a young age, he had imparted much wisdom to Norita, as much in life lessons as he did in leadership. As his only child Norita was sole heir the Empire.

What would you do? Norita asked, trying to imagine her father going in to meet with the Conclave. He had such grace in politics, she always felt the need to live up to his standards. *Why am I stressing over this so much? There's nothing I can do to prepare, I don't know what they want... Because it's important. Because this is the single most important meeting humanity has ever had.* She let out a long exhale. *Stop it. You'll do fine.*

After finishing her stretches Norita proceeded to have a shower. There were no water restrictions aboard the Bastion, much to Norita's surprise with the incredible size of the station and number of people aboard. She turned on the nozzle and a strong stream of hot water came running from the shower head. She stepped into the stream, closed her eyes, and stuck her face under the water. The bliss of the fresh water running across her face helped calm her nerves and made her feel much more awake.

She luxuriated in the feel of it. For the past several months with the tight water restrictions on the Saisei, the shower felt especially good. Sponge bathing had been their only method to clean their bodies; full pressured water felt like it was washing away months of grime. She stood there, almost in a meditative trance, enjoying every second.

Once Norita had finished showering and got dressed, she walked into the common room to find Takeo was awake. It was still early. The station ran on a 26-hour clock; a 26-hour day was the median daytime hours from the various planets of all the main species that lived aboard the station. It was in the 7th hour according to the station's clocks.

"I'm sorry, did I wake you?" Norita asked, surprised to see him awake.

"No, of course not. Just habit to be up now, my body has learned to follow the military hours over the years," he said matter-of-factly.

"Right. That makes sense. I suppose we all get our own rhythms in life," she said as she finished drying her hair with the towel.

Their appointment with the enclave wasn't until the 15th hour. Just like the day before, it felt like they had nothing but endless time on their hands. "Do you want to be alone to prepare?" Takeo asked.

Norita shook her head gently as she began to brush her hair, "No. There's really nothing to

prepare. I'll go stir crazy waiting alone. Maybe...
maybe we should go for a walk. We do have 8 hours
before the meeting, after all."

"Fair enough," Takeo said.

The two of them finished dressing and then
left their room to explore the station.

|

"Hey!" Raiden called to Freya.

Freya turned to see him as he jogged up the
walkway to join her at the patio table she sat at, just
outside a small bistro. The walkway was large, over
20 feet across in this area, so restaurants sprawled
out tables for patrons to enjoy the views. Small
vendors had stalls littered everywhere, and various
performers, some in troupes, some solo acts,
performed along the promenade.

They were meeting for breakfast in the
entertainment district. It lived up to its name. There
were incredible murals from the best artists from
across the galaxy decorating the white buildings.
Playhouses, digital entertainment, interactive games,
and performers of all kinds, made this wing of the
Bastion the liveliest of them all. Yet for all its energy,
and the business, it was as relaxing as it was
enlivening.

Raiden took a seat across from Freya. "Hope you weren't waiting long," he said, picking up the menu off the table.

"Nah, just got here," Freya lied, smiling, just happy to be with her friend. "So, what was the big rush yesterday?"

Raiden took his eyes off of the menu to look up at Freya, "I found water for the Saisei," he said, beaming.

"Yeah?" she said, surprised.

"Enough to completely resupply the ship," he nodded.

"Damn, nice job. I'm gonna have to up my game. Can't let you get to *Captain* before me," she grinned.

"Always a competition, huh?" he said, letting his eyes lower back onto the menu.

"You know it," she jived.

They sat in silence as they decided on what to eat. The waiter came over and took their orders, and their menus. A moment later their server returned with water, a coffee-like hot drink, and some qas berry juice. Raiden grabbed the hot drink and drank deeply, feeling instantly replenished.

Freya picked up her cup and sniffed it. It smelled nutty and bitter. She tilted the cup and the thick liquid slowly oozed around like molasses. She cringed at the idea of it but saw Raiden drinking it down, and decided to bravely take a sip. The hot liquid touched her lips and had none of the taste of the bitterness she had smelled, and instead had a rich taste which reminded her of a toasted walnut.

While it was thick, it wasn't sticky and was surprisingly easy to drink without leaving a lingering coating in the mouth. She swallowed, licked her lips, and set her cup down. Looking up, she saw Raiden still drinking his, his eyes closed, an expression of enjoyment on his face.

"Guess you adapted to this place fast," she said, smiling.

He opened his eyes, almost feeling embarrassed, "Oh, uh, yeah, haha! I didn't even think I was going to drink this stuff when they first gave it to me, but it's great. Better than coffee, once you get used to it. It's made from some sort of super nutrient rich nut or seed or something that's got sustained energy. Just a few days of this and I've never had so much energy in my whole life. No crash cause there's no caffeine," he explained, then took another gulp.

"Sweet," Freya said, impressed, and drank more of hers. After a few gulps she set the cup back down, "Yeah, I guess I could get used to that."

They sat in silence for a moment, and Freya looked around, taking in the sights, then looked back at Raiden, "So, any news from the General?"

Raiden shrugged, "News about what?"

Freya rolled her eyes and mimicked his shrug, "*Anything?* We're all grounded while we're stuck docked here."

"Are you serious?" he asked, not hiding his annoyance.

Freya sighed, crossed her arms, and gazed at the floor. *Shit, another fucking lecture...* she thought. "Look, I'm sorry," she started to say, trying to backtrack. But she wasn't sorry, she just didn't want to hear him berate her.

"We've just found the most amazing discovery of, of... of fucking ever, and you're complaining that you can't go fly? *Really?* What the hell is out there that's better than this? Nothing's ever good enough for you, Freya, is it?"

"You know that's not what I meant," she tried to explain.

"No? Then what did you mean?" he challenged her.

Freya went to speak but saw their waiter coming and decided to wait. Casually the waiter placed their food down in front of them and wished them a good meal. Freya watched him walk off, waiting for him to be out of earshot.

"I," Freya felt at a loss for words. *Shit! How did this spiral so out of control? I don't care that we're grounded, I don't care what the orders are, I just... I didn't know what else to say...* her mind felt noisy, and she felt frustrated. "I... look, really, I didn't mean anything by it. I just feel like... I'm not sure like I'm a bit out of place. It's been a lot to process." *Why is it so hard to talk to you?* Freya wondered. *We always talk about everything...*

Raiden stared for her for a minute without saying a word. It was rare for them to fight. Freya was always so strong, but right now she looked meek and defeated. Her arm still in the sling, he felt a pang of guilt for yelling at her. *She's been through a lot lately, I shouldn't have snapped...* he thought. "Look, it's OK. Sorry, I took it so seriously. Let's just let it go," he said.

"Right," she replied.

"So, what did you do on the station yesterday? It's massive, I felt so lost at first," he said trying to change the subject.

Freya picked up her utensils, "Well after you left, I," before she could say another word her comm clicked on.

"Hey Freya, I just got out of customs, where are you?" Koji's voice asked.

"Sorry," Freya said to Raiden, then clicked on her comm, "Hey, I'm just having breakfast with Raiden, we're in the entertainment district. Just look for a big waterfall that feeds into the main aqueduct and you'll see us."

"On my way," Koji said.

"It'll take him a while to get here," Freya said, then took a bite of her breakfast. They'd both ordered a mix of eggs and grilled meat that came with a sautéed leafy green. The eggs were pungent. She ate a bit of the meat, which was aromatic like pork, but hearty like beef.

"So, you two...?" Raiden asked, starting to eat his breakfast too.

"Yeah," Freya nodded.

"Serious?" he inquired.

"No. Not yet, anyway," she said casually. "Whatever this is let's get it for the Saisei," she said tapping the meat with her utensil.

"I'll get right on that," Raiden chuckled.

"Well, you kinda are the lead negotiator now," she winked at him.

"Oh, hell no!" he said, and they both laughed.

Just as they were finishing up eating breakfast Koji walked up. Raiden watched him and Freya, and the playful joy between them. He felt happy for them, and yet somehow excluded. After a few minutes, they walked off to explore the station together, and as Raiden watched them leave he felt more alone than he had felt in years.

|

Norita stood in the corridor leading to the Conclave. It was an immaculately designed part of the ship; the corridor's ceiling swooped up, leading to the chamber doors that were over 20 feet high. Takeo sat nearby, waiting patiently. They were to be called in at any moment.

The pacing helped Norita to get the hyper-energetic energy out of her body, and to focus her thoughts. *Just calm down,* she told herself, annoyed by her nerves. The massive doors swung open, and an Ethlana attendant came to guide them inside.

Takeo stood up and began to walk a pace behind Norita. They walked through the massive doors and into the inner sanctum. An arched walkway, over a water feature teaming with exotic fish, led up to a wide curved platform. Around the arch of the platform was a raised area with seating where the Conclave assembly members sat. The attendant walked as far as the edge of the walkway and then extended their arm indicating for Norita and Takeo to continue forth.

Norita and Takeo walked to the center of the platform and then bowed respectfully to the Conclave. When they stood back up fully, they could see nods of appreciation and acknowledgment. There were 5 members of the Conclave present. As it had been explained to Norita prior to their arrival, while the Bastion had political representation of all sentient species, the Conclave was made up of the 5-founding species who'd found the station first and who put forth the most resources and personnel to run it.

The 5-founding species were the *Ethlana*, the *Veata*, the *Baas*, the *Chuchana*, and the *Veick*. The Ethlana had substantially more resources and people to devote to running the station. Their culture was affluent, and prized wisdom and innovation above all else. With their 700-year life span, it was no wonder their influence was so widely accepted.

The Veata was an insect-like species. They walked on 4 legs and had 2 arms, their bodies bottom heavy. Their appearance struck Takeo as being exactly like that of a praying mantis. The quick-twitch head movements they made left the General feeling uneasy.

Baas' came from a cold homeworld and were covered with fur. Their stature was short, most of them standing no more than 3 feet tall. While they looked like a sort of dog-bear hybrid, their minds were sharp, and their people incredibly resourceful.

The Chuchana was by far the most unusual species on the entire station. They were advanced beings, who explored the far reaches of the mind and spirituality. In the millennia's they'd spent exploring thought, they'd slowly evolved more and more away from the physicality of their bodies. So much so that they no longer required food, and like plants, they were able to extract nutrients from sunlight through photosynthesis.

The Chuchana looked like jellyfish and floated in the air. Their ability to float was attributed to their incredibly light physical structure, and the natural helium produced by the gases of their bodies. On the Chuchana homeworld uranium and thorium were incredibly abundant, and the life forms that evolved on that planet all gave off helium gas to some extent. Their many years of dedication to matters of the mind had also allowed them to develop telekinesis, which was rumored to be how they moved with such precision while afloat in the air.

To make matters even more interesting, the Chuchana had no mouths. Originally the Chuchana had communicated through movement to one another. Over the years, with their incredible minds, and after learning language from other species, they now communicated solely through telepathy.

Finally, there were the Veick. From what Norita had read, despite their reptilian-like appearance, in many ways, they were more human than any of the other alien species. Their cultural and political values were similar, and their commerce system also mirrored humanity's. They were thoughtful and well spoken.

Each of the species had an appointed speaker at the Conclave: Saaya for the Ethlana, Ouct for the Veata, Ent for the Baas, Ecoatay for the Chuchana, and Zar for the Veick. Norita had memorized their faces and names the day before. Standing before them all now, her anxiety lifted. The Conclave was a peaceful and serene place and the faces of the speakers welcoming and kind.

"We are honored to welcome you to the Bastion," Saaya said.

"It was passed on to us that this is your first contact with other sentient life, is that right?" Zar asked.

Norita nodded, "Yes."

"Astounding," Zar said. "Please, tell us about you and your people."

"Well," Norita began, thinking about where to begin. "I'm Empress Norita Hiroshu, and my bloodline has served to help lead humanity for many generations. Though I am my people's leader, we are a democratic society, where everyone's opinion is heard and valued. My people, humans, we're now nomadic, although we weren't always. Our home planet is very far from here, and as far as we know it was destroyed after we left. We had to evacuate our planet well over 200 years ago when it could no longer support life, so our ship, the Saisei, it is our home. Though given the chance we'd like to find a planet to colonize," she smiled, hoping to have summarized everything well.

"Such a long time in space to have not drifted into other inhabited worlds," Ouct said curtly.

"I'd be happy to upload our flight path," Norita replied. "I'm sure if it wasn't for the wormhole if we'd have spent many more lifetimes without encountering any other life forms," she shrugged.

"The worm hole you came through hasn't been used for centuries. All the resources from that quadrant have been well mined," Ent chimed in.

"We would be grateful to be able to add your star charts to our galactic map to help complete the areas of space you've traveled through," Saaya said hopefully.

"I'll have them sent over after our meeting is concluded," Norita nodded.

"Thank you," Saaya smiled.

"You're most welcome. I have a question," Norita started.

Please ask anything you wish, Ecoatay's telepathic voice sounded in all of their heads. It threw Norita off guard momentarily, the experience strange; like thinking a thought, except it wasn't her thought and felt forced.

Norita swallowed her discomfort, "Thank you. I, well, before we purposefully sent our ship through with Lieutenant Saito that was intercepted by Xan's ship, another ship came through the wormhole about a day beforehand. A man named Link, Link Rose, he's a fugitive..."

Saaya looked to Zar questioningly. Zar pulled up information on his console, "There is no record of a second ship," he said after examining the logs. His fingers continued to work deftly on the interactive screen, "There's no file for any being registered on the Bastion by that name either."

"We'll check the sensors. Please send us the time logs so we know what times need to be checked," Saaya said definitively.

"You have my thanks, I will send that along with the star map data," Norita said. "This station is a marvel. I've been intrigued to learn more about it. I can't seem to find in the records who built it?"

"That's because no one knows," Ouct said.

"My people found this station, though none of our records indicate they ever discovered who the builders were. Due to the expansive size of the Bastion, we assume it was built in space. The first of our people to arrive found no traces of life forms. Materials and wooden objects left behind were all carbon dated; we have no exact date, other than to know this station is over 50,000 years old," Saaya explained.

Takeo and Norita looked at one another in surprise, "That's remarkable," Norita said.

"The computers contained nothing?" Takeo asked.

"The computer systems were recorded by the first arrivals as having been wiped clean of all data base information. The automated systems were all that was set up, and all systems set up for running and maintaining the Bastion were working, as far as we know, for thousands of years unmanned. It is a mystery we've been trying to solve, without luck, since we arrived. Perhaps one day we'll learn the answer," Saaya told him.

Our people believe the builders ascended long ago, Ecoatay's words blurted into their minds.

"Then where are their bodies?" Ouct scoffed. It was clearly a topic of heated debate between them.

All beings are composed of energy at their simplest state; they could have dissipated into pure energy, Ecoatay put forth.

"Unlikely," Ouct spat.

"Wherever they are, they are no longer here," Ent stated, trying to keep the peace.

"A mystery yet to be solved, we understand," Norita smiled. "I must say, the Bastion is a marvel, a true haven amongst the stars. I can't help but think some of my people will want to settle here if that's possible?"

"They'd be welcomed," Zar said.

"We must discuss representation," Ouct said, his tone still indicative of his impatience.

"Yes, we were getting to that," Saaya responded to him in her soothing tone. "The Bastion, as I'm sure you've learned by now, is a safe haven for all peaceful sentient species. It is our custom on the Bastion to have a representative for every race. For matters aboard the Bastion, intergalactic trade, and decisions impacting all of us, a speaker for each species is necessary for the diplomatic decisions that affect us all. In order to represent your people as they join into our galactic community, we ask that you appoint a representative."

"Oh," Norita said, stunned by the request, "I, uh, yes of course. I'll need some time..."

"There is no need to answer now," Zar reassured her, "When your representative has been selected they will be welcomed aboard the Bastion and provided with a permanent residence."

"That's most kind of you. I must say, I am inspired by the peace you've fostered here. So many different races, and so many cultures with such varying values... but you've truly made it work."

A common goal breaks down all barriers, Ecoatay communicated. The wisdom of his words rang with truth.

"That's right. Running the Bastion, and subsequently keeping the wormholes running with convoys, it is a large effort. One that's too big to be the burden of one species alone," Ent agreed.

"We're honored to be welcomed into this incredible alliance," Norita said, meaning every word of it.

"I'm afraid we're out of time. Your accommodations are yours to continue to use while you are aboard. We still have much more to discuss and will contact you shortly to arrange another meeting. There is much to do as you and your people learn of the Bastion, it's people, and laws. While we must ask for you to continue to keep your people on rotations coming aboard the Bastion due to your large numbers, we welcome you to stay docked while we continue to integrate your culture and your people who wish to stay onto the station," Zar concluded.

"Thank you," Norita said and bowed. She wished there had been more time, she had had so many more questions. The speakers in the chamber all returned her bow, and then she and Takeo took their leave from the Conclave.

Chapter 13: Cultural Exchange

It had been 3 weeks since the Saisei had first docked with the Bastion. After Norita and General Yamamoto had left their initial meeting with the Conclave they had called the council of the Saisei into session. There had been much debate, but in the end, Norita had convinced the councilors to go along with everything the Conclave had proposed. Norita returned to her quarters on the Bastion and had lived almost exclusively aboard the station since then. It felt like the first real vacation she'd had since she stepped into her position as Empress.

The water Raiden had negotiated for had been delivered to the ship. The resources he'd committed in exchange, mostly a variety of livestock and plant life that was foreign to the aliens, were traded. It was a huge relief for Norita to know they were finally properly supplied.

Crew rotations continued without pause; the joy of getting off of the Saisei to explore the Bastion had overcome everyone. And as a new species, many of the residents aboard the Bastion requested day passes to board the Saisei to meet the new additions to the galactic family. While it took some doing to convince the council, and arrange security details, Norita was thrilled that the cultural exchange had been initiated.

Over 20,000 members of the Saisei population had applied for permanent residency aboard the Bastion since the announcement had come through that humanity was welcome to stay. Norita was thrilled about the population alleviation for the Saisei; food, water, and air production were all carefully calculated and painstakingly maintained to support such a massive crew. Over the past 50 years, they had exceeded ideal population levels, and disincentivizing families from having more than one child had proved difficult.

Though despite the respite it would provide, she couldn't help but question why her people wanted to leave. *Is it our way of life? My leadership?* She asked herself. Deep down she knew it had to be the prospect of a new exciting life. The Bastion was wonderous, and after a life restricted to the Saisei, the youth especially were eager to expand their horizons. It had created a monumental amount of paperwork, however, which Norita had the council forward to the station for her to work on.

A few of the aliens who had visited the Saisei had sent in requests to come on tour when the ship was ready to depart the Bastion. Long discussions with the council and with General Yamamoto had ensued, but in the end, they felt compelled to agree. They had been welcomed, resupplied, and treated as honored guests on the Bastion. Extending the same kindness in return only seemed right. As the quarters of the people leaving the Saisei to live upon the Bastion became available, the handful of alien applicants began to move their belongings aboard, gleefully anticipating the new adventure.

Councilor Merrick Uda had come aboard the Bastion several times since their arrival. On his 3rd visit, he met with Norita to tell her he wanted to volunteer to be humanity's permanent ambassador on the Bastion. While it pained Norita to let him go, for she had always found his level-headed diplomacy to be a wonderful addition during council meetings, she knew he'd be the perfect representative for them among the galactic officials and approved his request.

Norita was due to meet with the Conclave again the next day and was happy to know she could finally report that they had a representative chosen. It had been an eventful 3 weeks as everything had come together. At tomorrow's meeting, Norita was eager to finalize the arrangements for her people to stay aboard the ship.

|

Suki sat in her bedroom, on her bed, leaning her back against the cool metal of the wall. Scattered across her bed were the military handbooks uploaded on various data pads, the files opened for reading. She also had a data pad in her lap which she'd been taking notes on. Now she simply sat in the quiet of the room, eyes closed, her mind tired.

It was October 11th, the day before her birthday. Her house was quiet, and she couldn't help but remember last year how busy it had been the day before her birthday. Her mother had been cooking tirelessly the entire day, making a cake and confections, and perfecting a glaze for a whole chicken her father had spent a month saving extra wages for. Space for livestock was incredibly limited on the Saisei, so soy and other plant-based proteins were all they ate most of the time. To get any type of meat was a real rarity.

The whole day she'd heard the clanking of pans and lots of commotion outside of her bedroom as her mother decorated and tried to create the perfect party set up for the next day. Suki felt guilty, remembering how annoyed she'd been at the incessant sounds. She had been trying to read and complete a book report for school that day, and her concentration had been constantly interrupted with her mother's party planning. Thinking back now she couldn't believe how she'd taken it all for granted. Now the perfect silence in her home was deafening.

Suki felt a twinge of pain build up in her eyes, and she couldn't fight back the tears when they came. She let out a slow exhale and gave into the grief. Death was a strange thing, it came and went so suddenly. Some days she'd been fine, and others lost to her memories. She put her hand over her chest and applied pressure. She'd read a long time ago that it helped calm the nervous system, and ever since her mother had died and her father had gone AWOL she'd used it to help herself calm down faster.

Once she'd finally calmed down enough that the tears had stopped, Suki opened her eyes. It took a few moments as the tears dried for her eyes to be able to focus fully again. She stared straight ahead at the opposite wall and her desk. There were several data pads, her computer, a cup of water, and a digital pen that lay on her desk. Her eyes lazily looked at them out of focus.

Without reason, she stared at the pen. She studied its shape and let her mind take a break from the chaotic thoughts. All day she'd been thinking about her birthday and signing up to be a pilot. The flight guides were tedious, but she'd studied them fervently every day since she'd received them.

By noon she'd felt exhausted, her brain overtaxed and had tried to take a nap. But she couldn't sleep. After laying wide awake in bed for over an hour she took up reading again. Now, mid-afternoon, time felt like it was at a standstill. All she wanted was for the next day to arrive; it had been all she could think about since the day she'd gone into the recruitment office.

She'd gone aboard the Bastion once, but quickly felt overwhelmed. The sheer size of the station and all of the unfamiliar faces made her feel uneasy. It was as if she felt like a child again, and just wanted someone there with her to tell her it was alright. But no one was there. Her nerves were still frayed from the loss of her mother, and the lack of information about her father's whereabouts, or even if he was still alive. After a short walk on the station, she found herself heading back to the safety of the Saisei.

Suki suddenly felt how dry her throat felt when she swallowed. She was exhausted, just as she always felt after a good cry. Her eyes lazily drifted over and looked at the cup of water. She wanted to get up to get it and yet she didn't want to move. She imagined how good it would feel to drink the water as she stared and the cup, and suddenly the cup began to move across the desk towards her.

"Holy shit!" she exclaimed and leaned forward. The glass immediately stopped moving. She blinked several times and wondered if it had really moved at all. Suki scrambled to her feet and walked over to the desk to look at the cup, which was now sitting ever so slightly perched over the edge of the desk. The cup had left a trail from its condensation on the desk. *It did move!* She thought surprised and excited.

As incredible as it was she felt unsettled. *How the hell did I do that? Did I do that? Did the ship just move? ... no, nothing else moved. But... how?* She stared at the cup again trying to move it, but nothing happened.

Suki went back to her bed and sat down. After a few moments, a thought came to her and she remembered the accounts from her history book, *How we Brought Down the C.D.F.P.,* about two of the women and how they used an ancient power called 'Magick' to make things happen. Suki grabbed one of the data pads and did a quick search to bring up the book. She sifted through the pages for nearly an hour before she found what she'd been looking for.

"Yu-Lee..." she muttered aloud after finding the name she'd been looking for, and then searched the name in the Saisei's online directory. Several short articles that had been written by her on paper and uploaded to the database as photographs had popped up and Suki read through them all:

Universal Energy: Insights into the Power of the Mind

After a life of dedication to understanding the ways of magick, otherwise known as life force energies, it's become clear to me the simplicity of it all. Everything is composed of energy; rocks, trees, animals, humans, air particles, the moon and stars – everything. This is true of all matter in the Universe.

In studies from scientific practitioners, we have learned that our brains fire neurons when thoughts are generated. This occurrence is a form of energy. Like energy attracts like energy, and therefore our very thoughts can become manifest.

It seems some are more naturally prone to be able to use their thoughts to create physical results, though all are capable. While I'm still studying the reason behind this inherent ability in some, it is my theory that their belief in their ability to conjure what they wish is simply stronger. If thoughts create our reality, surely doubt detracts from the ability to create as efficiently as those without doubt.

When one is in tune with life energy, extraordinary things can happen. I've witnessed, and caused, many incredible acts of magick in my life. Changing the weather, levitation, psychic abilities... there appears to be no limits to what we can attain through the use of this Universal energy.

Of all my students over the years, Suako was certainly the most proficient, in one instance she was able to walk on air. Her early death was extremely unfortunate. I wish we could have seen just how far she could have taken her powers. Her natural talent and connectivity to the Universal energy was far beyond that of my own.

In conclusion, practice and faith in ones' abilities appear to be the key to exponential development of these skills. For those naturally gifted, there's no telling how far their abilities could take them. Practice and time will tell.

Suki looked up from the data pad, "Incredible," she said. She looked again to the cup perched precariously on the edge of her desk. She let out a slow exhale and focused only on the cup. For several minutes she stared at it and nothing happened. Then she remembered she was thirsty, she never ended up having a drink from the water glass, and she imagined a refreshing drink being taken from the cup. All of the sudden the glass nudged forward and fell onto the floor, spilling water everywhere.

"It worked!" Suki squealed with delight and wonder as she sprung up from the bed. She stepped in the puddle of water, "Oh shit!" she ran out of her bedroom to grab a towel. While she rifled through the linen closet she thought about it all carefully in her mind. *It's when I thought about drinking, not moving the cup, that it happened... hmmm. I remember reading about how amputee soldiers outfitted with electronic prosthetics had to imagine the end result they wanted to get the limb to do what they wanted, instead of trying to move the limb itself. This must work the same way,* she reasoned.

Suki dashed back to her room and mopped up the spilled water. After the floor was dry she grabbed the cup and walked into the kitchen to refill her it, and she drank deeply, quenching her thirst. When she was done she felt better. She set the cup on the countertop and looked at it for a long time, her mind pondering the possibilities of this newfound power.

|

"...Gin? Gin are you still with me?" Dr. Adonis Murakami asked.

Adonis sat in a large reclining chair with a data pad in hand with which he was taking notes. Gin sat in a chair a few feet away, his eyes distant, as he stared blankly ahead. They were in Dr. Murakami's office, which was just off of the main wing of the hospital.

This was Gin's second therapy session with Adonis. In the first session a week ago, Gin hadn't said anything and had sat silently until the time had run out. His dedicated despondency had led them to keep him under 24-hour surveillance. The scar tissue from Gin's suicide attempt was healing well, but emotionally he'd made almost no progress.

Dr. Murakami had been a therapist for over 20 years. Over that time, he'd seen a staggering number of members out of the military in his office. The structure, the rules, and sometimes the fallout of situations gone bad, had brought people to him.

While the Saisei was an incredibly peaceful ship to live aboard, at least up until the insurrection, everyday happenings lead to emotional strife. Pilot error in training missions, dealing with the public, firearm malfunctions; despite the lack of war, inevitably challenging situations arose. Since the insurrection, however, his schedule had been booked solid by military personnel and civilians alike, coping with the aftermath of the terror and loss.

Today in their session Gin spoke, albeit minimally. He made small talk and asked about the Bastion. Adonis had told him about what his visit had been like and had tried to describe the experience in as much detail as he could, all while studying Gin's responses to the information he was receiving. Adonis was thrilled to note Gin's interest in the Bastion when Gin had asked about it; to him, it indicated progress and a desire to move onto something new.

Dr. Murakami had been telling Gin about the agricultural features aboard the Bastion when he saw Gin's gaze suddenly become distant. "Gin, what is it?" he asked, hoping to gain some insight.

Gin sat there silently, sitting in his thoughts. After several minutes, and with great effort, he found the words, "Rei… Private Davis, when I first met her she... she said she always wanted to be a botanist. She loved plants, but she just never had a green thumb. She said she killed every plant she ever tried to care for," he smiled, and laughed awkwardly, but was clearly pained and his eyes welled up with tears. "She would've loved to have seen the Bastion..."

"I'm sure she would have," Dr. Murakami said compassionately. "Tell me more about Rei."

"We were on shift a lot together. Almost everyone who signs on to the military applies to be a pilot, but she was like me, she didn't want to fly. She wanted to help people. And she was funny as hell, had a real great sense of humor... did the best impressions..." Gin trailed off.

"She sounded like a great person," Adonis said kindly.

"She was," Gin said, feeling flat.

"You know, it's entirely normal to feel how you're feeling," Adonis said in all seriousness.

Gin looked at Adonis and felt angered, "Normal?" he asked, his voice venomous.

"Quite," Adonis said nodding, "loss of life is one of the most challenging things to live through, it's hard for our minds to accept that something that was always there is no longer here. Even more so when we felt a sense of obligation to protect the person who died."

Gin said nothing. He felt guilt weighing heavily on him. Waves of anger, grief, and regret washed over him. He felt his saliva thickening, making him feel sick, and his eyes felt the string of encroaching tears.

"The hardest thing to accept," Dr. Murakami continued, "Is that it's not our fault. Our minds can accomplish the most brilliant things in life; even after all our technological advances, our brains are still the most advanced computers we know of. But like computers, our brains have an uncanny ability to process information. When we look back on an event, a trauma, something we 'compute' to be an error, our mind will go over and over it again and again in an attempt to see a solution to the problem. We mull it over, again and again, seeing all of the possible ways we could have changed the situation for a better outcome. But the problem and the outcome are done already complete and we can't 'reset' our lives to try it again. It's already happened, there's no going back to change it," Adonis explained.

Gin felt fear creep up on him at the thought of living like this endlessly, "How do I stop it?" he asked, his voice weak.

"We have to accept what's happened to move on," Adonis said simply.

"And how do I do that?" Gin asked, desperation in his voice.

"Forgive yourself, because it wasn't your fault, and even if it had been, you can't go back and change it. What's done is done. If we don't learn from the past then it was in vain, but if we can use what's happened, no matter how hard it was to live through, we can create a better future. If we refuse to move on, that's when we become doomed to repeat our mistakes.

"The only thing matters is right now, this moment. There's a quote by an old philosopher: *If you are depressed you are living in the past. If you are anxious you are living in the future. If you are at peace you are living in the moment.* We have to choose to be present, to pull our thoughts back from drifting to the past or the future," Adonis explained.

Dr. Murakami had a tendency to go on tangents, and it left Gin's head spinning. His thoughts felt heavy, like trying to see through a thick fog. He tried to digest what Adonis had said. *Create a better future...* those words had jumped out at him, and he held onto them while the rest of what Adonis had said drifted away from him.

Gin looked Adonis dead in the eye, feeling as if a new life, a new purpose, had been breathed into him, "I'm ready."

|

Raiden entered the Bastion's docking bay, on his way heading back to the Saisei after yet another shore leave came to an end. He found himself continuously drawn to spend more and more time aboard the station. As he walked casually down the walkway towards the Saisei he noticed Captain Xan a few hundred feet away and began to head towards her. He hadn't seen her since she'd first met him on the Bastion, and he felt compelled to thank her for her kindness.

As he drew closer to Xan, he noticed she was having luggage brought off of her ship. She was also out of her captain's uniform, wearing causal fatigues. Her sleeveless top revealed her arms, beautiful hues of blue shimmering skin under the passing light of ships coming and going.

"Hey, Xan!" Raiden called when he got close.

She looked up to see him waving at her, "Oh, Raiden, hello!" she said, pleased to see him.

"I never got a chance to thank you for all of your help," he said, a bit winded from his quickened pace to reach her.

She smiled, "Just part of my job. But in any case, you're welcome."

"I haven't seen you since we first met," he said, probing for more.

"My job was in the skies, helping the traffic. Travel here is, well, I'm sure you've seen just how busy it gets," she said, indicating all of the ships that flew past them.

"It's a wonder anyone can stay on top of it. Taking a vacation?" he asked, pointing to her luggage.

"Hmm? Oh, no. I've been accepted into the elite *Black Shadow*," she said, a hint of pride in her voice.

"Black Shadow?" Raiden asked.

"I keep forgetting how new you are here. The Black Shadow are handpicked soldiers for the Conclave. They are selected as the best of the best and granted special privileges and resources.

Essentially, they are the eyes and ears of the Conclave. There are less than 100 Black Shadow soldiers at any given time," she explained with excitement in her voice.

"Wow, that's amazing. Congratulations!" Raiden said, extending his hand to shake hers.

She stared at his hand, unsure what to do, "What are you doing?"

"Oh, uh, haha, sorry guess this is a human thing. We shake hands, sometimes as a greeting, other times to relay thanks or best wishes. May I?" He asked, looking to her hand.

"OK," Xan said, her curiosity aroused.

Raiden took her hand in his, squeezed it firmly, and then began to shake. She picked up on his rhythm and shook back. He smiled at her, "Yup, you got it"

"Interesting. I think I liked it," she said, and they released their grip.

"So, are you moving onto the Bastion then?" he asked.

"No, well temporarily I will, but I'll be assigned my own ship. We serve the Conclave, and in order for the Conclave to serve the people best, they need to have sight beyond that of the station," she said.

Raiden nodded, "That makes sense."

"I'm sorry I can't stay to talk longer, but I'm due to report in shortly," she said.

"That's OK, I need to get back to my ship anyways. Congratulations again, you deserve it," he said and began to walk off.

"Goodbye," he heard her call front behind, and he turned to wave goodbye.

As Raiden walked back to the Saisei he couldn't help but let his imagination run wild with thoughts about the Black Shadow division. It seemed so secretive, powerful, and seductive. It was also an incredibly prestigious honor to be chosen to join the ranks of them. He wondered what kinds of missions they went on.

After boarding the Saisei, and signing onto the system, he headed towards the army barracks to change his clothes. The hallways along the way were teeming with excited visitors. He passed by a group of Veick who had just come out of the concourse, each carrying shopping bags full of treasured items. Raiden smiled at them as he passed by, but they were so enraptured by their experience they hardly noticed him. Somehow that made Raiden even happier, *This is incredible,* he thought, loving every second of intermingling with new races.

Once Raiden opened the door to his quarters he felt his fatigue catch up to him. *How long since I slept?* He wondered. He remembered he went aboard the Bastion 2 days prior in the evening, and he'd stayed at a hotel the first night. But last night he had been too excited to sleep. He knew how fast the shore leave time slipped by and didn't want to waste a second. It made it easier to avoid sleeping when the Bastion never slept either; shops stayed open and people walked around at all hours.

He looked at the clock, and it was only mid-afternoon, but he could feel his bunk beckoning him to come to it. He took off his jacket and flung it onto the floor as he walked toward the bed. He thought about taking his pants off, but he was so tired, he just ended up crawling into bed with them on. It normally took him a long time to fall asleep, but in that moment, under the warm sheets, he drifted off quickly feeling pure contentment.

A few hours later Raiden came to, and while it hadn't been long, he felt fully rested. He went to the bathroom, stripped of his clothes and got into the shower. The warm water was invigorating. He had gotten used to long showers aboard the Bastion and luxuriating in the experience. While the Saisei's water reserves were full, aboard the ship he could never bring himself to take a long shower.

As he got out and toweled off, he could feel his stomach grumbling. He checked the time, and it was almost 1800 hours. He quickly finished drying off, and got dressed in fresh clothes, then left his quarters to head down the hall to ask Freya to come to dinner.

The past few weeks they hadn't seen much of each other. The duty shifts were constantly changing and fervently kept full staff to keep an eye on the visiting aliens. On top of that with regular shore leave, and Raiden maximizing his free time on the Bastion, their schedules had rarely lined up. He wasn't sure if she was on duty, but her room was on the way to the mess hall, and he never enjoyed eating alone.

Raiden walked up to her door, "Hey, Freya, you home?" he asked, giving a quick knock on the door, and then tried to open the door to let himself in as usual. It was unlocked, and he felt happy knowing she was home. As the door opened, he kept talking, "I thought we could grab dinner..." he stopped dead in his tracks.

Koji and Freya had been in the middle of having intercourse on her bed, and Freya was clamoring to pull a blanket over them. "Raiden, what the hell? Get the fuck out!" she yelled at him, red-faced. She was clearly angry about the intrusion and slightly embarrassed.

"I, um, shit, sorry," Raiden said and stumbled back out of the room awkwardly, closing the door. Raiden just stood in the hallway staring dumbfounded at the door for a moment. After a few people walked past and gave him strange stares he shook it off and started to head towards the mess hall.

He had known Koji and Freya had been seeing each other, and while he knew that had meant they'd been having sexual relations it was entirely another thing to see it firsthand. While he'd only seen the naked entanglement for a second before Freya had hastily covered up, it was as if the image had burned into his mind.

Freya had been upright on top of Koji, her body blocking him from view. Freya's back faced Raiden when he'd walked into the room, shiny with sweat, and contorting as her body moved. When she'd heard him and turned briefly to see him her face was full of shock, and he'd seen her breasts for an instant, luxuriously pale cream with pink nipples. Her sling had been off, and the bandage as well; the healing gunshot wound bright red and painful looking from the heightened blood flow.

Raiden had seen Freya naked before plenty of times in the locker rooms as they'd prepared for missions. But to see her with Koji, he felt a tug-of-war between lust, disgust, and jealousy. *It's Freya for fuck sake's, what's wrong with you? She's like your sister!* He could hear his rational mind yell at him. *But she's not your sister...*

By the time Raiden walked into the mess hall his appetite had completely vanished. He thought about going back to his quarters but didn't feel like being alone. So instead he kept walking to try to clear his head.

Eventually, he ended up in the atrium. He took a seat on a bench that faced the expansive windows. Groups of people walked by, many alien visitors marveling at one of the most prominent visually alluring spaces on the whole of the Saisei. Outside of the window, he could see the docks and the vast amount of people coming and going from the station. It was strange, after a lifetime of this room facing nothing but open space, to feel so confined. But despite the lack of a celestial view, he felt at peace.

It dawned on him that this was one of the few times in his life he hadn't felt gripped with concern on some level. As the last harbor for humanity, a single ship drifting through what seemed like endless space, their very existence had always seemed to be teetering on a knife's edge. *Why'd they only send one ship?* Was a question he always asked himself. *Wouldn't it have been safer to send multiple ships? Wouldn't humanity have had a better chance to survive?*

As a child in school, he'd remembered asking his teachers about it. He never got a concrete answer, although one of his teachers had conjectured, "I think it came down to time and resources. Building this ship was a monumental task on a planet on the brink of collapse. It's a wonder they were even able to build the Saisei." It was the only well thought out answer he found acceptable, though it did little to allay his concerns.

Now sitting here in the atrium, knowing human beings were moving aboard the Bastion, and a few traveling to other worlds, he felt like he could finally breathe deeply. Now, even if the Saisei fell to some calamity, humanity would live on. He let out a long exhale.

Raiden had always felt the need to take responsibility for the ship. It was one of the reasons he tried so hard and applied himself without reserve. As much relief as he felt knowing humanities future was secure, he also felt at a loss. *Now what?* He asked himself. *I don't know...*

|

"...with so much commotion some minor theft was to be expected. Thank you for handling it so swiftly, and for keeping me updated," Norita spoke into the comm.

"Not a problem," General Takeo Yamamoto's voice responded over the speaker. "Honestly, I'd expected it to be worse. Things have been rather smooth overall."

"Any other updates?" Norita asked.

"We got the report from the Conclave in response to our query about Link Rose's ship, about wormhole activity for the time period's we requested."

"That's great!" Norita exclaimed.

"Well, not really," Takeo responded.

Norita heart sunk, "What do you mean? What did they say?"

"The wormhole never opened," he said.

"What?!"

"That's what I said. They have dedicated logs and sensors over this entire region. The wormhole never opened, and no ship ever came through," he told her.

"It just doesn't seem possible," Norita said, sounding defeated.

"The only thing that their sensors picked up on were some temporal anomalies around the wormhole during that time. It's not much to go on, and maybe it's nothing, but I've forwarded the information to Dr. Takei and his team to investigate further," Takeo informed her.

"Thank you. Well, I need to get going, I'll be in touch for our next check in tomorrow. Goodbye," Norita told him and clicked her comm off.

Just then a knock came to the door which startled Norita out of deep thought. She walked over hastily and opened it to find Merrick standing before her.

"Oh, Councilor Uda," she said, surprised.

Merrick stood before her, his calm energy emanating, "Please, you know I'm not for formalities any more than you are."

"Sorry, Merrick. It's nice to see you! Come in, please," she said and stepped out of the way to let him enter. Merrick walked in and she closed the door behind him. "How is everything going with the move?" she asked.

"Finished yesterday, everything's in my new quarters, I just have to unpack it all now," he smiled, "Thank you for asking."

"Of course. You're going to love it aboard the Bastion, this place is a hub of wonder," she said, meaning it.

"I'm surprised you didn't volunteer to stay as our ambassador yourself," he said.

Norita felt caught off guard, "What do you mean?"

"It's quite obvious you love it here, you've barely set foot on the Saisei since we've arrived," he said.

Norita felt her face flush, "Oh... well, I, you know there's been..." she struggled to find the right words.

"I'm not judging, I think you deserve a respite, but I felt you should know many of the counselors have been gossiping," Merrick explained.

Norita sighed, "Thank you. I can't say I'm surprised to hear it either."

"Don't let it fluster you, those windbags can talk until they're blue in the face," Merrick said, and they both laughed.

"I don't know what I'm going to do without you. You were the only level-headed person in the room during any debate," she said, and affectionately gave him a hug, "But I'm so happy for you. There's no one better to be our liaison."

Merrick hugged her back, "That means a lot. And hey, maybe hold some elections? Get some new blood in the room."

"You know, I just might do that," Norita smiled. "I'm sorry I can't stay to chat more, I have a meeting with the Conclave I have to get going to."

"Why don't I come along?" Merrick suggested, "I'll be the one dealing with them directly soon enough, and I'd appreciate the introduction."

"See, this is why you're the right choice for this job. You always consider all the angles and know the right thing to say," she nudged him playfully with her elbow and winked at him.

Merrick chuckled, "Let's hope the Conclave sees it that favorably."

Norita quickly went to the bathroom, straightened out her clothing, and then grabbed a few data pads she needed to take along for the meeting. Then she and Merrick left her quarters together and meandered down the walkway towards the assembly hall. It was relatively quiet in the political wing today, with very little foot traffic. It created for a somber feel. The sounds of the birds in the trees and the flowing water of the aqueduct was that much more prominent.

"This place feels like paradise," Merrick said, admiring the views.

"It certainly feels that way today. It never gets bad, really, although I can tell you to watch your step when it's a busy day here; politicians from any race seem to parade around with the same level of self-entitlement," she whispered in a giggle.

Merrick laughed, enjoying Norita's company very much. He had always respected her as a leader, with her down to earth attitude. *Why do politicians always have to get so high and mighty on power, and so bitterly argumentative?* It was an ongoing pet peeve for him.

Reasonable, level headed discussions, had always been Merrick's vision in politics, but in reality, he'd seen that less than 1% of the time when dealing with the Saisei council. The prospect of new minds, with hopefully new outlooks, was the main allure for him to come aboard the Bastion. If he could instill real change that would positively impact lives, he could feel content that he'd contributed to the greater good.

"So, where do you think the Saisei will head when you finally disembark from the Bastion?" Merrick asked.

"Oh," Norita hummed, "To be honest I haven't been focused on it much, though I guess it's coming up isn't it? The Conclave will be issuing us a list of planets we could colonize. It seems pertinent for us to set a course to go check them out when we're ready to leave."

"Human beings back planet-side... that'll be interesting," Merrick said, imagining it.

"It's strange, isn't it? I've dreamt about living on a planet since I was a girl. Imagining the blue sky, wide open spaces... but, to be completely honest, it terrifies me. What do we know about living on a planet? Dealing with weather? And then there's disease, and our bodies adapting to the natural biology of whatever planet we build on, and real gravity... I don't know..." she sighed.

Merrick nodded, "it will be a challenge. But," he stopped walking, and Norita stopped next to him, and then he pointed up at the simulated blue sky with its wisps of cloud, "this isn't even real, and you haven't been able to pull yourself away for weeks. Whatever the risks, and the difficulties in making it work, it will be worth it."

"Thank you," she said, looking him in the eye. "You're right, it will be worth it," then she giggled, "See? Always knowing the right thing to say."

They walked jovially the rest of the way to the assembly room. Once they reached the anti-chamber, the attendant was there and ready to walk them in immediately. Merrick found himself in just as much wonderment as Norita had felt the first time she'd walked through those massive doors.

They walked up the short pathway and then stood before the speakers. Norita bowed, and Merrick matched her movement. An array of introductions and congratulations for Merrick began the meeting. After that Merrick stood stoically next to Norita and said very little as he watched her converse with the speakers.

Merrick had always been an introvert and loved to study human nature. As a boy, one of his mentors had said to him, "Speak little and listen much. That is the way of the wise man." He had taken the advice to heart, and it had always served him well.

As a student of human nature, Merrick found it incredibly easy to influence others when he knew what made them tick. He was the voice of reason, and they trusted him implicitly. That same mentor had taught him about subtly mirroring the behavior of anyone he spoke to, which created a subconscious feeling of familiarity in the other person. If the person you're speaking to has their arms crossed, cross your arms too, the concept was simple and powerful.

The Conclave had an air of harmony, something Merrick was intensely grateful for. But even among these speakers, there were subtle power struggles. Most obviously Ouct, whose poor manners, and obvious disdain and lack of patience ground on the nerves of the others.

Norita was in the middle of uploading some finalized paperwork about the personnel moving aboard the Bastion when suddenly the intercom came on, "Speakers, this is control room 2, I'm terribly sorry for the interruption, but we have a situation."

"My apologies," Saaya said to Norita and Merrick humbly.

Norita shook her head, "It's quite alright, we understand."

Zar hit the button to respond, "What is it, control?"

"We have an unidentified ship that came through one of the *Heaven's Eyes* at the far reaches of our solar system," the control room attendant replied.

"Why do you need *us* for this?" Ouct asked, annoyed.

"Well, sir, the scans are coming back with an Ethlana signature, but visual is unlike anything we've seen before. They're not responding to our hails. We're not picking up any power readings, but it's on direct approach full speed towards the station," the control room attendant explained.

"Which wormhole did it come through?" Ent asked.

"I'm sending you the coordinates now," the attendant said over the speaker.

A second later the information popped up on their terminals, and each one of the speakers stood looking stunned.

"This can't be right," Ouct huffed.

"When's the last time an expedition went through there?" Ent asked.

"I don't ever recall one, at least not in my lifetime," Zar said.

"It's been a few hundred years," Saaya said, "But... there's nothing out there, it leads to the edge of our galaxy, to dead space. The last expedition reported back within a month of going."

"The ship is on a direct trajectory for the station, what do you want us to do?" the attendant asked.

Something about that ship feels wrong, Ecoatay interjected.

"What's the ETA before it reaches the station?" Zar asked.

"It's coming fast, just over 3 hours," the attendant replied.

"We'll send a ship to intercept, headed by a Black Shadow Operative. Standby for further instructions," Saaya said, then turned off the intercom. She then turned to Norita and Merrick, "I'm sorry, but we'll need to reschedule."

"Of course," Norita said, and bowed.

Merrick and Norita turned and took their leave.

Chapter 14: The Derelict Ship

Norita and Merrick didn't speak until they were out of earshot from the attendant who led them out of the waiting room. "That was odd," Norita said, finally breaking the silence. They walked at a heightened pace back towards Norita's stay room.

"Very," Merrick agreed.

"I haven't had much time to read about all of the destinations that the Heaven's Eyes lead too from here. Have you?" Norita asked.

"No. I've been trying to learn cultural information to prep for life aboard the station," Merrick replied.

"Dead space at the edge of the galaxy... Whichever one they were talking about, it must lead exceptionally far away from here. We ran long-range scans and added star maps from the Bastion's data stores to our information banks on the Saisei when we arrived, and this is a massive region full of planets and stars," Norita said, trying to imagine just how far these wormholes might reach.

"The Heaven's Eyes are supposed to route destinations throughout our galaxy," Merrick added, "As far as we know there's no limit to the distance they can reach. It stands to reason they could extend as far as where the dead space between our galaxy and the next begins."

"It's certainly possible. I'll need to talk to Dr. Takei about the maps," Norita replied.

They barely said another word until they arrived at Norita's quarters. Merrick bid her farewell and left to unpack in his new home. After a few moments of pacing within her quarters, Norita sent a quick transition to General Yamamoto, "Takeo, prepare a ship and get one of your best pilots ready. I'll be there shortly to explain. I'll meet you in your office." She then left her room and sped off towards the docking port.

|

It had been nearly 30 minutes since Norita had exited the meeting with the Conclave by the time she made it onto the Saisei. She walked with haste through the corridors on her way to meet General Yamamoto. Something in her gut told her this was important.

When she arrived at his office she found the door open, and he was waiting for her at his desk, with Raiden sitting across from him. Norita instantly felt better seeing both of them in front of her.

"Thank you both for meeting me on such short notice," she said as she entered the room. And closed the door behind herself. Norita sat down and as quickly as she could she recited what she had heard in the Conclave. "...so, what I want to do is send one of our ships as well to investigate," she explained.

"It does sound strange, but the Speakers are already sending people to investigate, they might see us as interfering by sending a ship of our own," Takeo said.

Norita shook her head, "I can't explain it, but I just have a feeling, we need to do this. We'll say it's an escort, a 'thank you' for accepting us as citizens on the Bastion. Leave the politics to me," she said to Takeo, then turned to Raiden, "I want to know what's happening on that ship. Maybe it's nothing but... I need to know."

Raiden locked eyes with her and nodded reassuringly, "You got it, ma'am."

"Go launch," Norita said and stood up, "I'm going to go explain our 'gift' of assistance."

|

Raiden hurried from the General's office down to the docking bay. His ship was ready when he arrived. Raiden secured his helmet, and after a quick inspection, he got in the ship and prepared to launch. The Saisei's bay doors opened up to the massive port of the Bastion, and Raiden carefully navigated his way through the port and out into space. It felt different being out in open space this time, still liberating, but he somehow felt like he was leaving home.

The ship sent out by the Conclave had already departed, so he headed at full speed towards the coordinates that had been uploaded into his flight path. After 10 minutes he was finally able to see the ship in the distance. Is was a small vessel, but larger than the solitary fighter ship Raiden flew in.

He sent a hail, "This is Raiden, from the Saisei, here to offer an escort."

"Nice to have you along," he heard Xan's voice reply.

"Xan?" he asked, surprised.

"Haha, yes, who'd you think?" she replied, clearly amused.

"I don't know. I was told a member of the Black Shadow was heading the mission, but I guess I thought it'd be someone else," he said.

"There aren't many of us, Raiden. I was the only one at the Bastion," she explained.

"First mission as an operative, huh? Well, I'm honored to get to see you in action," he said warmly.

"Thanks," she said.

"So, what's the plan?"

"We're on an intercept course. Once we reach the ship we'll try to make contact. If that fails, we'll dock for an emergency boarding," Xan told him.

"Got it," he said.

Raiden continued to follow Xan on course for the rogue ship. It wasn't long before it was on their sensors, and then within sight. Raiden amplified the image of the ship on his computer monitor. The ship was still far off, so the image wasn't pristine, but even so, it was clear there was something off about it.

"What the hell?" he murmured as he squinted at the video feedback.

The derelict ship was visually unrecognizable as any Ethlana ship he'd seen. The hull was full of holes, but not from any kind of battle, but rather it looked as if the metal had been eaten away. Black-brown tendrils encompassed much of the ship and looked almost as if they were alive. The ship was dark, blending in with the black backdrop of space. It sent a shiver up Raiden's spine.

As they got closer on their approach vector Raiden began to see the disfigured ship with his own eyes. *What could have possibly caused this?* He wondered. It was beyond strange. In all his life Raiden had never seen or heard about any organic tissue surviving in the vacuum in space, and yet here, before his eyes, he could tell the tendrils encapsulating the ship were very much alive and moving.

Once they were close they changed course to match that of the derelict ship. Xan's ship tried sending out hails on a variety of frequencies, but after 5 minutes of failed attempts, she announced it was time to board. The secondary docking port on the derelict ship was unusable due to the tendrils, so Raiden and Xan agreed he would dock with her ship and they would then dock Xan's ship with the derelict ship and board together.

Raiden quickly positioned his ship, aligning it to Xan's, and with perfect precision matched her ships speed and then docked. He climbed down the attaching hatch which opened into the main cockpit where Xan and two other crewmen were operating the ship. Xan was securing her helmet when Raiden came in. She turned to look at him, "Ready?"

"Let's do this," Raiden said, with a sharp nod.

The pilot of Xan's ship carefully took them in to dock with the derelict ship. Xan and Raiden stared out the window at the ship as they came into contact with it. The thick black-brown tendrils on the hull seemed to be pulsating. "Do you see that?" Raiden asked, feeling nauseated by the sight.

"Yes," Xan replied, her eyes transfixed on them.

Clunk! The ships connected. "I'm extending the hatch door now," the co-pilot said. There was a loud creaking as the heavy metal exterior door opened.

Xan looked to Raiden and tilted her head, indicating for him to follow her. They made their way to the hatch, and Xan opened up a weapons locker near the door. She pulled out a weapon that looked like some sort of advanced assault rifle. Just like the Ethlana ships, their weapons were a stunning white chrome. Xan passed one to Raiden and quickly showed him how to use it, "I'm hoping we don't need it, but if we do..."

"Better to be prepared," Raiden agreed.

They holstered the rifles and made their way through the hatch. With the holes throughout the derelict ship, they were in zero gravity. Both Raiden and Xan activated the magnetic plating in their boots to hold them against the floor.

Even with their helmet flashlights on full luminosity, the derelict ship was incredibly dark. The tendrils that engulfed the exterior of the ship were much sparser on the inside. *That's so odd... maybe they survive through photosynthesis? But... they'd have died in dead space then...* Raiden tried to wrap his mind around it all.

One of the tendrils had wrapped itself around a bulkhead. Xan approached it and examined it. Up close there was no doubt about it, it *was* pulsating. "It looks like an oversized vine," Raiden said in awe.

"Yes, or like some sort of amphibious tentacle. Whatever it is, it's alive," Xan said while examining it.

"How could anything survive extended space exposure?" Raiden asked.

"I have no idea. I'm taking a sample," Xan said and grabbed a small vile and a knife hilt, which when powered on, created a plasma blade, from her utility belt. She stuck the tip of the blade into the tendril to cut off a piece, and without warning, the tendril swung violently, hitting Xan in the chest. Xan was sent back from the blow, falling to the floor, the wind knocked out of her.

"Ouff!!" Xan hollered as she hit the floor.

The fall hadn't hurt; the lack of gravity making it less intense, but it was the scare that left her feeling rattled. The flailing persisted for a few more seconds before the tendril returned to its previous position. Raiden rushed to Xan's side, "Are you OK?" he asked, looking at her.

Xan sat there in shock for a moment, "What in the world? I, yes, I'm fine... I've never seen plant matter act like that."

Raiden helped her back onto her feet, "I can't say I've seen anything on that scale either. We had this plant on our home world though, a *Venus flytrap*, and they ate insects. When the insect would touch a certain part of the plant it would close and entrap the insect. Though those plants were small, nothing like these things."

"It was almost like it had a nervous system," Xan said. She looked at her blade, and it was covered in a thick gooey substance from the tendril. She carefully tapped the goo into the vile, then put on the lid and stuck it back on her belt. "Let's hope the scientists can explain it when we get back. Whatever the case it seemed reactive to touch, so avoid making contact with it," she said.

They continued to make their way slowly and carefully through the ship. Holes had been ripped through the ship everywhere, all decks were breached. They carefully avoided contact with the tendrils that were along the walls, floors, and ceilings. The old metal creaked as they made their way.

"Did the Speakers give you any more intel?" Raiden asked.

"What do you know?" Xan inquired.

"Just that no one uses the wormhole that this ship came in through anymore because it leads to dead space and that this ship read as Ethlana on the scans," he told her.

"That's as much as they could relay to me as well. The last expedition through that wormhole was a long time ago, with deep space ships. The plan was to traverse the expanse to get to the next galaxy, the *Phoenix Galaxy*. The ships were all outfitted with cryo chambers, and the idea was for automated travel and a computer system that would wake the crew up as soon as the vessel encountered anything. While the ships were preparing for launch the Ethlana government decided it was too dangerous and ordered the ships back. The ships came back, but I guess not all of them," she explained.

"How'd they miscount the returning ships?"

"They probably didn't, they likely just kept it out of the media."

Raiden nodded, "That makes sense. So, theoretically, this ship has been flying in dead space for several hundred years?"

"Yes," Xan nodded.

"That's likely not enough time to make it across the void between Galaxies... it's definitely not enough time to make it there and back again. What the hell did they encounter?" Raiden spoke his thoughts aloud.

"I'm hoping they can tell us," Xan said plainly.

"What?" Raiden asked, confused.

"If we're lucky some of the crew may still be alive in the cryo bay," Xan explained.

Raiden went to speak but didn't know what to say. He followed closely behind Xan as she led the way through the ship. He could feel his heart pumping, and he wondered if they'd really find anyone alive amongst this chaos.

They pushed on towards the cockpit. The tendrils seemed to be more abundant the closer they got to the front of the ship. They carefully navigated their way through, doing everything they could to avoid touching the tendrils. Xan tread carefully as they went, her eyes fixed forward. She felt relieved when the cockpit was in sight.

"The cockpit is right ahead," she said and pointed.

Xan sped up her pace and stepped on a rusted-out portion of the floor, which gave way beneath her, making her trip. She fell sideways, and her torso landed against the tendril covered wall. In an instant, the stationary tendrils jumped to life and wrapped around her body.

"Xan!" Raiden shouted in shock as he watched it happen.

Xan struggled but the tendrils were alarmingly strong and were beginning to crush her, "Help!" she gasped, terrified.

Raiden ran up to Xan and tried to pull the tendrils off of her, but their grip was too tight. His mind raced, and then he remembered the rifle. Raiden backed away and took the rifle from his holster and took aim, "Xan, try to stay still," he said.

"Just do it!" she screamed.

Raiden steadied his grip and fired several shots, hitting each tendril that had wrapped itself around Xan. One by one the tendrils recoiled and dropped Xan. Raiden ran up and grabbed her, then pulled her away to safety. The tendrils reached out trying to grasp her back. Raiden and Xan stared at them in horror.

"You OK?" he asked.

"Yes, I'm OK," she said, wheezing as she tried to catch her breath, "Come on, let's go."

They tiptoed the rest of the way to the cockpit. Xan sat down in the pilot's chair and tried to use the controls, but nothing was working.

Raiden turned to her, "Sensor scans said the power was off."

"I thought that was a misread. The engines are working, which the power should be on here," Xan replied.

"Could be an issue along the circuitry, those tendrils have carved up the ship," Raiden speculated.

Xan stood up, "We're going to have to make our way to the engine room and do a manual shut down."

"Right, lead the way," Raiden said.

As quickly as they could manage they made their way towards the back of the ship, and then down an access port to the lower level. Xan followed a diagram she'd downloaded before they'd arrived on the ship. The lower level was much more intact. Tendrils still made their way through it, but the damage was much less severe.

"It seems like the tendrils like to actually be exposed to space," Raiden said, wondering why, but relieved that they were able to walk uninhibited in this part of the ship. "Are there any life forms you know of that live in space?" he asked.

"Single-cell organisms, bacteria, viruses, they can survive frozen on asteroids. But complex plants and animals? No, not that I've ever heard of," she replied.

They reached the end of the corridor, where the hallway split right and left. A plaque on the wall indicated the engine room was to the right and the cryo stasis room to the left. "Come over here, this way," Xan said, heading to the right. They made their way down the hall and entered the engine room.

When they walked inside the engine room it was as pitch black as the rest of the ship, but they could hear the hum of the engine. Unlike the rest of the lower level, the engine room was rife with tendrils. Raiden and Xan stepped carefully, desperately trying to avoid stepping on any of the tendrils that lay across the floor. Xan made her way up to the engine's manual interface.

"It's not powered," she said, after several attempts to use it.

"I thought you said it was interfaced with the engine itself?" Raiden asked.

"It is," Xan said, not hiding her concern.

"So, there's no way to turn it off?"

"Not unless we can find a way to power this up."

"Alright," Raiden said, "Where's the damn power regulator on this ship?"

"Engine room's the power hub, so it should be on one of the walls in here," Xan replied.

Raiden glanced around the room. The walls were completely covered in a sheath of tendrils, the writhing brown-black of them looked sickening to him. "We can't get to the walls, there's too many of these things in here. Does your blueprint have that kind of detail?"

"No, this is an old ship, it's just a basic schematic," Xan sighed.

Raiden walked up closer to the engine and took a look over it. It didn't take long to see that the tendrils were intertwined within the engine as well. "I don't understand how this thing is still running, everything else is off," Raiden started running the scanner on his suit. To his surprise, he was picking up massive electrical sources, "Xan, I'm picking up massive amounts of electricity, not just from the engine, from the whole room. Run your scanner."

Xan turned on her scanner and walked slowly around the room collecting data. "I'm picking up the same thing. The power is flowing, it just must be interrupted along the circuits," she surmised.

"Can we hook up an alternative power source to the engine interface?" Raiden asked.

"We might be able to hardwire something in. Why? What are you thinking?" Xan asked.

"Our suits have battery life to run basic functions, we could reroute the power source to work the interface for a short time," he said.

"OK, let's do it," Xan said. She knelt down in front of the interface and removed the front panel. She looked over internal components, a biotechnological system, carefully, "Looks like they used the same basic ferrofluidic systems format that we still use our ships now, I should be able to rig it up," she said as she pulled out a handful of tubes.

Raiden waited patiently as Xan set everything up. He felt uneasy like he was being watched. He tried to push it from his mind but couldn't help feeling like he couldn't wait to get off of this ship.

"Give me a hand," Xan said.

Raiden tiptoed past the tendrils nearby to get to Xan, then crouched down next to her, "What can I do?"

"I need to open up the panel on the arm of your suit to access the power source. Hold these tubes while I open it up," she said passing him the readied tubes.

"Will it be compatible? My suit's power system uses copper wiring," Raiden said.

"Yes, at least temporarily. Ferrofluids are magnetic, so they'll hold the wire in place, and conductivity won't be an issue," Xan explained.

Raiden held onto the tubes and did his best not to move. Xan was an adept worker. Raiden watched her as she efficiently and meticulously went about the task at hand. He tried to imagine being on this mission with Freya and had to stop himself from laughing when he couldn't help but picture her just trying to blow up the engine out of frustration.

"What is it?" Xan asked.

"What?" Raiden said, not sure what she meant.

"You smiled, what's funny?"

"Oh, haha," Raiden blushed, feeling caught, "Nothing, just thought of a friend that's all."

"A romantic friend?" Xan questioned.

"No. No, not at all. Just a good friend," Raiden said, still feeling the sting at seeing Freya with Koji in bed together.

"There, I've got it rerouted," Freya said, and Raiden's helmet flashlight turned off. She took the tubes from Raiden and deftly attached them to the wires from the power source of his suit. The tubes held onto the copper wires just as Xan had said they would and created a sturdy bond. Instantly the screen lit up that interfaced with the engine.

"Great job!" Raiden congratulated her.

"Thanks. Stay still so the wires don't pull loose," she instructed as she stood up to use the panel. She only got a few keystrokes in before the screen slowly faded dimer and dimer until it turned off entirely. "What in the world?"

"What happened?" Raiden asked.

"I don't know, the screen dimmed and then went off," Xan said. She looked down and tested the connection from the tubes to Raiden's power source and everything had held properly. She then ran a scan and discover Raiden's power source had been drained dry. "The power reserve in your suit is completely gone. My scanner says the battery is dead," she said.

"What?!" Raiden said, shocked.

"That shouldn't have happened... Let's go see if any of the crew are alive in the cryo chamber. If there's any survivors maybe they can explain what's happening," Xan said. "Follow close behind me, we'll share my helm light."

They made their way down the hall and into the cryo room. Just as they entered the room an alarm went off on Xan's suit, she clicked it off. "We're only an hour away from the Bastion now, we have to hurry," she told Raiden.

The cryo room was less infested with the tendrils than the engine room had been, but still, the eerie life forms had engulphed much of the space. Many of the cryo pods were broken or damaged, with tendrils running through them and the unlucky inhabitant within.

"It's like a horror movie," Raiden said, looking at one of the unfortunate impaled crew members, mummified by the cold of space in an expression of agony.

"It would have been a bad death," Xan said.

One by one they checked the pods that were still intact. Most of them had their power or circuitry disrupted by the tendrils that tore through the walls. "It's a graveyard in here," Raiden sighed.

"I found one, weak bio-signs, but they're alive!" Xan exclaimed.

Raiden quickly made his way over to her. The cryo pod was running on minimal reserves, but it had been enough to keep the occupant alive. "How are we going to get them out?" he asked. The entire ship was breached, there was no oxygen.

Xan smiled, "I guess we've got a few things to teach you humans." She pulled an octagonal black metal object from her belt and held it out for Raiden to see, "This is a device we use to create an energy barrier, it acts as a hermetic seal. The molecules that form the barrier are subatomic. Gasses can't pass through, but solid matter can."

"That's amazing! We have airtight seals, but out of materials like rubber," Raiden said.

"Originally so did we. Once we discovered the ability to harness energy in new ways, well, let's say it's a useful advancement. We can calibrate the size we need on the fly, and it isn't inhibited by physical objects in the way, it fills in the space around them," she explained, then checked the readings on the cryo pod. "It looks like it's still pumping a plentiful amount of oxygen, when we open the pod it'll be enough to fill the area with breathable area until we can get them into a suit."

Xan set the black hexagon on the floor at the base of the pod, adjusted the dial on it, and then turned it on. A beautiful flash of red light exploded from the small device to create a large sphere. The sphere's energy was all connected by beautiful red hexagons. Xan adjusted the size more precisely to encompass the entirety of the cryo pod.

"There's lockers against the back wall, can you check them to find a space suit we can help this crewman get into once they're out of the chamber?" Xan asked.

"On it," Raiden said and set off to search.

While Xan waited she studied the control mechanism on the cryo pod. It was low tech, using an old-fashioned seal that could be opened manually in the event of a ship-wide power failure. *Smart*, she thought. *If only the same idea had been applied to the engine.*

A few minutes later Raiden came back carrying an intact space suit, "Most of them are shredded, but this one's good."

"OK, we're ready," Xan said and initiated the waking sequence. *Hiss!* The airtight seal on the cryo pod released. The cool air released is a mist of white. Raiden helped Xan lift the large transparent-plexiglass front of the pod up, on its stiff hinges.

The crewman was slow to wake. His blue skin was extremely pale, and now that they could see him, it looked like he'd been in a fight before getting into the cryo pod. Bruises and lightly healed lacerations were all over his forearms. His eyes began to flutter.

"He's starting to wake up. Help me get him in the suit, it's as cold out here as it is in the pod," Raiden said.

Xan and Raiden both picked up the pants of the suit and approached the crewman. The man was beginning to wake up and regain awareness, and he looked scared. Xan turned to the man and grabbed his hand in hers and squeezed tight, "We're here to help. My name is Xan, and that's Raiden. We need to get you in this suit to warm you up, OK?"

The man hesitated for a moment, and then slowly nodded his head once. They proceeded to get him dressed. The man was clearly in no condition to move, his body stiff and freezing, so they moved his limbs as was needed. Raiden was amazed at Xan. She had an uncanny ability to instill trust. *Just like the first time I heard her voice...* he thought, impressed at how this scared man became instantly docile.

After a few minutes, they finally had the man fully dressed, and he was beginning to warm up. Xan turned off the energy barrier and placed the hexagon back on her belt. "Where are we?" the crewman asked.

"We're close to the Bastion," Xan said.

"What?! Yena, how long have I been asleep?" The man said, fear in his voice.

"'Yena?'" Raiden asked.

"Yena is one of our Goddesses," Xan told Raiden, then turned to the man, "You left known space nearly 400 years ago."

The crewman began to tremble; they could see it even through the suit, but neither knew what to say to comfort the man. He tried but couldn't suppress his sobs. Raiden couldn't imagine what it would be like waking up hundreds of years in the future.

"What's your name?" Raiden asked him.

"I, I'm Vex... I'm a scientist, an ecologist, I was supposed to study the planets we'd find and visit once we'd crossed the void," he said meekly, looking around the room. "Oh hell! Is everyone else dead?"

"I'm afraid so. I'm sorry," Xan said.

"We don't have much time," Raiden said to Xan.

Vex watched them both, "Time? Time for what?"

Xan looked Vex in the eye, "We need your help. The ship's powered off, everything except for the engines, but we can't access them through the control panel. We're headed full speed towards the Bastion, we need to shut this ship's engines down."

Vex shook his head, "They won't let us."

Raiden and Xan shot a look at each other. Then Raiden looked to Vex, "'They?'"

Vex pointed around at all of the tendrils, "They're... some sort of conduits. They use electricity, they consume it, re-disperse it, I don't know..."

"That explains why your suit's power reserves were completely drained when we tried to use it as a power source," Xan said to Raiden.

"Shit, we fed it?" Raiden said, alarmed.

"I have a lot more questions, but they'll have to wait. We have to take this ship out of the sky. We can't risk it intercepting the Bastion," Xan said.

"A couple well-placed shots to the engine should take it out," Raiden added.

"That won't be enough to stop them..." Vex morbidly added.

Xan thought for a moment, "OK, Raiden. We're going back to our ships, then we'll reposition and shoot out the engines. We'll head back up together, then I want you to get Vex onto my ship. I'm going to get the flight record from the cockpit, and then I'll hurry back to my ship. That'll give you enough time to get your ship online and to dislodge the docking clamps," Xan explained her plan.

"The cockpit's infested, you shouldn't go alone," Raiden said, feeling anxious.

"It's OK, I'll be careful. We have to hurry, let's go," she insisted.

Speedily they made their way back to the access hatch that led up to the main floor. Vex's body was stiff, but fear was a powerful motivator. Raiden and Xan helped him along the way. Once they were on the main level Raiden and Vex parted ways with Xan.

Xan hustled as quickly as she could to make her way to the cockpit. Another alarm went off, *30 minutes, damn…* she hurried even more. On the way, she opened a comm link to her ship, "This is Xan, prepare for takeoff. I'll be there in a few minutes."

"Roger," the pilot responded.

As she approached the cockpit she took special note of the placement of the tendrils and trod lightly. It was oppressive in the cockpit, lightless, with the dark throbbing tendrils making the small room feel even more confining. Xan took deep steady breaths to calm her nerves.

The flight recorder was lodged in the main hub of the pilots' control panel. One large tendril had burrowed its way into the control panel, scarcely missing the flight recorder. Delicately she plied the flight recorder free, making sure not to disturb the tendrils nearby. Once she had it she quickly stored it in a pouch on her suit and turned to leave.

That's when it dawned on her, *The tendrils use and redirect energy. They heavily linked into the engine, and now this one in the main control panel... they're not just powering the ship, they're flying the ship!* She spun around and stared at the tendril with newfound horror. *They're sentient!*

Xan unholstered her gun and aimed it at the tendril in the control panel. She took a deep breath, steadied her aim, and then open fired. The shock as the tendril was shot caused it to veer the ship off course. The gunfire was so concentrated it finally cut the tendril in half. The mutilated tendril flung about in the air wildly, like a fire hose let loose.

Just as Xan was about to leave she suddenly saw the severed tendril's end light up with electrical current. She could hardly believe her eyes as the tendril began to regenerate. It then plunged itself back into the control panel, sparks flying, and readjusted course for the Bastion.

"Fuck!" Xan yelled and then turned to run for her ship.

In her haste she misplaced a step, tripping over a tendril, falling to the floor and dropping her rifle. The tendril then grabbed her leg and began to squeeze with intense pressure. Xan clamored with all of her strength to reach her rifle, grabbed it, and then struggled to flip onto her back. She aimed quickly and shot the tendril until it released its grip on her. Without wasting a second Xan got to her feet and fled for her ship without looking back.

⁇

Raiden had gotten Vex onto Xan's ship safely, and then hurried to his ship. He had barely turned on his engines before he heard Xan's voice come in on his headset, "Get in position!" she commanded. He could hear the fear in her voice.

"Just about to disengage my docking clamps from your port, in 3, 2, 1..." he hit the switch and his ship jolted as it came free. "There, I'm loose. Heading into firing position now."

Raiden flew in an arching circle until he rounded behind the derelict ship. He armed his missiles and waited for Xan's ship to disengage. He saw the seal break, but when the ship began to pull in the docking bridge it wouldn't budge.

"What's happening? You OK over there?" Raiden asked.

There was no reply for several long seconds, and then, "We can't detach. Can you see if debris is blocking the retraction or hooked onto us?"

"Taking a look," Raiden said. He pulled up his monitor and zoomed in on the docking bridge. "Son of a bitch!" he exclaimed upon seeing that the tendrils had intertwined on the exterior of Xan's ship. They were already making their way past the extended docking bridge and onto the main body of the ship. "Xan, the tendrils, they're making their way across your hull!"

Suddenly Xan's ship went dark. Raiden held his breath as he waited for an answer. A minute later Xan's voice came over his headset again, "We've lost main power already. Those things don't waste time. We're trying to reroute but... it doesn't look good."

Raiden's mind raced. The Bastion was approaching in the foreground faster and faster. "We can't let those things on the Bastion," he said.

"I know, if we only had more time..." Xan sighed. "...We're abandoning ship. We've got life pods we'll eject on. It's up to you to destroy both ships, Raiden. The escape pods have beacons, so come give us a tow when you're done. Got it?"

"Understood," Raiden replied.

Raiden watched and waited until he saw all four life pods launch from Xan's ship. He then repositioned behind the derelict ship and locked on his missiles. "Here it goes," he said to himself, then hit the button to launch. The missiles sped towards the back of the derelict ship where the engine propellant came out of. Just as they were about to hit the target the derelict ship swerved, and the missiles hit the far wing of the ship instead.

The explosion sent the ship reeling, but it quickly recovered and resumed course. Raiden's jaw dropped as he saw it happen. *That can't be!* he thought, shocked.

There was static in his ears and then he heard Xan's voice, "Raiden, it's alive! I can't explain it, but those *things* are aware! You need to swoop in close and take them out!"

"Roger," Raiden said and shook off the miss. He took in his ship as close as he could while still being able to avoid getting caught up in the blast and then fired again. The derelict ship attempted to swerve but there wasn't enough time for it to dodge the missile. The engine block erupted in a massive explosion, bringing the speeding ship to a slowing glide.

The drastic change in speed, with Raiden chasing after it full tilt, caused him to narrowly miss colliding into the back of the ship. "Fuck!" he yelled as he yanked the steering as far right as he could. His heart was thumping in his chest like a drum beat.

Raiden peeled back around to take a run at Xan's ship. While both ships were halted he knew they couldn't take the risk of the tendrils activating the engines of Xan's ship. He got a straight shot and fired, taking out the engines on her ship. For the first time in hours, he took in a calm breath. Once he was certain both ships had been incapacitated he set his radar to pick up on the escape pod beacons and set course to pick them up.

Chapter 15: The Aftermath

The derelict ship exploding so close to the Bastion was already becoming somewhat of a legend. Countless thousands of Bastion residents, and ships coming and going in the vicinity had witnessed the heroic display first hand. Since the incident, which had happened 2 days ago, it was all anyone was talking about.

Raiden, Xan's crew, and Vex had all been quarantined since arriving back on the station. Given the extreme biomatter they'd encountered, lead scientists and doctors on the Bastion deemed in necessary not to let them out until they were sure they hadn't any hazardous DNA on them. It had been an arduous 48 hours for them as they waited while test after test, and decontamination after decontamination procedure was executed.

Raiden had used the time to document what had happened on the derelict ship in a report for Saisei's military command. Xan had followed suit with making her records for the Conclave. Vex remained oddly quiet and reclusive through all of it. Despite the ships being decommissioned away from the Bastion, his fear was palpable and left the rest of them feeling uneasy.

Dr. Takei waited anxiously in his lab for the team to be released. Word had reached him about the sample that had been taken from the unknown beings, and he was eager to run tests. It had been a long time since he'd been so excited to work on a project.

It had been a long recovery after the terrorist incident with Niko Adai before the doctor had felt safe returning to his lab. He'd developed a sudden fear for crowds of people. He neglected to see any of the psychologists on board about it; he knew his fear was unfounded and was determined to push through it alone. If there was one thing Seto was proud of, it was of the power of his mind.

He'd never particularly enjoyed being around other people to begin with. Interruptions were always the bane of any intellectual endeavor. But after seeing the politicians that were crushed to death like cattle in a pen, his discomfort grew.

While Dr. Takei waited for the specimen, unsure of how many more hours or days it would take for a sample to arrive, he focused on xenobiology. It had been a main focus of his ever since they had come to the Bastion and were given access to swaths of information. There were many technological advances as well, but Dr. Takei was a methodical man and intended to make his way through one of the sciences at a time.

Seto studied each species with great interest. He found himself very curious about these Ethlana and their unusually long lifespans. It got him to wonder if there was a way to instill that kind of DNA coding into humans. *What I could do with hundreds of years...* he thought, imagining it. *As a human a meager 70, 80, maybe 100 years if I'm lucky, it's not enough to scratch the surface of science. Great minds need time.*

As he continued to look into the matter he found a lot of the subspecies on the Ethlana homeworld also lived much longer by comparison to other planet's subspecies. Both flora and fauna thrived. And it was apparent that even though many of the Ethlana people lived off-world, some never even setting foot on their homeworld in their entire life cycle, they still retained their extended life.

It may have origins on their home planet, but it's biological now, hereditary. Fastidiously he took notes and submitted a proposal request for several DNA samples from various beings from their planet. The digital documents were thorough, but there was nothing like seeing with ones' own eyes to shed new light and perspectives on learning how things worked.

|

Freya had holed herself up in her quarters for the past 2 days. She'd heard about the emergency expedition Raiden had gone on not long before the massive explosion had happened. She hadn't seen it, but she'd felt the shockwave.

After the intel had come in that he had survived, and the initial relief she felt had faded, anger overcame her. She wanted to know why he didn't tell her he was leaving, not even over the comms, which he could have done if he had to leave in a hurry. They were supposed to tell each other everything. *Is he mad about me and Koji? And why is it always that Raiden gets picked for the best missions?* She was mad at him, and mad at the system, and at General Yamamoto. *I'm JUST as good as Raiden... No, I'm BETTER than Raiden...* the thoughts raged in her mind.

She took out her aggression through exercise; the pent-up energy needed an outlet. She did push-ups despite the stinging sensation of her healing arm until she couldn't feel anything but the burn of lactic acid in her chest, then did sit-ups until she couldn't breathe. The pain helped to clear her busy mind.

Koji had come by to check on her the day before. She let him in, grasping for him, and saying nothing. They had had rough, passionate sex, and then she had kicked him out of her room. The sexual release had been relieving, but all too soon her troubled thoughts bubbled back to the surface.

After 2 long days, she finally found a sense of calm. She knew what she had to do. *No more petty rivalry, no more outbursts, no more fucking up opportunities,* she told herself. *I am the best pilot, and I'm going to prove it.*

|

Hiroshi had just excused class for the day, and the students were filing out the door while he packed up his briefcase. Suki pushed her way past the steady stream of students to walk into the classroom to see Hiroshi.

"Hey," she said as she approached his desk.

"Oh, Suki," he said, surprised to see her as he looked up. "I haven't seen you in a while, how are you?"

"Good, thanks for asking, Mr. Kasai," she said, and held out her hand with 3 data pads, "I just came to return these to the school."

Hiroshi took hold of the data pads and set them on his desk, "You know, just because you've graduated doesn't mean you can't come by for continued learning."

Suki nodded, "I know and thank you, but I can't. I just enrolled as a pilot in the military."

Hiroshi looked at her with a stunned expression on his face for a moment before he replied, "I, I have to say, I'm surprised. You're such a smart young woman."

"You can't be smart in the military?" she said, on the defensive.

"No, not at all. It's just, you've always excelled at book learning. I guess I always imagined you'd have been much more interested in science, or even history," he shrugged.

Suki felt bad for her anger. She loved literature, and reading, and learning, and she knew he was right. But she'd made her decision, "It's a new kind of learning," she said, trying to convince herself as much as him, "You'd be surprised how hard flying is."

Hiroshi smiled, "I don't doubt it. Good luck."

Suki smiled back, happy to have his support, and then turned around and walked out of the room. She meandered slowly through the corridors. Tomorrow was her first official day of training in the military academy. She had studied the manuals front to back 3 times over. She knew she was ready, it was just a matter of diving into the actual work.

The last few days she'd managed to pack up all of her belongings. She was to be assigned a bunk in the military district, and no longer needed the full residence. It would be provided to another family in need of bigger housing. She felt good about getting out of there, her home had too many memories in it now.

She decided to head for the concourse. It would be her last free day in a long time; new recruits were locked into a 6-month training regiment, and free time would be next to none. She entered the concourse, and it was bustling as usual. It was a major hub for all of the visiting aliens coming over from the Bastion. *I guess they all must want souvenirs to take back home... makes sense. I used to ask dad to bring me back rocks from the planets he got to visit...* she had to stop her train of thought before she got teary-eyed.

Suki made her way over to her favorite dessert stand. They made the most delicious soy ice cream on the entire ship. Nearly everything on the Saisei was soy, it was easy to grow, cheap protein, and cattle were at a premium. Real dairy was a rarity, and a major expense, just like meat.

Once it was her turn in line she ordered her favorite, plain vanilla. She was handed a bowl with 2 perfectly rounded scoops. After she paid, she wandered around, slowly eating her ice cream with pure enjoyment.

More and more people were coming into the concourse. It was approaching lunch time, and with the majority of restaurants located here, it would be the most crowded part of the ship. Suki decided to leave to walk back towards her quarters.

Walking down the halls, still blissfully enjoying her ice cream, she walked past a man in his early 20's, slender, with stark black hair and pale skin. Instantly she felt a surge of energy that rippled up her spine and gave her goosebumps. She turned around to look after him, to find him standing there, equally shocked, staring back at her. His eyes were a shocking indigo.

Neither knew what to say, but Suki felt uncomfortable, so she spoke first, "Hi, I'm Suki."

"Blaine," he replied, his voice deep and smooth, "you sensed it too?" he asked.

"I, um... something, yes," Suki said, feeling even more uncomfortable.

Relief swept over Blaine's face as if a great weight had been lifted, "You're the first person I've even run into that also has the *power*."

"Power?"

His smile faded, "You don't know, do you?"

"Um..." Suki felt exposed and nervous with others walking past them, "Can we go talk somewhere else... somewhere private, with less people?"

"Of course," he said, then he turned around, and began to walk away.

Suki stared after him, feeling stunned, wondering if this was some sort of strange waking dream. She thought about turning around to go back to her quarters, her unease with the situation nagging at her. She found her legs involuntarily began to walk as she hurried to catch up after him.

Blaine led her down many passageways until he found an access hatch. He deftly removed covering panel and began to crawl through the hatch. *Where the hell is he taking me?* Suki wondered. She knew she could ask, but she didn't. They hadn't spoken a word the entire trip. She couldn't explain it, but she trusted him implicitly. She could sense him. *Is it his thoughts? Feelings? I don't know...*

After making their way down the shaft they emerged into an area where they could stand upright. It was a section of the ship only engineers ever came to. The small circular space surrounded a major hub for the energy relay that powered primary systems. There was a gentle hum in the air from the massive amounts of energy passing through the conduit.

Blaine sat down cross-legged facing the conduit. Suki sat down a few feet away from him. "I can't say this is exactly what I had in mind when I said somewhere more private," she said.

"I know... but no one ever comes here but me, except maintenance teams on the first of the month," he explained. "This place is unique. You can feel it can't you? The incredible abounding energy here?"

Suki quieted her mind to focus on sensing the space, "Yeah, I can. How'd you even find this place?" she asked.

Blaine grinned, "I used to like to explore every nook and cranny of the ship as a boy."

"How did you discover your, uh, 'power'?" Suki asked, hugging her arms around her knees.

He stared at the conduit as he spoke, "I was 6, it was the first week of kindergarten, and we were learning the alphabet using those metal blocks that have the letters inscribed on 'em. Well, the teacher was having us all look for the letter S and to have it displayed upright on the block. I was looking through my blocks trying to find it, and finally saw the S facing me, I pictured it being upright in my head, like the teacher wanted it to be, but before I got to it to move it the block flipped," he shook his head, "I was amazed and excited, and I started screaming 'did you see that?!' ... I tried to tell them what happened, but the kids laughed at me and my teacher told me to stop making up stories. I knew from that moment on that I was different."

"6 years old? Wow..." Suki said, taking it in.

"How about you?" he said, turning to look at Suki.

"I just found out, really. I was thirsty, and I made a cup move. I never had anything like that happen before. It was the same thing though, I imagined drinking, and then it moved," she said.

"Played with it since?" he asked, his eyes glinting in the low light.

"A little. It's not consistent."

"It gets easier. Then you can do more."

"More?" Suki asked, her curiosity piqued. "Like what?"

"Move bigger things, mess with the lights, hear what someone else is thinking... there's no limits far as I can tell," he shrugged.

"How'd you learn to do all of that?" Suki was fascinated.

"A lot by accident. But after a while I just started trying stuff, to see what I could do. Watch," he told her. Blaine pushed himself forward onto his knees, closer to the conduit. He closed his eyes and put his hand out an inch away from the conduit.

Suki watched closely. At first, she didn't see anything, but after a few minutes, she could see the tiniest blue-white particles of electricity appear between his hand and the conduit. Slowly they grew bigger and bigger until free-flowing electricity coursed between his hand and the conduit. Suki watched in awe.

Blaine pulled his hand away and cupped it, and the electricity came with his hand. It flickered, jumped, and sparked, in a perfect sphere. He opened his eyes and looked at Suki, "We have no limits."

"How?" was all she could utter.

"It's just energy. Everything in the Universe is just energy. Thoughts attract their physical counterparts, and like attracts like. If you can think it, it can happen," he said simply, with pure conviction. "Hold out your hand."

Just like Yu-Lee wrote in her paper… she thought. Suki felt nervous but determined to understand, so she extended her hand with her palm facing upwards. Blaine moved his hand towards her, the electrical ball flashed and flickered as he moved it.

"You are energy. This is energy. Harness this energy in your hand with your mind," he told her.

After letting out a long exhale to calm her nerves, Suki focused her thoughts. She looked at the electricity, wild, yet contained, and imagined it in her hand. Doubts of her ability and fears of being shocked crept up in her mind, but she kept pushing them out, and imagined holding the electricity just as Blaine had done. *I am energy. Electricity is energy. I can hold it,* she kept telling herself over and over.

Suddenly the electricity began to migrate from Blaine's hand to Suki's. It didn't hold shape as a perfect sphere, but it held together, and it didn't shock her. Suki stared at it with gleeful amazement.

"I did it," she exclaimed.

"Now disperse it," he instructed.

"I'm not sure how..." she said.

"Remember, we're all just energy. That means you can transmute it into air," he said.

It all makes sense! She thought at the realization. She pictured in her mind the electricity disappearing and becoming air particle energy. The electricity dissipated and shrank until it finally vanished. Suki looked at Blaine with gratitude.

"Nice work," he said.

"Thank you!" she exclaimed, full of joy.

"I only wished we met sooner. I guess that's life. It's nice not to be alone anymore," he said.

Suki's smile faded, "I wish we had met sooner too. I'm starting my training as a cadet to be a pilot tomorrow."

Blaine didn't hide his disappointment, "Oh."

"I won't have much free time for a few months. But what's a few months?" she said, trying to cheer him up, "And any time I do have, well, I'll find a way. I, this is going to sound weird..." she said, trying to find the words.

"What?" he asked.

"I just... I can't explain it really, but, I feel like I've always known you. I just lost my mom, and my dad... fuck, who knows where he is. I've never made friends easily, people are hard to talk to, but you... I feel like I could tell you anything and you wouldn't judge me," she told him.

Blaine looked Suki dead in the eye, his indigo eyes commanding her complete attention, "I've spent most of my life alone. People who don't know, don't understand what we can do, they fear this power. I've kept to myself because of that. I can honestly say I've been waiting my whole life to find you."

He reached his hand out toward Suki, indicating for her to reach out her hand. She extended hers, and he took her hand and held it firmly. They sat in silence simply enjoying each other's company. They were two lost souls who had finally found each other amidst the chaos of life.

Chapter 16: The Last Expedition

Finally, after three days of being locked in quarantine, Raiden, Xan, Vex, and the rest of Xan's crew had been deemed safe for release into the general population. The newfound freedom was short lived for Xan, Raiden, and Vex, as summons to attend the Conclave Speakers for a debriefing beckoned them to make haste. After a quick meal, shower, and a change of clothes, they were off to the assembly hall.

Vex took in the sights like a child experiencing something new. Xan and Raiden had noticed him looking all around, and they kept quiet to allow his mind to digest it all. When they were near the consulate, Raiden asked, "Has it changed a lot since you left?"

Vex shook his head, "No, that's just it... it looks exactly the same."

"What? Really?" Raiden said, surprised.

Xan thought about it for a moment, "I guess that makes sense. The maintenance never really changes anything, just keeps it all running. Most of it is automated."

"Even after hundreds of years?" Raiden asked.

"I doubt this place has changed much at in thousands of years, maybe not even since when it was originally built. The only thing that changes are the people who visit," Xan said.

They walked into the waiting room outside of the assembly hall where the Conclave awaited them. Within 5 minutes they were escorted in. As they approached the center of the room where they would stand Vex couldn't help but nervously whisper, "I've never been in here before." His anxiety was tangible.

Raiden put his hand on Vex's shoulder, "It's OK, don't worry."

"Thank you for coming so promptly, I can imagine you're exhausted," Saaya said to them as they approached.

We will try to keep things brief, Ecoatay channeled his thoughts to them all.

"We read your account Shadow Xan," Zar said, "and yours Lieutenant Saito. Your findings were... most disconcerting."

"Vex, we are pleased to meet you. I'm sorry for your ordeal," Saaya addressed him.

"Thanks..." Vex said barely audibly.

"That explosion was too close to home," Ouct sneered.

Xan bowed deeply, "Sincerest apologies, Speakers. The situation was most unusual."

"The flight recorder was worth the risk," Ent said, as much to Ouct as to Xan.

"Have you managed to recover anything off of the recorder yet?" Raiden asked, eager for news.

"It's still being processed," Zar told him.

"Vex, I've been wanting to hear from you. Your expedition, the tendrils, what happened? After your ship went through the wormhole it didn't relay anything more," Saaya asked.

Vex took a moment before he began to speak, "It's a long story," he sighed.

⁂

Nearly 400 years ago...

"...0700, don't forget," Captain Cain said to Vex. Cain was Ethlana too, with very pale blue skin, like snow hinted by a blue-black night sky. He had deep laugh lines and a weathered face from a life well lived. Cain was in his 500's, but spry as ever.

"Yeah, yeah, I know, I just gotta grab the rest of my bags. I'll be back tonight," Vex told him.

"No, you won't, you'll remember there's someone else, or somewhere else you need to say goodbye to before we leave. And that's OK. Last time you'll ever see this galaxy after all," Cain had laughed in his robust voice.

Vex laughed too, although it was entirely out of nervousness. Vex was only in his 90's, barely an adult in Ethlana society, and Cain's boisterous nature intimidated him. It didn't help that he'd been fighting second thoughts about leaving on this expedition all week. He had just finished rigorous training in ecology, and it was the opportunity of a lifetime to be the first ever scientist to travel to a new galaxy and to document all of the new life they'd encounter.

"0700, or we leave without you," Cain said and walked off.

Cain may have been overbearing, but he was right. Vex found himself endlessly wandering throughout the Bastion that night. He didn't sleep and wasn't tired. After Cain had said it would be their last time there Vex couldn't bring himself to leave. When the crack of dawn rolled around, and the computers automated the sunrise, Vex finally went to collect his bags and boarded their ship at 0637.

Vex hurried toward the storage lockers to pack stow his belongings, dodging between the crew who were hurriedly doing their last checks before departure. Vex was near to the locker room when Cain caught sight of him. The uproarious laughter was unmistakable, and while Vex was aboard on time he couldn't help feeling like he had been caught.

"Told ya' you wouldn't be on 'til morning, lad," Cain said, chuckled, and patted him on the back before heading off to the cockpit.

Vex finished putting his belongings in storage and then went to the observation room. Their ship was small but comfortable. The minimalist ship needed to reserve energy stores for the exceedingly long voyage it had to undertake, while still being a livable space once the crew emerged into the neighboring *Phoenix* Galaxy. It had been an engineering feat that Ethlana's top designers had rivaled to achieve.

Their ship had built in gravity generators, but they weren't to be used until they crossed the void, so during the launch, all crew members had to be strapped in for safety. Docked at the Bastion, the intense gravity emitters of the station gave the ship mild gravity until their departure. The observation room was a semi-circle on the lower deck right beneath the cockpit. A spread of 20 bolted down seats with safety belts were there for the crew.

Vex entered the observation room and took the first available seat he saw and strapped himself in. Seconds later the Engineer, Zev, sat down next to him and buckled in. "Excited, kid?" Zev asked as he tightened the harness.

"Yeah," Vex said, nodding, trying to convince himself as much as Zev.

"Hey, it's alright," Zev said, sensing Vex's anxiety, "No one's ever done anything like this before. It's alright to be scared. All these people," he said, looking around the room, "their bravado is all for show. They're scared."

"Thanks," Vex said, feeling slightly less alienated.

"Want to know a trick?" Zev asked.

"Sure," Vex said, leaning back in his chair.

"Fear and excitement go hand in hand, they're two sides of the same coin. Instinct tells us to fear the unknown, it's basic survival. That's how our ancestors avoided being eaten alive way back when. But as we learn, overcome, achieve, and expand our knowledge, that's exciting. Every time we conquer something new it's that exhilaration that keeps us going to push our boundaries. So, lean into the excitement of it," Zev told him.

"I will," Vex said, inspired by his words.

The launch went smoothly, and they were on course for the far wormhole. Several other ships launched at the same time. The expedition had 30 ships in all scheduled to cross the expanse to reach the Phoenix Galaxy. Once their ship had pulled away from the Bastion Vex could feel the lack of gravity and his butt lifted up off the chair, his harness was the only thing holding him down.

They made good time and rendezvoused with the other ships on the other side of the wormhole. Once they emerged through the wormhole they found that ahead of them lay a sea of utter darkness. The dead space had no planets, no stars, no light; it was, in the truest sense of the word, a void.

Behind them, the bright galaxy they'd all called home seemed that much harder to leave. Life was teaming across all the planets around all the stars. But the decision had been made, and they stood steadfast in their convictions.

All ships were doing their final checks before departing. Once they were on course the crew would all enter into cryogenic sleep. One crew member would remain awake for 30 days, to maintain systems, and ensure the crew remained safe. After 30 days they'd wake the next crewman on the rotation schedule and get into their own cryo pod. This safety precaution was also beneficial to the crew members to get their bodies moving. With 30-day rotations, each crew member would only be woken up every few years during their several centuries journey across dead space.

Like everyone else, Vex was waiting for the command to head to the cryo room. The time dragged on and the crew was becoming restless. Staring out into the void was discomforting, to say the least. The only thing to break up the unending blackness of dead space were a couple of ships visible through the window that lay before them.

Vex was trying to meditate, but the underlying murmuring and tension in the room made it hard for him to concentrate. He looked at Zev who had fallen asleep in his chair. *Lucky,* Vex thought as he looked at Zev, wishing that he could fall asleep so easily.

Another hour passed by and Vex was beginning to feel that something was off. Not long after that the ships within the view of the observation deck turned around and flew out of sight behind them. *What the hell is going on?* Vex wondered.

It was then that Cain came on over the intercom, "We're ready, time to get in the cryo pods, everyone." No one else seemed disturbed by the other ships leaving. The crew, cranky from waiting, simply unbuckled from their seats, turned on their mag boots, and made their way down the hall.

Zev had slept through the announcement, so Vex shook him gently until he woke up. Zev yawned and rubbed his eyes, "Time for cryo now, kid?" he asked as he stretched.

"Yeah, but..." Vex wasn't sure what to say.

"What?" Zev asked.

"It's been hours, and the other ships just left," Vex told him.

Zev looked at the clock, "We should've made way by now... but these things happen, sometimes checks take a while. Don't worry kid, captain says we're good, I trust 'em."

Vex nodded, feeling reassured, "Right."

They made their way down the hall and into the cryo room. The majority of the crew were already in their pods. Vex walked over to his assigned pod and looked at the control panel attached to it and was trying to remember how to set the sequence.

Zev noticed the perplexed look on Vex's face and walked over to him, "Need a refresher?"

"Please," Vex said.

Zev showed him exactly how to input all of the data to set up the pod and Vex was incredibly grateful. He wasn't sure how he was so lucky to have made friends with Zev so easily. He'd always had a hard time talking to new people.

Vex climbed into his pod, and then the door closed. After a few seconds, when the door connected to the pod, all that he could hear was the *hiss* as the airtight seal made perfect suction. It was incredibly tight quarters within the pod and Vex had to choke down his claustrophobia. Zev tapped on the plexiglass, "Sweet dreams," his distorted voice echoed oddly hollow inside the pod.

"Thanks," Vex said and watched Zev walk away.

A moment later the pod activated, and the chamber became cold. Pure oxygen filtered in, which at first felt incredibly stimulating. It didn't take long for Vex to feel the effects and to fall into a deep dreamless sleep.

Time after time Vex was woken up to do his 30-day rotational shift to maintain the ship. The 30 days were a blessing and a curse. He had always reveled in solitude, but no contact of any kind except for the day he was woken up by another crewman, and the final day where he'd wake up his replacement before going back into cryo sleep, was a bit more than he could bear.

After his 6th cycle, he'd read through all of the books he'd brought and started to pilfer through his crewmates bags to find more entertainment. There was very little to do while waking; while they were called maintenance workers, the ship was essentially self-sufficient. A waking sentient being was merely a precaution in the event of an emergency or power failure.

Vex was in the midst of his 21st cycle when the proximity alarm went off. He had been napping and the high-pitched frequency had snapped him awake abruptly. He headed for the cockpit in a sprint while covering his ears against the noise.

When Vex arrived he quickly turned off the alarm and breathed a sigh of relief. He scanned the void with his eyes, but as always, there was nothing to see but never-ending darkness. He cut the engines to be safe and plopped himself down at the helm to go over the sensor scans.

The motion sensors did detect some movement, however, the readouts varied greatly. Multiple detections from one, a single object from the other, he was beginning to think the sensors were malfunctioning. *I'll have to leave a note for Zev to fix them next time he's up,* he told himself. He ran an infrared sweep of the area ahead of them just to be safe, but it came back showing nothing was there.

Vex reengaged the engines, resuming their course, and wrote out the note for Zev about the sensors. He stood up and stretched, looking out upon the void. "There's nothing here but us," he said, feeling the finality and isolation of it.

He turned around and walked out of the cockpit, eager to resume his nap. He walked through the hall unenthusiastically. The depression had set in strong. They had been warned before they left on the voyage about the mental effects of extended cryogenic usage, but the reality of it was a lot harder to deal with than he'd expected. His past few cycles he couldn't wait for his 30-day rotations to be over so he could get back into his pod. *How many more cycles before we get there? I don't even want to think about it...*

As he was halfway down the hall suddenly he heard a loud *thump!* And the ship jarred hard to the left which made Vex lose his footing with his magnetic boots. His body was flung hard into the wall knocking the air out of him. He floated there dazed for a moment. The ship continued to jar, *thump... thump, thump!*

Vex shook his head, and then pushed off the wall hard so his feet touched the floor and grabbed on. He made his way quickly back to the cockpit, fighting the tremors every step of the way. He clamored his way into the pilot's seat and quickly shut down the engines. He breathed a brief sigh of relief when the jarring had stopped.

He stared out again into the dark abyss ahead, *Did we hit something?... Maybe the engine destabilized?* His mind raced trying to decipher the problem. As usual, there was nothing but blackness to look out at, but then, the darkness moved. "What the fuck!" Vex nearly fell out of his seat.

Vex rubbed his eyes. *Am I seeing things?* He wondered, his heart pounding in his chest. He continued to stare, there was nothing, and he was beginning to doubt himself, and then…. Movement! The joy of knowing he wasn't losing his mind quickly wore off and became uneasiness about whatever it was on the ship. His mind raced about what to do, but he was out of his league. He needed help.

Rushing down to the cryo bay, Vex bit back his panic. *What is that? The sensors were right after all… how did anything else get this far into dead space? And it was moving! Oh, Yena!*

Running into the cryo room he went up to the captain's pod first and initialized the waking sequence. Once it was underway he ran over to Zev's pod to wake him up too. It seemed like it was taking forever this time for them to wake up. After a moment the seal gave and slowly the captain's pod opened.

Cain came to rather quickly, and without warning, vomited all over the floor. He wiped the bile from his mouth, "Urg, this never gets easier…" Then he noticed it was Vex who had woken him, and that

Zev's pod was beginning to open. His ears were acutely tuned to his ship, having spent most of his life in space, and he could tell the engines were off, "What's going on?"

"I, we, there's something out there, in dead space! We just ran into it... I don't know what to do," Vex told him, glad to not be alone anymore.

Zev's pod finished opening and he woke up and stretched heartily, "Nothing like a good nap," he said, wholly unaffected by cryogenic sleep.

Cain's eyes darted to Zev, "How you enjoy this I'll never know."

"We have to hurry!" Vex exclaimed.

"What?" Zev asked, confused.

"Kid says the ship hit something," Cain said casually while climbing out of his pod, his legs shaky.

"Really?" Zev said and looked to Vex. Vex's pale serious expression said it all. "Well, shit," Zev said and got out of his pod.

The captain and the engineer quickly dressed, with Vex trying to rush them. The older men both tried to keep their calm composure; they'd seen unusual things in space many times over the years, but Vex's distress was hard to ignore.

"Keep it together kid, the Universe is full of surprises," Cain told Vex.

The three of them began making their way up to the cockpit. Along the way, the lights began to flicker. "That's odd," Zev said, "how bad was the collision?"

"I, uh, not that bad, I don't think, just jostling," Vex said.

"Maybe a relay came loose," Zev said.

They walked into the cockpit and Cain sat at the helm. He pulled up the sensor logs, "That's weird," he sneered.

"I thought the sensors were malfunctioning," Vex said. "Look," he said pointing out the window.

"At what?" Cain said, seeing only the darkness.

"Just wait," Vex told him.

A few seconds later it moved. "What the hell?" Cain said in a loud whisper, standing up to get a closer look. It moved again, "Yena! It's alive!" he exclaimed.

"This certainly takes the prize for the weirdest thing I've seen in space... how can anything live out there? It's a total vacuum. There isn't even any light out here," Zev said, wracking his brain for answers.

"We can figure out the 'why' later, I want this shit off my ship and to resume course," Cain said sternly.

"How?" Vex asked, perplexed.

"More importantly what after that? The sensor feedback is garbled, it can't make sense of whatever these things are. We don't know how many are out there," Zev said.

"We have to go out and see for ourselves. We'll take the floodlight and use our eyes," Cain said gruffly.

Vex felt a shiver run through his body at the idea of having to go out amongst those *things*. He had a sinking feeling in his gut he couldn't shake. "We're not enough," he blurted out. Zev and Cain looked at him questioningly. "We, uh, need more crew, people to go out and pry those things off while we process the data in here and try to get accurate scans," he said, his brain grasping for any excuse not to have to leave the ship.

Cain grinned, "Knew we brought you along for a reason, kid. Alright, you two get things set up in here, I'm going to go wake up some more of the crew and lead the team on the hull of the ship. I'll loop my helm feed for you to figure out," Cain said and got up to leave.

"How are you going to get those things off the hull?" Zev asked.

"Zap 'em off," Cain said as he left.

30 minutes later Cain had 5 other crewmen awake and suited up ready to exit the ship. They had equipped themselves with shock rods which had been brought to be used as non-lethal defensive equipment to fend off wildlife while they established colonies in the next galaxy. They entered the airlock and sealed it off. Each of the crew attached their safety harness, which connected back to the airlock and would keep them from floating off into space if they lost their footing.

Cain radioed the cockpit after he finished attaching his own harness, "Ready to depressurize," he told them.

"Confirmed," Zev's voice came back, and he began the depressurization sequence.

It took less than a minute for the oxygen to be sucked out of the room. Cain then opened the exterior hatch, and one by one the crewmen made their way out onto the ship. Cain was the last one out, and when he set foot on the hull he was taken aback by the vast number of the tendrils that had attached themselves to the ship.

"How is it?" Zev asked.

"Oh, one minute," Cain replied and turned on his helm's camera feed. He then turned on the floodlight he'd brought out with him. For as far as the eye could see these ugly brown-black tendrils filled dead space. "It's like being in the middle of a school of fish in the ocean," he said as he panned his head around to get a full view on the hull. "You seein' this?"

"Yes," Zev said, his voice grave.

"They look like the tentacles of a fish or some sort of engorged worm," Cain said, looking closely at one.

"It looks like they have suction of some kind, like some sea creatures do, by the way that they're able to hold on," Zev agreed.

"We're completely surrounded!" Vex cried out as he watched the incoming video footage, his fear getting the better of him.

Cain could hear Vex through his headset, "Kid, keep it together," he told him. Cain walked along the hull. The other crewmen were in place and readying their shock batons. "Alright, have at 'er, men," he told them.

The first crewman who was in place set the stun baton to the highest setting and zapped the tendril that lay before him. The tendril didn't let go of the hull like they had expected and instead buried itself deep into the ship's plating. "It's eating its way into the ship!" the man called out, in shock. Another crewman shocked another tendril, and this one snapped up with alarming speed and grabbed the stun baton right out of his hands.

The third crewman to attempt to dislodge a tendril hadn't been so lucky. After stunning it, the tendril latched onto his leg and began squeezing with excessive force. The man was screaming at the top of his lungs as he felt the *crunch!* of his bones breaking. Cain ran over to help as fast as he could, but before he could make it the tendril had made its way up the man's body and across his midsection and chest. Cain shocked the tendril with his baton, but it only seemed to make it act more hastily. The crushing continued, and one after another, the man's bones snapped.

When the tendril got hold of the crewman's arm and broke it the break was so severe that the bone pierced through his space suit. The man began gasping as his oxygen flooded quickly out into space. His screaming was frantic until finally, the pressure collapsed his lungs and the broken ridged bones of his ribs pierced his heart. There was a disturbing gurgling as he choked to death on his own blood before he was fully silenced.

"Back in the ship!" Cain commanded.

The crew hastily made their way back to the airlock. Cain thought about trying to free the dead man's body from the death grip of the tendril but thought better of it. *I'm sorry. Rest easy now...*

Cain followed up the rear and got in the airlock. It didn't take long to pressurize. Once they were back inside of the ship their panic and fear were palpable. They stripped off their spacesuits. Cain told everyone to come to a meeting in the observation room in 15 minutes.

Before the meeting, Cain needed to clear his head. He went to the nearest bathroom, locked the door, and ran cool water which he splashed on his face. He let his mind digest everything that had happened and tried to push the horrific images of the crewman's death out of his mind. He took a few deep breaths, put on a brave face, and went out to lead his crew.

When Cain walked into the observation room, he heard the men's terror as they spoke, recanting the events outside the ship. "Keep it together," Cain said as he entered the room. "The worst thing we can do is lose our heads. This is just a problem we have to find a solution for," he told them.

"But..." one of the crewmen, distraught and scared, went to argue.

Cain cut him off, "What happened was awful, but we'll mourn later. We need to stay focused right now. If we can figure out what happened and a way to counteract these things, then we'll be in the clear."

"I may have some insight," Zev chimed in.

"Go on," the captain told him.

"I went to go and check if we had a loose relay to see if I could get the lights to stop flickering. There's nothing wrong with our electronics, but when I was looking I saw our power reserves are down. You saw how those things reacted when you shocked them? I think they absorb electrical energy," Zev said.

The crew scoffed, but Cain hushed them, "How bad are the reserves?"

"Down to 70% but I don't know when the drain began. Could be coincidence, but for now, it's a working theory," Zev said.

"I don't believe in coincidence," Cain said.

A silence fell over the room. They were all deep in thought. A couple of the crewmen were on the verge of nervous breakdowns. The lights were flickering more rampantly now.

Amidst the silence, a loud screeching of what sounded like grinding metal filled the room. Everyone covered their ears and looked around. When the noise finally subsided, the crew all got to their feet.

"They're breaking their way through the hull," Zev said.

"Everyone, we need to fend these things off, they can't get in the ship. Stab them, shoot them, burn them, do whatever it takes to stave them off!

I'm waking the rest of the crew," Cain instructed and then led the charge out of the room.

Vex stuck with Zev; he was the only person he trusted. Despite the precarious situation Zev was level headed and focused. They headed down to the engine room together. They could hear the other crewmates fighting off the tendrils, with the clanking of metal echoing through the corridors.

When they got into the engine room Zev immediately checked the power readings, "61%," he said, alarmed.

"It has to be them. Your theory is right," Vex affirmed.

Zev nodded, and radioed the captain to let him know about the change, "Another 9 percent down, in less than an hour."

"Yena... of course. Alright, we're doing our best to get them off. Do everything you can to keep them from getting into the engine room! If they get in there, we're dead in space," Cain said.

"Good luck, Captain," Zev said.

The realization of dying in the void made Vex involuntarily throw up. He continued to dry heave after. His body trembled, and he felt a heavy dizziness. Zev helped him stabilize on his feet.

"It's OK, kid. Common, we need to arm ourselves, just in case," Zev said and led the way to the locker room and used his key to open up a small weapons locker. He passed Vex a projectile rifle and took another for himself. Most of the weapons they'd brought used energy and plasma, making them utterly useless against these tendrils. He shut the locker and relocked it. They made way to get back to the engine room.

Once they got back they set themselves up in a defensive position in the engine room, weapons ready. The loud creaking of the ship being pulled open resonated through the walls. Vex shuddered with every sound, dreading the one that would signal the first tendril penetrating into the engine room. He closed his eyes tightly and wished for it to all be a bad dream.

Just then the hull breach alarm went off and yellow lights began to flash all over the ship. Vex's eyes shot open and his heart raced.

"Shit!" Zev yelled above the alarm.

The engines came back online. Cain's voice came in over the intercom, "They're tearing the ship apart! All of you, get in a spacesuit immediately! I've resumed our course, full speed, to the Phoenix Galaxy. We'll get through the hoard then get any of these leftover bastards off of our ship. The..." Cain was cut off as the loudest and eeriest sound of screeching metal came through the ship deafeningly, amplified by the intercom. Cain was sucked out into space through a massive breach. The intense suction from the breach could be felt all over the ship.

"Hurry!" Zev yelled over the chaotic dissonance.

As quickly, and carefully, as they could they made their way toward the cryo bay where extra space suits were stored. Once they were there they dressed as fast as they were able. Vex breathed a sigh of relief, surprised he was still alive. The ship shook constantly as they plowed their way through the field of tendrils. Vex looked to Zev, who was securing his helmet, "What now?" Vex asked.

"Whatever we do we have to act fast, our suit's oxygen reserves won't last forever," Zev said, then took a minute to think. "The captain said he set us on course again... I think our best option is to verify the course is laid in and to set the computer to wake us up when we arrive."

"What about the tendrils?" Vex asked.

"We can't do anything about them out here, nothing is working," Zev said pragmatically.

"We can't go into cryo with those things loose on the ship! You said it yourself, they're consuming the power!" Vex said emphatically.

"Get it together, kid! We're in the middle of nowhere with nothing to fend them off with. Even if we cleared a few, we're flying through an endless sea of them now, it won't matter. This is our only chance of survival. Those things seem to have some self-awareness, so my guess is that they won't completely drain the power. If it's their food source they'll keep it going," Zev told him.

Vex's head was spinning. *How'd this happen? Why did I sign up for this?* he asked himself. He looked at Zev with distraught. "OK," he said, feeling out of body.

Zev nodded, "Good. I'm going to make sure everything is set with the ship. I need you to round up the crew and get everyone back to the cryo room."

The two men parted ways to set out on quickly setting their plan into motion. Vex had this horrible feeling that if he went into cryo sleep he'd never wake up again. He pushed it to the back of his mind; there was no choice after all.

The ship had become what looked like a scene from a horror movie. Tendrils had burrowed in through the ceiling, walls, and floor. Their black-brown appearance made Vex feel nauseous. *This is all your fault... if only you hadn't ignored the proximity alarm and had looked more closely at the sensors!* He felt a deep anguish pull at him.

He found several crewmen fighting the tendrils to no avail. Zev had been right, they simply had no means onboard the ship to ward off these invaders. He told the men of the plan and they had hurried off to the cryo bay.

Then the lights went out entirely. It was pitch black and he couldn't see a thing. Vex stopped in his tracks when it happened, terrified of stepping on a tendril by mistake. He fumbled with his helmet until he got the flashlight working. Vex closed his eyes tight, wishing for it to all be a bad dream, but when he opened them nothing had changed.

He made his way carefully through the ship and sent everyone back that he could find. He found a couple more crewmen who had been crushed to death and he cringed when he saw them. *I'm so sorry,* he thought as he looked upon them.

Vex turned the corner in the hall to get to the last few rooms of the ship only to find one of the crewmen had been ripped to pieces by the tendrils. His legs, torso, arms, and head, all held by tendrils spread across the hall. Vex was paralyzed by the sight. There was blood everywhere. Bits of brain, intestines, and organs were floating in the zero-gravity environment, the blood droplets cascading in an arc; like a macabre art exhibit. His fear got the better of him and he turned and fled.

Tunnel vision set in, and all Vex could think about was getting to the cryo room and getting into his pod as fast as possible. In his haste, he missed his footing and tripped over a tendril on the floor. Vex screamed, imagining the torn apart man, and fearing the worst would befall him. He kicked the tendril on the floor with all the force he could muster before it could grab him, then scrambled to his feet and continued running without looking back.

When Vex made it into the cryo room he was heaving to catch his breath. A cold sweat had broken out all over his body. He looked around and saw that most of the crew had gotten back safely and were getting into their pods. Zev was checking everyone's pods to make sure there wasn't any damage when Vex walked in.

"Good to see you made it back safely. You checked everywhere?" Zev asked.

"Yes," Vex lied, unable to bring himself to tell Zev about the horror he'd uncovered and how he'd been too scared to check those last few rooms. "Did you find the captain upstairs?"

"No, he's gone. The breach, it was massive..." Zev sighed. "Alright, we shouldn't waste time. Quickly get your suit off and into your pod. Remember we're badly breached, so exhale entirely before you take your suit off and then and quickly get into the pod. I'll do the rest," Zev told him.

"Right," Vex said. Just as he was about to take off his suit they heard the loud *clank, clank, clank!* of heavy footsteps from down the hall. Vex and Zev both looked to the door.

"I thought it was all clear?" Zev questioned.

"I, yes..." Vex felt caught but didn't know what to say.

The crewman's footsteps got louder and were awkwardly spaced out. When the man arrived in the doorway they saw his helmet was broken, the faceplate shattered, and rushed over to him. "It's OK, we've got you," Zev said, grabbing the man's arm to help stabilize him. That's when Zev saw the man's face was devoid of color; the once blue skin was now a pure white, and his eyes were entirely black. Zev let go of the man and backed away, pushing Vex back too.

"What's wrong?" Vex asked.

"I don't know," Zev said.

Then it happened. Like a thousand needles pricking into their brains, images flashed in their minds. A deep guttural sound accompanied the images; whether it was a scream or a war cry they couldn't tell. The images appeared so fast they couldn't make sense of them. The only thing they knew with any certainty was that the feeling behind them unmistakable; it was pure hatred.

"Make it stop!" Vex yelled, the experience was excruciating.

Zev pushed through the pain in his head and ran full speed at the crewman and tackled him to the ground. Instantly the images and the sound ended. Zev tried to pull the man's helmet off, but it was stuck. He turned the man's head to the side and saw a tendril had burrowed through the helmet directly into the man's brain. Instinct kicked in, and Zev used all of his strength to bash the back of the man's head, and the tendril in it, onto the floor until the tendril had been emulsified. Then he pulled off the helmet, revealing the pure white skin.

"What in Yena's name?" Vex said when he saw the man.

The back of the man's head had been hollowed out by the tendril. "It was using him like... like some kind of puppet," Zev said, disgusted.

Vex rested his hands on his helmet, wishing he could put them on his forehead for relief, "My head is killing me," he cringed.

"Could you make sense of what you saw?" Zev asked.

"No... just, it was bad. All of it. Death, pain..." Vex said trying to remember.

"Yeah..." Zev said, perturbed. "Alright, common, time to get into cryo."

Vex undressed and got into his cryo pod. When the door sealed he breathed deeply. He stared out the plexiglass opening at Zev who was setting up the sequence on the control panel. Zev looked up at Vex before he turned it on, "See you on the other side, kid."

"See you there," Vex said, wondering if they'd ever make it. Just then, from the corner of his eye, he saw the man with the white skin's foot tremor. "Zev, look!" he called out, afraid.

Zev turned around to see the body convulsing. Zev was starting to walk over to it when the dead man suddenly stood up and lunged toward Zev. "Fuck!" Zev yelled, narrowly dodging the man's attack. Zev spun around and ran for his rifle which he'd set down across the room.

Vex watched in horror, banging on the glass, feeling trapped. Zev grabbed the rifle and turned around to take aim, but the white man was too close. Vex could see another tendril sticking out of the crewman's skull. *They're unstoppable!*

Zev wrestled with the crewman who seemed unnaturally strong. After an intense struggle, he managed to kick the man back and fired a concentrated volley of bullets into his head, ripping his face to shreds. The man stumbled back and fell to the floor.

Shakily Zev made his way back over to Vex. "Are you alright?" Vex asked, seeing how out of sorts Zev looked.

"I'm… alive. Let's put it that way," Zev said, intending a joke to break the tension, but it fell flat.

Zev was inputting the last few keystrokes on the computer and Vex's pod was beginning to fill with cool air. Condensation started to form like a mist on the window. Just as Zev was finishing the sequence the crewman's body began to move again, crawling along the floor. Vex could no longer see clearly through the window and didn't notice anything was wrong until he heard the *thud!* when Zev had been pulled to the floor.

"Zev?" Vex called out.

There was no response, but he heard the fighting and the rifle go off again. Vex began panting heavily, *What's happening?!* Vex could faintly see the shadowy outline of Zev's hand reaching up to tap the panel one last time. The sequence was completed, and the pod was set into the final stages of initiating cyro sleep. Then the darkness overcame him, and he drifted into a sleep that would last hundreds of years...

Amanda Rose

Chapter 17: Aftermath

Vex stood before the Conclave stoically. A silence had befallen the room as he finished recounting the events from his expedition. Xan and Raiden had stood by Vex's side throughout, listening as he told the tale. It wasn't what anyone had expected and had left them all feeling chilled.

"Thank you, Vex. That was quite the ordeal you lived through," Zar said compassionately.

Vex nodded, tears streaming down his face, "Yes... thank you. Whatever happened to the other ships?"

"They'd been recalled," Saaya told him. "It was deemed too risky to make such an extensive voyage until we'd improved on our technology. Captain Cain ignored the order."

Vex nodded to indicate he understood. The Speakers reviewed their notes from the events Vex had described. Raiden placed his hand on Vex's shoulder while they all waited, and whispered, "Good job." The touch of another being felt so foreign to Vex which made him cry even more, he was grateful to finally be home.

"Now, Vex, you mentioned that engineer Zev was plotting the course to continue across to the Phoenix Galaxy, correct?" Ent queried.

"Yes," Vex said.

"When our rescue team discovered your ship, it was locked on course for the Bastion. Did you actually see the coordinates entered?" Ent continued.

"No, Zev and I went separate ways to prepare for the voyage. But Zev had told me when we met up again that the course had been input for our continued journey," Vex explained.

"When people fear death they always think of getting home to safety," Zar said. "He was probably just embarrassed to tell you that he changed course for the Bastion."

"No, Zev wouldn't do that! We saw how fast those things took apart our ship, we'd never risk bringing them back! Never! Especially not Zev," Vex said with conviction.

"Yet here you are," Ouct said snidely. "You admittedly lied to a superior before. What's to say you both didn't agree to set course for the Bastion once you knew the captain had died? And reanimated corpses? The story is preposterous."

I sensed no deception from him, Ecoatay communicated.

"Vex is right," Raiden interjected, "when I shot at the ship it course-corrected. Those tendrils were flying the ship."

"How would they possibly know where the Bastion is? And why would they come here?" Ouct argued.

"If I may," Xan started, "those things have rooted themselves into all of the ships main systems. They may not appear dynamic, but they are sentient. The way they conduct energy and react, I have no doubt they accessed the computer data in some way. As for coming here, I can only speculate that if they consume energy, and we have it in abundance at the Bastion, it was to seek out a substantial food source."

"That seems to line up with our knowledge so far. The scientists should have more information for us as they study them," Zar said.

A surge of panic swept through Vex, "Study them?! You didn't destroy them all?"

"It's alright, calm down. The ships and debris from the explosion have been contained in a force field. We have brought back a few specimens to better understand these creatures," Saaya informed him.

"Didn't you hear a word I said?! Those things will kill us all! They need to be incinerated immediately!" Vex yelled, outraged.

"We've taken all necessary safety precautions," Ent tried to explain.

"It won't matter! Oh Yena, not again," Vex fell to his knees and sobbed. He was a broken man, plagued with fear and regret.

"It's been a long day. Vex, get some rest. Thank you," Saaya said, excusing him. The attendant came in and escorted Vex out. Uneasiness set in on the room. "Xan and Raiden, as Zar mentioned before, we've read your reports. They seem to be congruent with Vex's story."

"If you want to know if he's telling the truth, then yes. I believe everything he told us is what really happened out there," Raiden said.

A disturbing conclusion, but I agree, Ecoatay transmitted.

"Suggestions?" Zar asked.

"Well," Xan began. "I think Vex may be right about incinerating the remaining tendrils, to prevent any mishaps. However, knowledge is our greatest strength. So, with extreme care, if our scientists can gather as much information as possible, and if we tractor out the debris further from the station, for the time being, I think that's our best option."

"Raiden?" Zar inquired.

"I'd feel safer knowing they were all dead. But Xan is right, if we can understand them better we may have a defense against them if we need it in the future," Raiden concurred.

"Wise counsel, indeed," Saaya said to them, "we'll begin working on arrangements for the debris to be taken further from the station. Your work on this mission was exemplary, both of you. Which brings us to our last point of business today. Raiden, it did not go unnoticed by Xan, or this council, that your actions contributed to the direct success of this mission. You acted with valor in the face of the unknown and saved the Bastion from a direct collision which could have been catastrophic. In light of these heroic actions, it is with great honor that I extend to you an invitation to become a member of the elite Black Shadow."

Raiden stood momentarily speechless. He felt the conflict within himself. He had always been, and always imagined being, a pilot for the Saisei. He felt like a protector to his ship, and yet ever since they'd arrived at the Bastion, he'd felt like that responsibility was much less dire. He also couldn't imagine leaving the Bastion. He knew the Saisei would eventually disembark to pursue colonization in some nearby system, which wasn't much of a life for a pilot.

"Permanent quarters will be provided to you on the Bastion, and you'll be assigned your own ship, should you accept," Zar told Raiden with a small smile on his face.

"...I accept," Raiden said, exhilarated. He couldn't help feeling a pang of guilt like he was abandoning his ship, but deep down he knew he wanted this more than anything else he had ever wanted in his life.

"Congratulations!" Xan's cheery excitement overcame her.

"Yes, Congratulations!" Ent said, and everyone in the room clapped. Raiden could feel himself blushing, but he didn't care, he was so overcome with joy.

"Go enjoy some free time you two," Zar smiled, "We'll inform you when your quarters are ready, Raiden."

"Thank you," Raiden said. Xan and Raiden both bowed and then left.

|

Dr. Takei had finally received his sample of the tendril, which had been delivered that morning. He had been pleasantly surprised when he received an entire portion of a tendril, and not just a scraping as he'd originally expected. He had locked himself away in his lab for hours and had left strict instructions that he was not to be interrupted. He'd gotten to work immediately, getting his tools ready and preparing his thesis. Then he pulled out his audio recorder to track findings as he went.

Now that the lab was set, he was ready for the real work to begin. The tendril specimen he'd received was the tip cut off of a full one; 5 inches long, about 9 ounces to work with. Seto had placed the container the specimen had arrived in within a hermetically sealed incubator when it had arrived, that would prevent the possibility of air contamination. The doctor pushed his hands into the built-in rubber gloves on the side of the incubator and then proceeded to pick up and open the sealed bio container that the tendril had been delivered in. He gently shook out the specimen until it slid out of the container.

Seto picked up the tendril to touch it, "Firm to the touch, the skin feels like that of a fish."

Dr. Takei set it back down in and grabbed his scalpel. He made an incision at the tip and ran it lengthwise down the tendril, it was difficult to cut through. He then used his forceps to pull the skin back. The inside of the tendril was a complex interconnected webbing of circuitry, presumably a nervous system, that was all held in place by some sort of jelly-like substance. "No muscle tissue, or basic bone structure," Seto said, wondering how they moved. In many aspects, the tendrils resembled earthworms, but even worms had some muscle tissue to use to move.

He stuck his forceps into the jelly to get to the circuitry. The second his forceps touched the inner webbing Seto got a strong electric shock; so strong it penetrated through his rubber gloves. "Urg!" he immediately let go and pulled his hand back. After taking a moment to rub his hand to alleviate the pain he leaned in to look at the inner workings of the tendril. "The theory about these creatures storing electricity within their body proves to be true. The inner workings of the body are hyper-conductive. It seems likely these tendrils use the electrical current to generate their desired movement, however, there is no brain that I, or the scientists I've corresponded with on the Bastion, have found. How they act on anything but instinct is as of yet, unknown."

Seto took his scalpel and grabbed a slide. He took some of the jelly-like substance on the tip of the blade and then delicately tapped it onto the slide and pressed the two pieces of glass together. He then slid the slide into an advanced scanner that acted as a microscope, with a digital feed that showed him the magnification readouts on his computer in real-time. Seto pulled his hands free of the rubber gloves and went to his computer.

It was surprising to Dr. Takei to see that the jelly was much like a thicker version of blood. Much like human blood, it stored plasma and cells, but that's where the similarities ended. "Bloods cells come from bone marrow, but you have no bones, hmm," Seto spoke aloud to himself as his mind began churning through possibilities. *And the thickness of the jelly may be a way to resist the colder temperatures, to survive space. I'll need to run temperature tests,* he mentally noted. *With no* circulatory system, they must be born or grow with enough of these cells for their life spans.

The cells within the blood-like substance were translucent and brown. The tendrils seemed to have no use for oxygen and survived in dead space for an unknown amount of time, perhaps millennia, without it. The cells were conduits, but not for oxygen dispersal as humans need. They contained a nucleus, unlike red blood cells in humans, making them most closely resemble white blood cells; but they were abundant. White blood cells make up a mere 1% of blood in humans, but Dr. Takei was seeing more than 20% of the tendril blood was made up of these cells. *White blood cells normally live for less than 24 hours... if these beings have superior disease-fighting cells we may be able to use them.*

The rest of the blood was made up of platelets, the small cell fragments that help heal and coagulate blood. Just like the cell count, the platelet count was incredibly high. "They have a remarkable ability to heal," Seto said, impressed. The sheer medical possibilities for this kind of accelerated healing capability was staggering. *Of course! The density of the blood acting like a gelatin, the abnormally high platelet count has caused this,* he thought.

Seto worked late into the night running tests, putting cells under observation and jotting down his thoughts and findings. He batted around one idea after another on how to properly study the superconductive inner webbing of the tendril but had yet to decide on the safest method. His hand still stung from the initial shock. Eventually, Seto fell asleep on his desk.

The next morning Seto was awoken when one of his alarms began to go off. He came to and shut it off, then checked on the results from the experiment he'd run. He'd set a portion of the jellyblood into a deep freeze for several hours. He removed it and allowed it to thaw, and then checked it under the microscope, "It's like it never happened," he said in awe. The tendrils could go into a perfect hibernation under extreme-cold condition and be revived with ease.

Dr. Takei stood from his seat, stretched, and yawned, then walked over to start a pot of coffee. After turning the machine on his eyes lazily glanced around the room while he was waiting. He looked to the tendril in the incubator and his heart skipped a beat when he saw it. The incision he'd made, cutting it open, virtually in half, had completely healed; it was as if he'd never done it. He walked over to it to give it a closer inspection. "Remarkable!" he exclaimed. *The high cell count, the accelerated healing, it makes sense... but to see it! Astounding!* He thought.

Seto felt elated at the new finding and documented it. As he did so he suddenly realized that the tendril was now appearing to take up much more space within the incubator. He remeasured and weighed it and found it had grown by an inch and gone up by 3 ounces. His mind began piecing it together, *It's regenerative. It must be able to regrow itself!*

He paced and began to record his findings, "...High leukocyte and thrombocyte counts, higher than any I've seen in any life form, even throughout the extensive database from the Bastion, proves to provide these beings with incredible restorative capabilities. In 19 hours this specimen has not only completely healed itself from an incision extending the full length of it, but it's also grown. If we can utilize the DNA we may be able to regrow limbs for amputees and fend off illness and fatal disease in ways we never could have imagined. Further research and time will tell, but the prospects are enormous," Dr. Takei recorded.

|

Raiden stood in General Takeo Yamamoto's office. The General was sitting at his desk and had a somewhat sour expression on his face, "I can't say I'm surprised, it's quite an offer…" Takeo said. "Won't be the same without you on Omega, though."

"I know, sir. It wasn't an easy decision…" Raiden tried to explain, still feeling torn.

Takeo cut him off, "Life has been nothing but constant change since we arrived here. You don't have to say anything. I'm proud of you! The first human Black Shadow elite soldier, now that's quite an achievement!"

Raiden smiled and felt like he was glowing. The General's opinion had always meant a lot to him. "Thank you, sir."

"I can't say I know exactly what's in store for us, for any of us, in these coming days and months, but I have a feeling we'll be in touch. Congratulations, Lieutenant, you earned it!" Takeo smiled, stood up, and extended his hand.

Raiden took his hand and they shook. "I'll do you proud," Raiden said.

"You do humanity proud, son," Takeo told him warmly.

Raiden walked out of General Yamamoto's office and set off towards his quarters to begin packing his belongings. He looked around the hallway, and it felt weird knowing he wouldn't be walking down them every day anymore. After a few minutes he heard footsteps running toward him from behind, and he turned around to see it was Freya.

"There you are!" she said when she finally caught up to him, then stopped to catch her breath.

"Hey," he smiled, happy to see her.

"I'm glad you're OK," she said, "they kept you in quarantine for forever."

"Yeah..." he nodded, "it sucked."

Freya's smile faded to a frown, "You didn't tell me you were leaving... you just left. I thought we told each other everything?"

Raiden felt caught off guard, "Oh, I, I'm sorry. Really. The General called me in and before I knew it they were setting me out to launch."

"And your personal comm was broken too?" she jousted.

"No. I just didn't think it was that important," he shrugged.

"Right," she said, her voice icy. "Well, I'm glad you're safe. If you'd died out there and I hadn't said goodbye... Anyways, I'll see you around," she said and was about to walk off, but Raiden stopped her.

"Freya, I'm leaving," he said as he looked her in the eye.

"'Leaving'? What do you mean?" she asked.

Raiden sighed. He'd been fretting about telling her ever since he agreed to take a position in the Black Shadow elite. "The Conclave, they offered me a position. I'll have my own command."

A look of shock came over Freya's face as the realization that her best friend would no longer be an active part of her life hit her like a punch in the stomach. "Oh..." she said, not sure what else to say. Suddenly all the anger and jealousy she felt towards him slipped away, and she felt guilty for being angry. She swallowed hard, "Congrats, man." She fought her pain, smiled, and pulled him in for a hug. "Always knew you'd be destined for great things."

Raiden held her tight. He could feel her trembling in his arms. Her breathing was strained, and he felt her chest rise and fall in short bursts as her breasts pushed against his chest. He nestled his face against her hair. "We'll see each other, as often as possible, I promise," he told her, meaning it, hoping it was true.

Freya was on the brink of tears, unable to speak, she nodded her head which rubbed against his chest. She took a moment to regain her composure before pulling out of the hug. "When do you leave?" she asked, trying to keep her voice from cracking.

"A few days," he said.

"Drinks tonight?" she asked.

Raiden smiled, "You got it."

Chapter 18: The Visions

It was the middle of the night when Blaine arrived home from work. Much like the way he lived, he worked in the shadows, doing odd jobs around the ship. He did just about anything that needed doing that didn't require him to interact with others; stocking shelves, cleaning, inventory, and so on.

After a quick dinner, Blaine went into his bedroom, sat on his bed, and began meditating. It was something he had learned to do long ago to quiet his mind and cleanse himself of all the energies from other people that he'd picked up on each day. His empathy allowed him great awareness, but it left him susceptible to mood swings. The emotions of the people around him colored his own feelings, and so he did his best to keep to himself.

As soon as he got comfortable and closed his eyes he felt at peace. He let the thoughts from the day dissipate and was freed by their release. He focused on his breathing, in through his nose, and out through his mouth. It reenergized him. The longer he sat in silence the easier he found it to keep random thoughts from creeping in. Every session was different, but today, he felt an especially strong clarity.

A half hour passed by, and with each passing minute, Blaine slipped into a deeper meditative state. He almost felt like he was in a trance, which was a state he rarely achieved. He luxuriated in it. With his eyes closed, the blackness of his mind's eye drifted thoughtless through the haze. As his mind and spirit became freer and freer within the confines of his body, the blackness started to take form, like smoke dancing into imagery.

He came to see, or rather *feel* or *sense* the tendrils. It was unlike anything he'd ever experienced. Their inherent beings were like husks; soulless hallow pawns in a grander scheme. Blaine tried to steady his breathe, to see clearly. He could feel how the tendrils had come into being, not born, but created. Their existence was one of agony. They were conduits for electricity, they lived on it, but the currents ran along a nervous system, causing unfathomable pain. He sensed their time in space, waiting indefinitely, frozen, unable to move, but awake. It was horrifying. As Blaine delved deeper into the consciousness of the tendrils he found himself feeling trapped, alone, and cold.

Blaine traveled further and further into their psyche. *Slaves...* he realized and felt pity for their wretched existence. As if a veil had been lifted he then saw the tendrils' creators who came from the Phoenix Galaxy. He saw their minds and felt their power, the overwhelming strength of it startled him. They were beings who understood the power of the Universe, energy, and the ability to bend it to their will. They wielded their power without mercy.

Desperate to understand, Blaine kept searching for answers. He couldn't see their motivations, and it was as if they were hidden just behind a fog that he couldn't see through. He felt like he was running around in a maze, unable to find the right way to go. Then images began to flash in his mind, quickly and incoherently. Blaine cringed against the sharp pain he felt as it happened, and tried to focus, to see what they were, but it was a blur. A moment later the images ceased, and he saw, plain as day, a pair of malicious eyes staring at him.

Blaine opened his eyes and threw his back against the wall. He was hyperventilating and sweat ran down his face. He was trying to catch his breath and breathe through the fear. The eyes, they *saw* him; they had seen into his mind, and Blaine knew that they knew what he had seen.

|

Xan woke up from a dead sleep in a cold sweat. She shot up to seated, her heart racing, and she placed her hand on her chest to try to calm herself down. After a moment she got up from her bed and went to get a glass of water. She chugged it down, refilled it, and drank deeply again. "What was that?" she then asked herself, trying to make sense of her wild dreams.

She had not just seen a great darkness, but she had walked among it. There had been a cascade of imagery and places where she witnessed war, torture, and despair. In her dream, she had been running, trying to escape it, but it had enveloped her, and that's when she had awoken with a start. It had shaken her to her core. The Ethlana had natural aptitudes for psychic abilities and astral projection. She tried to dismiss it as just a nightmare, but deep down, she knew it was real...

|

Vex sat on the edge of his bed with his head in his hands. He'd just thrown up and his body felt vile. The heel of his left foot tapped nervously on the floor. He had witnessed the annihilation of his homeworld *Aeros* in his dreams, and it had felt so real, that now that he was awake his mind couldn't accept it.

He'd ran from the bathroom after vomiting to check the news to make sure Aeros was still there. It was, but it hadn't allayed the sinking feeling he had in his gut. He'd seen an intense battle in space above his planet, the tendrils attacking Ethlana's fleet, and then a bright blinding light, and the planet exploding into a million pieces. Vex shuddered as he recalled it in vivid detail.

They're in my head, he thought, perturbed by the tendrils. It had been an excruciating experience recounting the events that had happened on his expedition into dead space. *I'm imagining things...* he tried to tell himself. The imagery was all too real, like a dejavu yet to happen.

Vex replayed the nightmare in his mind and tried to slow it down. The ships attacking his planet were like none he'd ever seen before, and yet they looked so incredibly familiar. He wanted to understand why. The more he tried to get a clear sight, the harder it became to recall how they looked.

"Dammit!" he yelled, opening his eyes. Vex was tired of living in constant fear. He wanted nothing more than for his nightmare to be over, but it was just beginning.

|

The first few days as a cadet Suki had found to be much like being in school. They'd spend most of their time reviewing materials and studying. It would be over a month before any of them got in a cockpit, and many more before their first flight. It was 0600 hours and they'd made their way into Bay E to practice pre-flight exterior ship checks. Suki stood amongst her fellow cadets as their flight commander walked them through the drill.

Suki was having a hard time concentrating. The night before she'd been having nightmares, though she couldn't recall any of them. She'd tossed and turned the entire night.

On the other side of the bay from them, Zavion and several of his engineers were fixing up some of the ships. Suki found herself gazing over at them and watching them work. "Cadet Rose, am I boring you?" Ken Adama asked, staring Suki down. Ken had recently been promoted to Private 2nd Class, and as part of his new duties, he was to instruct new cadets on flight basics.

Suki felt her face flush, "I, no, sir!"

"Eyes front then," Ken said sternly, and then continued his lecture.

Suki kept her eyes on Ken, but her mind wandered. Ken had been in the middle of running down the pre-flight checklist when Blaine suddenly came storming through the door and ran towards Suki. Ken saw him and stopped his lecture. The students turned to see what Ken was looking at. When Suki saw Blaine and the seriousness to his face, she felt her heart skip a beat.

"Excuse me, this is a closed session, you can't be here," Ken said, but Blaine ignored him.

Blaine ran right up to Suki and grabbed her by the shoulders, his eyes even more intense than normal. He stared into Suki's eyes and she felt like he was staring right into her soul, "You saw it didn't you?!" he asked frantically, desperation in his voice.

Suki, wholly unprepared, was entirely confused, "I, what? Saw what?"

"They're coming!" Blaine yelled.

"You need to get out of here!" Ken said marching up to Blaine.

"What's going on over there?" Zavion called from across the room and began to walk over.

"Suki, we have to warn them, warn everyone, they're coming! Oh, god, they're going to kill us all... it was all a trap! You saw it, didn't you?!" Blaine's words were urgent and fearful.

Suki stood there, shaking, feeling his fear. *Does he mean those dreams?* She wondered. Ken separated Blaine from Suki and stood between the two, facing Blaine. "Leave. NOW! Or I *will* call security to have you dragged out!" Ken said with authority.

Blaine stumbled back, "Suki, you *know*," he said with finality.

"Listen to him, son. Time to go," Zavion said to Blaine.

Suki nodded, and Blaine finally left. Ken straightened his uniform, then faced the cadets, "Back in line." Everyone rearranged themselves with eyes front. "Thank you," Ken said to Zavion, who nodded in recognition and then returned to his work.

Ken walked in front of Suki, "Cadet Rose, what was that all about?"

"I don't know, sir," she told him.

Ken stared at her questioningly before returning to the front of the room to continue his lecture. Suki's mind raced, *What did I see?* She tried to remember the chaos of her nightmare, but it was all a haze. The look in Blaine's eyes had left her feeling spooked.

|

Dr. Takei was finishing up a lab report in his office when *Knock! Knock!* Dr. Xena Nakamura knocked on the door and startled him. Seto spun around in his seat to see her standing in the doorway. Xena stifled a giggle at seeing the surprise on his face, "I'm sorry, didn't mean to barge in."

"Need something?" he asked.

"My curiosity is getting the better of me. What've you found out about the tendrils?" she asked.

Seto turned around and grabbed a data pad off his desk and handed it to her. Xena took it and began to read through it. "So unusual..." she said as she reviewed it. Once she got further in she looked up wide-eyed at Seto, "They regenerate?"

Dr. Takei nodded, "Yes."

"How fast?"

"I last recorded at 48hours, it had tripled its size from when I'd received the sample," he told her.

"Show me," she said, dying to see it.

Dr. Takei led her into the lab and showed her the tendril within the incubator and the comparative photos. Xena looked at them all with intense fascination.

"I had no idea you were interested in xenobiology," Seto said.

"Any biology," she smiled, "I reveled in the joy of biology class growing up, animals, humans, even plants, it didn't matter. I like to know how living things work. Xenobiology is just that next step, I only wish there was more time to study outside of medical practice... hmm, this really is strange though, isn't it? White blood cells with no expiration date that don't come from bone marrow... Do you have a slide I could look at?"

"Over there," he pointed at the computer which still displayed the scans feedback.

Dr. Nakamura walked over and sat down in front of the computer and began to play around with the magnification. She took her time, adjusting the sites, and processing what she saw. She increased it to its maximum magnification. "They're unnatural," she said at length.

"Of course, I've never seen anything remotely like them," Seto agreed casually while reading some notes.

"No, I mean they're artificial," she explained, sounding concerned.

Dr. Takei furrowed his brow, "How did you come to that conclusion?"

"Look," she said, tapping the computer monitor. Seto walked up behind her and looked. "You can see they're spherical," she said.

"That's not wholly unnatural. Spherocytosis occurs in humans," Seto rebutted.

"In red blood cells, not white. But let your eye adjust," she instructed.

Seto exhaled and tried to let his eye fully relax to look at the cell. The translucent nature of it made it challenging to fully perceive. After a few moments, he wasn't seeing anything new. He looked at Xena, "What is it?"

"It's not just a sphere, it's a geodesic sphere. Perfect symmetry between the triangles creates the sphere and makes it an abnormally strong structure!" she exclaimed. "Here," she said, taking over.

Xena used the computer to amplify the image and then she enabled the 3-dimensional enhancement. Once it was blown up on the screen there had been no doubt, it was a geodesic sphere. Seto gazed upon the screen and couldn't believe he'd missed it.

"Nothing like that in nature exists. There's no reason this creature should have these qualities. It's a product of genetic engineering," Xena said with absolute certainty.

"That explains everything, and why the DNA sequencing kept giving me an error," Dr. Takei said, all of his findings now making sense to him. The newfound understanding quickly gave way under the weight of the repercussions, "This is a feat of genetic engineering beyond anything I've ever read about. But if they were created, someone had to have put them out there in the middle of the space between our galaxies."

"That thought is incredibly disturbing," Xena said grimly.

|

Xan had just helped Raiden finish moving the last of his belongings into his new quarters. Her own dwelling on the Bastion was a mere five-minute walk away from his, and she was happy to have a friend on board. After all of her years in the Ethlana military, she hardly knew anyone apart from the soldiers on the ships she'd worked on, and all of them never docked for too long at the Bastion.

They set down the last crate and then both sat on the floor to catch their breath. The endeavor of moving had been a bigger proposition than Raiden had ever realized. He was glad it was over, though dreaded the unpacking ahead.

"You have a lot of stuff," Xan said, looking at him with fatigue.

Raiden laughed, "Yeah, I guess I do. I lived on that ship all my life." He looked around at all of the crates they'd hauled in, "That's weird."

"What is?" Xan asked.

"This," he said, gesturing at all of the crates, "This is my whole life."

Xan laughed, "No it's not," she said and then tapped her head, "This is your whole life, your thoughts, and your memories. That's just stuff."

They said nothing for a moment and just enjoyed each other's company. A yawn then overcame Xan and she rubbed her eyes. Raiden saw how tired she looked, "Didn't sleep well?"

Xan shook her head, "No. I think Vex's story got to me, can't get those tendrils out of my head."

Raiden put his hand on Xan's shoulder, "It was intense on that ship too. Our minds like to play games."

"Yeah, maybe," she said, clearly not convinced.

"What?" he asked.

"I just think we haven't seen the end of it. Have you ever had a dream that's come true?" she asked.

"Like a premonition?" Raiden asked. Xan nodded, and he thought for a few minutes before responding, "I think so. Once my pilot squad and I were doing some drills, and suddenly I had this feeling, almost like dejavu but not quite. Then one of the pilots, Masato, he was flying to my right and one of the thrusters on his ship gave out and his ship started spinning wildly. I knew I'd seen it before, I think I dreamt it as a kid. Why?"

"Our species really aren't that different. Ethlana are sensitive too. Most of us are highly empathetic, and, if we focus on it, we can develop our precognitive functions. It's not something I've spent much time doing, though. Military life, well, you know. But that dream last night… it was more than just a dream," she said uneasily.

"If there's one thing I've learned, it's to expect the unexpected. A few months ago, we humans thought we were alone in the galaxy, and now we know there's this massive intergalactic civilization. So, there's something out there? OK. But whatever it is we're not fighting it alone," Raiden smiled.

Xan nodded, "You're right."

Chapter 19: Science

Only a few days after the many scientists around the Bastion had received the tendril samples they submitted their preliminary finding to the Conclave. While speculation on the specifics varied, they had all drawn the same conclusion about the tendrils being genetically engineered. The information sat heavy with the Speakers.

A Veick scientist, Krass, suggested taking his research team through the far-reaching Heaven's Eye to the edge of the galaxy to better understand the effects of dead space on the tendrils. He requested to take one of the fully formed tendrils from the containment field that held them captive within Bastion space. The Conclave approved, and the science vessel departed shortly thereafter.

A confinement beam had been used to isolate and immobilize one of the tendrils as it was tractored behind the science vessel. The operation was going smoothly. They made good time on their way to the outlying Heaven's Eye and went through the wormhole that led them to the edge of the galaxy.

When they arrived on the other side of the wormhole the expansive black sea of absolute nothing was pervasive. "I've never been out here," Hark, Krass' lab assistant, said absently.

"Why would you? There's nothing this far out," Krass said as he readied the scanners.

They flew several hundred thousand kilometers out into the desolate black of the void. Once they were deep enough into dead space they release the tendril and backed the ship away from it, then began monitoring it. After several hours it was frozen and unmoving.

"It's affected by the cold... how did they attack the Ethlana ship if they were frozen?" Krass said, thinking out loud.

"They must be able to sense nearby energy sources and come out of hibernation when they need to," Hark said.

"And unthaw themselves at whim?" Krass pondered, "It must be related to their electrical nervous system. If they had enough reserves the electricity could be converted to enough heat energy to warm them. There's nothing like these in nature. Whoever conceived to create these beings did so with precision. If only we knew their purpose."

"Guardians?" Hark conjectured.

"Perhaps. They certainly act like a security system," Krass nodded.

They continued to monitor the tendril. After 26 hours no change had been witnessed. They decided to send out a small probe, which had its own power source, to test their theory on the tendril's preceptory senses. The probe sat within 10 feet of the tendril, and within an hour the tendril had begun to move and propelled itself toward the probe.

"How is it moving?" Hark asked as he watched.

"I'm not certain," Krass said, looking at the incoming data.

The tendril latched onto the probe and began to eat through the outer metal casing. It was working its way through the probe to get to the power source. "See how it lays its mass lengthways along the exterior of the probe? It has no head, no mouth, I think the skin itself processes the matter," Krass explained his theory.

"It's not growing, is it consuming it, or pulling it apart?" Hark asked as he zoomed in on the computer feedback.

Krass took the magnascope to view the tendril in action and viewed it with maximum 1000x magnification. Viewing the process down to the microns he could see it all clearly.

"Incredible! Hark, come see this!" Krass said.

Hark came to look through the magnascope and saw tiny sparkling metal shards flying off into space, invisible to the naked eye. The metal was passing through the skin of the tendril as the being broke down the metal plating of the probe.

"It's like it's a wood chipper for metal!" Hark said in awe.

The science team continued to watch and take readings and notes on the tendril over the next several days. The tendril had managed to absorb most of the probes power without draining it entirely. The seeming intelligence of a creature without a brain was most confounding. Without a complex brain for thought processes, they were unsure of how the tendrils made decisions and didn't act purely on instinct. Despite all of the tests they tried, that remained an unanswered question.

On the fourth day, without warning, the tendril flew the probe off deep into dead space. The crew scrambled to power up the ship in time to set a course before they lost it on their long-range sensors. They followed the tendril-driven-probe for nearly two full days before it suddenly stopped just as abruptly as it had begun. Then they picked up a strong frequency it began to emit.

"What in the world is it doing?" Hark asked as they listened to the low-pitched sound it created.

"It seems like it's searching. It may be looking for the other tendrils that are back through the wormhole," Krass speculated.

"It flew the wrong way," Hark said.

"We still don't know enough about how it processes information. It likely has no sense of direction," Krass said.

"Why stop here?" Hark wondered.

"It probably was using too much energy. They seem to be aware enough to be cautious with power levels. What I wonder is, why wasn't it emitting that frequency before? If it's searching, sending out a signal the entire time would have increased its odds of success. Maybe it's just not that intelligent," Krass shrugged. "My guess is it will continue to move on once it realizes there's no response."

But the tendril did not move on. For three days it didn't move and continuously emitted its frequency. Nothing else had changed. Krass and his team attempted to simulate the frequency in response, but the tendril did not seem to acknowledge it. After so long without any change in behavior Krass decided the next day they would recapture the tendril and tractor it back through the wormhole with them.

That night the crew was awoken to the sound of the proximity alarm. Hark, exhausted, got up from his bed and went to the cockpit to shut off the alarm. He checked the logs and the radar showed a massive incoming structure. He turned on the ships floodlights but couldn't see anything except for the tendril's encapsulated probe.

Hark felt his heart skip a beat; he'd read about the story of the lone survivor from the derelict Ethlana ship and how the tendrils had enveloped the ship and killed the crew. *Calm down,* he told himself, *that was after hundreds of years of traveling into dead space. We're nowhere near them.* He re-ran the scans and they came back the same. He felt a sinking feeling in his gut.

Watching and waiting, Hark continuously re-ran the radar scans every 5 minutes. After an hour it was clear there was something huge out there moving in their direction. *They're coming. How?* He wondered, his heart racing. Then it dawned on him, *They must have been following that derelict ship through dead space all these years! They were always coming...* His eyes fixated on the probe, *Oh no! And we just helped them find us!*

Hark turned the ship around and set a course for the wormhole at full speed. The ship was jostled at the sudden movement. Krass came into the cockpit a few minutes later, "What are you doing?" he demanded.

"They're out there!" Hark said, his eyes fixed forward on flying the ship.

"What are you talking about?" Krass asked, annoyed.

"The tendrils! The ones that were out in the middle of the void, they're here!" Hark yelled. He then pointed to the terminal next to him, "Look at the damn readings!"

Krass sat down in the seat next to him and went through the radar recordings. "This can't be," he said in disbelief.

"Don't you see? They've been on their way all these years! They're just slower than the ones that were on the ship, but now they're here, and that tendril we gave the probe to just told them where to go!" Hark explained.

"They can't be more than a few days away from meeting up with the probe," Krass said looking at the distance on the screen. On the radar, the tendrils showed up like a massive wall moving in. "There are *millions* of them," Krass swallowed hard.

"We have to warn the Conclave," Hark said with determination.

Chapter 20: Incoming

Norita had finished packing her belongings and was taking one last look around her stay room on the Bastion. She knew she would miss it, she already did; while her stay had been diplomatic it had felt like a much-needed reprieve. "All good things," she smiled half-heartedly.

The Saisei was due to launch in two days' time. All of the personnel transfers had been completed, the ship had been restocked with food, water, and fuel. The final rotation of visitation passes was all they were left waiting on. As soon as the rest of the passengers returned to the Saisei, it would be time to leave the Bastion docks.

Once they were ready to get underway, they would be making their journey through one of the nearby wormholes to the coordinates given to them by the Conclave. An unclaimed planet awaited them for colonization. The prospect both excited and terrified Norita. It had been the goal, after all, to find a new planet to make a home on but overseeing its development was never something Norita had thought she'd live to see. After a life in space, living on a planet seemed to be an intimidating prospect.

Norita took a moment before leaving the room, took a deep breath, and reminded herself she could do it. *Zavion, you better be ready for the engineering feat of a lifetime,* she thought and smiled to herself. She picked up her suitcase and walked out.

|

Koji left his quarters and was on the way to the hangar bays for flight drills. The Bastion had a pilots' course set up around an asteroid belt, that tested pilots' agility. Omega squad was suiting up to fly out to test out the course. After all this time, Koji was looking forward to getting back out to fly. He'd missed the feeling of freedom being in the cockpit had given him.

Just as Koji turned the corner of the hall he saw Gin walk by, "Hey, man! I haven't seen you around in ages. You doing OK?" Koji asked.

"...Yeah, thanks," Gin said, fidgeting with his sleeves. He was self-conscious of his scars, "Just checking in for duty. See you around."

"Yeah, same here. See ya," Koji said and watched Gin walk off. He'd heard the story second hand from Freya about how Raiden had found Gin half-dead, nearly bled-out, in his room. He wanted to say something more, to know if Gin was *really* alright, but he didn't know what to say. After a moment of hesitation, he turned around and again started to walk towards the hangar bay.

Freya's quarters were along the way. Koji debated on whether or not to stop to see if she wanted to walk down together. They'd hardly spoken in over a week. She hadn't been rude per se, just unavailable. Outside of their duty shifts, she slipped away. *Is she avoiding me?* He wondered. He knew she was taking the news about Raiden leaving the ship hard, but she had been distant even before that. *I don't know if I'll ever understand women,* he thought and sighed.

He got to her door and stood in front of it for a minute before he finally knocked. He waited but there was no response. He tried the handle, and it was locked. "Freya?" he called through the door, but no reply came. He tried knocking once more, but when the door didn't open, he walked on.

When Koji arrived at the hangar bay he found Freya was already there, doing her pre-flight checks. He walked over to her, "Hey," he said and waved as he approached.

Freya looked over to see him and her face lit up, "Hey!" she smiled. No one else had arrived from their squad in the hangar bay yet, so, she ran over to him, wrapped her arms around his neck and kissed him deeply. Koji was intoxicated by her. All of his feelings of doubt melted away in an instant.

"What was that for?" he asked.

"I missed you. And, I'm sorry. I've been an ass lately," she sighed. "I honestly don't know what I'd do without you. Thanks for dealing with me and all my crazy."

Koji placed his hand under her chin and tilted her head back, "We're in this together," he smiled.

"Whoa, need a minute?" Ken jived as he entered the room.

Koji and Freya took a step back from each other. "Very funny," Freya said and rolled her eyes. She walked back over to her ship to complete her pre-flight checks. Ken smirked, stifling a laugh, as he headed for his ship.

Koji couldn't help but keep his eyes on Freya. She had become his whole world. He wasn't sure how it had happened, he hadn't been looking for it, and had always seen Freya as one of the boys. But everything had changed, and now he felt incomplete without her.

|

For the first time in hours, Dr. Adonis Murakmi had a moment to himself. For the past week, a steady stream of patients had come into his office, panic struck, about the idea of leaving their ship to live on the new planet. Neurosis' were cropping up faster and faster. One woman had even had a full-blown panic attack in the middle of her session with him and had had to be taken out to be given a sedative to calm her down.

He rubbed his eyes, fatigued, and it was hardly noon yet. He still had 6 more patients to see before the end of the day. *Over 200 years in space, generations confined to a ship... no wonder they're scared. So many unknowns,* he thought. His mind mulled over the fears everyone had divulged, some quite unfounded, but others quite real. *How will our bodies handle real gravity? And our immune systems, are they compromised? We did alright on the Bastion I suppose,* he thought, trying to remind himself to be the voice of reason.

Yesterday he had had the last mandatory session with Captain Gin Koto. Unlike the rest of his patients, Gin was incredibly excited at the prospect of colonizing. It had given him a new sense of purpose. Adonis had worried at first that it was a guise or a form of escapism that Gin had been using to avoid his feelings, but it had seemed genuine, and he hoped it was.

Real air, land, a sky... a real home to go home to... I think I like the idea of that...

I

Hiroshi had managed to get one last rotation on the Bastion before the Saisei was to depart from the station. He had debated putting in a request to move aboard the Bastion, but the prospect of colonization was too intriguing. He imagined having a home, with an incredible view, where he could practice his art and have as much paper as his heart desired. He also couldn't imagine leaving his students. While teaching wasn't always everything he wished it could be, he felt a responsibility in shaping young minds.

While taking in the multiculturalism about the station he also had wanted to purchase some paper and art supplies before they left the Bastion. It was much more affordable, and the selection vastly improved compared to what the Saisei had to offer. He bought several large books with white and cream papers, pencils, pens, and paints. Hiroshi felt completely fulfilled after his shopping trip and excited to practice his art more often.

As he made his way back towards the docking bay he decided to stop at a nearby diner to have some more of the exquisite foods the Bastion was abundant with before departing. He had heard that the planet they would colonize wasn't a terribly far journey after passing through the nearby wormhole and hoped that would mean regular trips to the bastion on civilian freighters. *I imagine we'll have regular import and export with our new alien neighbors,* he thought while sipping on a hot cup of tea.

Crash! Just as Hiroshi was halfway through eating his lunch the entire station shook as a major sound shockwave rippled through the ship. Hiroshi sprang to his feet alert, *What in the world was that?* He thought startled. It had clearly come from the direction of the Bastion docks. Hiroshi settled his tab quickly, grabbed his shopping bags, and hurried off towards the docks to investigate.

When Hiroshi arrived, he found the Veick science vessel had crashed into the docking port. A huge crowd had gathered around to watch. No one had been hurt, but the ship was badly damaged, and the dock would need serious repairs as well. A small fire had occurred, but it had been put out before Hiroshi arrived, and all that remained were the black burn marks. The Veick scientists were being escorted out of the ship by the port's security.

"Let go of me! The council, I need to see the council!" Hiroshi had heard one of the Veick yelling at the security guard who tried to escort him.

Hiroshi didn't fully understand what had happened, but he knew it was time to leave. The crowd had grown significantly since he had arrived, and he had to push his way through the mass of people to get away from the crash site. Once Hiroshi was out of the crowd he made his way down the walkway at a heightened pace to get to the Saisei and he boarded quickly.

|

A few hours after the collision in the docks Norita was aboard the Saisei, in her room, unpacking her belongings. An incoming message beeped on her communicator. She tapped it on, "Hello?"

"Norita, it's Merrick," the voice came in.

"Merrick, how are you? I'm sorry you just missed me, I'm back aboard the Saisei," she began to say.

He cut her off, "There's a situation. When is the Saisei scheduled to leave?"

"Oh, don't worry, the ship that flew into the dock was nowhere near us. We weren't damaged at all," she said as she hung up her blouse.

"It's not that. Please, when do you leave?" he insisted.

Norita felt the hairs on the back of her neck raise, "About 50 hours from now."

She was about to ask why when Merrick cut her off again, "That's too late. You need to recall our people and depart immediately."

"Merrick, slow down! What is going on?" Norita asked, her anxiety creeping up.

"The Veick science team, the ones that were running the tests on that tendril in the void, their scans show there are millions of tendrils, *millions* Norita, coming towards the wormhole. It looks like they were following the Ethlana ship for hundreds of years... Based on these projections they'll start coming through the wormhole in about 40 hours. I've sent the data to your terminal," he said with a heavy voice. Norita stood there, shocked, unsure what to do or say. "Are you still there?" Merrick asked.

"Y, yes, sorry... This is..." again she lost her words.

Merrick was sympathetic, "I know. That's why you have to get out of here. I'm coordinating with the Conclave. They're recalling all Black Shadow operatives and calling in the fleets. The Saisei isn't armed, I don't want to strip your fighter ships, you may very well need them to defend yourselves, but..."

"I'll talk to General Yamamoto. We'll leave a squadron. If this battle can be contained here, that's our best defense," Norita said.

"Hm. Your wisdom precedes you Norita," Merrick said, some relief in his tone.

"I'll issue the recall to get our citizens back aboard the Saisei. We'll depart by tomorrow, that should get us through the wormhole before the tendrils come into this system," she said, trying to plan every contingency in her mind.

"Good luck, and Godspeed," Merrick said.

"To us both," Norita replied.

The comm clicked off and Norita felt wholly alone. Her mind worked quickly, deciphering problems and strategizing. She clicked her comm badge again and called General Yamamoto, telling him to meet her in her quarters immediately. She then contacted the staff coordinating shore leave and issued the immediate recall to go into effect.

Once Norita was sure she'd got the immediate actions underway to ensure their hasty departure from the Bastion, she sat at her desk and reviewed the data Merrick had sent. It was undeniable; the tendrils were coming. Their only defensive advantage was that their ships could fly faster than the tendrils could propel themselves through space.

Norita then pulled up the star map of the region. She had read the report Raiden had submitted, and the transcript from Vex's debriefing. The tendrils, without a doubt, could completely destroy the Bastion if they could make it all the way to the station. *And then?* She shuddered. *That would just be the beginning; millions of them could obliterate all space fairing vessels. And after that?* She took a deep breath and pushed the negative thoughts from her mind. *Stay focused, save your people!* She demanded of herself.

As much as she tried to stay focused, fear lurked in her mind. Millions of tendrils were on their way, and the consequences of what that meant were horrifying. An impending attack was inevitable. The invasion was coming...

Amanda Rose

To be Continued...

Characters Guide

Saisei

Norita Hiroshu: Empress and Descendant of Kairu

Takeo Yamamoto: Military General and Descendant of Mack

Lieutenant Raiden Saito: Omega Squad Pilot

Lieutenant Freya Tanaka: Omega Squad Pilot

Corporal Koji Akagi: Omega Squad Pilot

Private Masato Ito: Omega Squad Pilot

Private Ken Adama: Omega Squad Pilot

Captain Gin Yoshini: Ground Troop and Descendant of Mei & Kato

Private Rei Davis: Ground Troop

Koi Goto: Pilot in Command for the Saisei

Zavion: Head Engineer

Doctor Seto Takei: Lead Scientist

Hiroshi Kasai: Teacher

Suki Rose: Student

Link Rose: Suki's Father

Doctor Xena Nakamura: Medical Doctor

Doctor Adonis Murakami: Therapist

Niko Adai: Anti-Government Radical

Counselor Jona: Norita's aide

Counselor Merrick Uda: The People's Representative

Blaine: Magickal Adept

Conclave

Saaya – Speaker for the Ethlana

Ouct – Speaker for the Veata

Ent – Speaker for the Baas

Ecoatay – Speaker for the Chuchana

Zar – Speaker for the Veick

Ethlana

Xan

Venu

Vex

Vex's Expedition

Captain Cain

Engineer Zev

About the Author

ABOUT THE AUTHOR

Amanda Rose is an avid reader and storyteller. Working in a variety of mediums and genres, communicating new ways of thinking is her passion.

Amanda works as an online Health and Fitness coach, Law of Attraction Coach, Actor, Model, and Writer. Residing in Kingston, Ontario, with her husband and 3 cats, Amanda is currently working on her next novel. Get in touch with Amanda by visiting her website, www.AmandaRoseFitness.com

Amanda also loves to help others write their own books. Her course is available online through Udemy: **Get Published Workshop | Write, Publish, & Market Your Book**

Author's Other Works

- Fire Fury Freedom

- The Impending End

- A Strange Dream

- Manifesting on Purpose

- Manifesting Your Best Life

Fire Fury Freedom

"A veritable saga of a dystopian novel by an author with a genuine flair for detailed originality, and narrative driven storytelling, "Fire Fury Freedom" by Amanda Rose is an extraordinary and truly memorable read from cover to cover." -*Midwest Book Review*

Amanda Rose

Prequel to the Fire Fury Frontier Series

Fire Fury Freedom Book Description:

A dying planet on the verge of collapse…. tormented pasts that haunt the present… an ancient hidden magick…

The C.D.F.P. mega-corporation rules all, with unchecked power, and dark secrets…

The planet is dying, and they are the last hope to save it… Mack, an ex-soldier of the C.D.F.P. military division, and his mercenaries, standalone against the C.D.F.P. (AKA the Company), in the fight for humanities survival. Left unchallenged, the company has ruled over the East Green Continent with an iron fist for decades. The pollution they've caused has devastated the planet, destroying the ozone, and killing off plant and animal life.

Outside of domed cities the air is thin, and the sun scorches all; it's a veritable wasteland. In the past two decades the planet has reached entirely new levels of decay. Extreme weather patterns, and massive quakes, ravage the land.

Time is running out…

Mack and his mercenary troupe set out on a quest to stop the C.D.F.P. once and for all, and the planet will test them to their limits… But are they ready for the horrors they'll uncover? Can they alone stand up against the all-powerful C.D.F.P.?

Fire Fury Frontier

The Impending End

The Impending End Book Description:

It's 2005. Ayla Jefferson is 17, incredibly intelligent, sensitive, imaginative, and thoughtful. She's also contemplating suicide...

After a life long battle with mental illness plaguing her every move, Ayla is ready for death. Eerily calm, she says her goodbyes, and sets out to commit her final act.

But despite her stubborn conviction, life isn't as easy to let go of as she expected. Her hyper-imagination blurs reality and she finds herself getting lost in gripping memories. Mentally disengaged, Ayla's experiences are surreal, and discerning fact from fiction becomes harder and harder.

As the life she's so eager to leave behind begs to hold on, will she be able to leave it all behind?

A Strange Dream

Anthology of Short Stories and Poetry

A Strange Dream Book Description:

Death, Depression, Insomnia, Prostitution, Eating Disorders, Abortion, Convicts, Insanity, and Marital issues... This anthology of short stories and poetry explores the dark reaches of the mind and mental health issues.

The 9 short stories, including award winning EGGS and OUTSIDER, as well as runner up in the Canadian Writer's Guild Short Prose competition, DROWNING IN SILENCE, and 9 poems, take us on a journey from the surreal to the mundane. From day-to-day life to fantasy, the characters and situations explore many walks of life.

Manifesting on Purpose:

A 3 Week Guide to Transforming Your Life Through the Law of Attraction

Manifesting on Purpose Book Description:

It's time to take manifesting off auto-pilot, get behind the wheel, and start steering your life in the direction you want it to go!

Manifesting on Purpose clarifies why we manifest what we do, why we experience the same things over and over again, until we step in and weed out our own mental gardens.

Ever wonder how is it that 2 people can start off with the same opportunity, and one will become a massive success, while the other barely scrapes by? What's the defining factor?

What do successful people know that we're missing? We've been taught that the harder we work the more money, happiness, and success we'll have in life; but if this was the case successful people would constantly we run ragged, and be bleary eyed from lack of sleep, instead of enjoying lots of free time pursuing their heart's desires. So, what are we missing?

The Law of Attraction is always working, even when we're not focused on it. The Law of Attraction states that, "Like Attracts Like," we are all energy, so our thoughts get reflected back to us. Your thoughts create your physical reality. The problem? We're always thinking! Our thoughts, ungoverned, bounce around from idea to idea, and all too often, focus on the immediate problems in our lives, creating a feedback loop. Since we attract back what we think about, if we're focused on our problems, what's going to show up? More problems!

Your mind is your most valuable asset. Your thoughts literally create your reality. Your current situation is a reflection of your previous thoughts. Most people, however, do not consciously decide what they want, their subconscious belief systems run everything on auto-pilot; making most people feel as if they are victims of their circumstances.

YOU ARE NOT A VICTIM OF CIRCUMSTANCE!

You are in the driver's seat, you simply have to take control of the wheel! Take manifesting off auto-pilot and create the life you want!
"But I think positive thoughts," you say. Your conscious thoughts will always be secondary to your subconscious thoughts in the way of manifestation. Until you change your core beliefs to line up with who you wish to become, and what you wish to do, you cannot break the old cycles.

Are you ready to take control? Have abundance in money, love, health, freedom, experiences, and all other areas of your life? Then let's get started!

Manifesting Your Best Life:

How to Stop Wishing for Change and Start Living Your Best Life

AMANDA ROSE

How to Stop Wishing for Change and Start Living Your Best Life

Fire Fury Frontier

Manifesting Your Best Life Book Description:

Stop dreaming about a better life and start living it!

Manifesting You Best Life is going to show you that "Living Your Best Life" isn't just some cute meme on social media – it can be your way of life! The 21 nugget-of-wisdom chapters in this self-help book are for people who want to start living their best life, but don't know where to begin. It will give you the skills to take you from dreaming about your best life, to making it your reality!

You will learn:
•How to Identify what living your best life really means to you.
•The steps needed to stop wishing and start living your best life.
•How to use the Law of Attraction to support your efforts.
•Successful habits that will change your life.
•And how to create the life you've always wanted... And start living it NOW!

By the end of Manifesting Your Best Life, you will have a clear picture of what your dream life looks like, how to get there, and the tools and skills to make it into your reality!
Are you ready to begin?